Our Nipper

Best wishes from the
author

Terry Watson

OTHER WORKS BY THIS AUTHOR

THE LUCY TRILOGY:
Call Mama

Scamper's Find

The Leci Legacy

*

Before Lucy: prologue to The Lucy Trilogy

*

SHORT STORY COMPILATION:
A Tale or Two and a Few More

*

FOR CHILDREN:
The Clock That Lost Its Tick and Other Tales

*

NOVELLAS:
A Case for Julie

A Break for Julie

*

Coming soon
A Letter for Julie

Our
Nipper

Terry H. Watson

Ramoan
Press

Published in 2020 by Ramoan Press

ISBN Paperback: 978-1-9996502-6-1
Ebook: 978-1-9996502-7-8

A CIP catalogue copy of this book can be found in the British Library.

Published with the help of Indie Authors World
www.indieauthorsworld.com

IndieAuthors
World

Acknowledgments

Many thanks to my proof-readers, John and Drew, who in different ways kept this novel on the right road.

To Christine McPherson, whose sharp eyes professionally edited OUR NIPPER.

My thanks, as always, to Kim and Sinclair Macleod from Indie Authors World, for friendship and assistance with publication.

Finally, my thanks to Rebecca Forster, where the buck stops.

DEDICATED to the many people affected by the 2020 Coronavirus pandemic: to the workers who cared for the victims of Covid-19 both on the frontline and in the background, and to my NHS family members, John and Lesley, Catherine and Michelle. Proud of you.

PART 1

PART 1

PROLOGUE

The young man walked along the desolate street, anxiously looking at each of the dilapidated houses that came under the misnomer of Summer Grove. Each house was covered in overgrown wisteria, ivy, and similar climbing plants, as if attempting to conceal what lay behind the grimy curtains that covered dirt-congealed windows, some protected from the elements by newspaper or roughly hewn wood. Rubbish littered the once prosperous and pretentious street; discarded, broken items of furniture, and other household items made walking difficult, like a challenging obstacle course.

He stopped to read from the piece of paper he held in his hand and, satisfied that he was in the right area, continued his search for the elusive house. He trampled through autumn leaves that had fallen like a colourful carpet onto an unforgiving land. Trees that once adorned the area now struggled to rid themselves of the remnants of foliage, as if in doing so they eliminated memories of the past. He was oblivious to the scrunch beneath his feet as the dry leaves made contact with the firm soles of his shoes. The smell of the season had no effect on his senses as he moved on, intent on his task.

He stopped once more, re-read the paper, and replaced it in his jacket pocket. Reaching the door of one such grim house, he paused and took a deep breath to prepare himself for whatever lay ahead. His heart thumped inside his chest. He felt that it could be heard by passing public, but there was no-one around to witness the young man's anxiety or hear his beating heart. It was as if mankind had abandoned not only the buildings, but the very soul of the area.

Unwilling to use his pristine handkerchief, he rubbed the dark brass plate with a large leaf to reveal a notice and inscription that hinted of better days. He banged purposefully on the cast iron doorknob, the hollow, almost eerie sound seeming to reverberate throughout the house. He rubbed the grimy glass section of the door and waited. He saw movement within. He knocked again; this time more vigorously and with a determination that his search may be about to end. He was not leaving until he had fulfilled what he had come to do.

After a considerable time, the wooden door creaked open to reveal a dismal and dark hallway. An anxious looking woman held the door slightly ajar, as if to keep out unwanted visitors. She did not speak but waited for the well-dressed youth to either state his business or leave. She appeared to be of middle age or older; her well-worn dress was covered at the shoulders by a shawl that had seen better days. The dullness in her eyes spoke volumes of a hard life, a life perhaps void of meaning, of laughter and purpose. Her eyes never left the handsome face of the visitor. She waited.

'I've come for our Nipper.'

Archie Connor was admitted into the gloomy hallway, his eyes slowly adjusting to the dimness.

'Wait 'ere, sir. I'll fetch Matron. She's expecting you.'

In due course, the clip-clop of heels on the hard floor announced the arrival of a tiny, rotund woman whose grim face gave Archie the answer he dreaded. Another failure, another false lead.

He walked back along the road he had come, his shoulders hunched in defeat, his hands thrust deep into his pockets.

Where are you? Where the hell is our Nipper?

1

Elsie Connor, wracked with pain, coughed uncontrollably and spat blood-congealed sputum into a grubby container then wiped her mouth with a rag. Her twelve-year-old son Archie held the bowl and comforted his mother with every ounce of his being.

'You feelin' better now, Mam?' he asked anxiously, as he adjusted the flimsy bedcover over her thin body.

He pushed her matted hair from her worn face, gently patted her forehead, and planted a kiss on her wrinkled brow.

'You're a good lad, our Archie,' she whispered. Her body convulsed once more in pain, causing her to hold herself in such a position as if afraid that her inside would erupt. The pain became unbearable, and any attempt to hide it from her young son caused more stress as she forced herself not to cry out.

'Promise me something, Archie,' she pleaded as she looked into the fearful eyes of her first born. 'Promise me, son, you'll look after your sisters and take care of our Nipper when I'm gone.'

'Mam, Mam, you're scaring me. Don't go away, don't leave me with Da, please, Mam.'

He hugged her tightly, unaware that he was crushing her frail body.

Elsie took the hand of her boy and looked into his worried face, her once bright eyes now sunken and dull.

'Son, it's hard for you, but I have to speak while there's breath left in me body. I'm dying, our Archie. I'm not long for this world. I'll go content if I know you'll keep the family together.'

She coughed some more. 'Your da is a weak man; he'll not cope when I pass. He'll take to the drink and be no use to any of you. Our Nipper has drained me body, Archie. Four babies and three lost ones has done the life out of me. Say you'll do what I ask, then I'll have peace.'

'Mam, I will, I promise you. I'll look after our Ruby and Betsy and our Nipper.'

As she spoke, the baby lying in a urine-soaked box that was his makeshift cot, let out a painful cry.

'Give 'im here to me, son. I want to die with me babe in me arms. He'll give me comfort. Fetch the milk for him. He's a hungry lad is our Nipper.'

Archie gently placed the crying newborn in his mother's arms and gave him a make-do bottle of watery milk. He was too heavy for the sickly woman to hold comfortably. Archie placed his arms around him and supported his wriggling body as Elsie attempted to give him some milk.

'I think it's time, lad. Fetch your da from the beer house, but first go along to Mrs Young and ask her to kindly pop in, then go and fetch your sisters from Lizzie McCourt. I want to say me goodbyes to you all. And Archie love, down there by the fire is a loose floorboard; underneath is a rag with some money. I've managed to save it for you to help look after your sisters for a bit. It's not much, and your da knows nought about it.'

With tears streaming down his face, Archie ran out of the house to do as he was bid. He hurried to the next equally dilapidated tenement and sprinted up broken stairs, two at a time, until he reached the last door in the building.

'Mrs Young, Mam said could you come, cos it's time. I've to get me da out the doss house and fetch our Ruby and our Betsy.'

Doris Young, a lifelong friend and neighbour, felt her heart go out to the kiddies she had helped deliver into the cruel world of dirt and poverty of early 20th century London, where neighbour helped neighbour and shared their time and limited goods. She wiped her hands on her wrap-around apron, hugged the weeping boy, planted a kiss on his grimy forehead, and spoke gently.

'Do as your mam wants. Run to the Frog and Pond and tell your da I said he's to get home right now and not dawdle, then go and fetch your sisters.'

Doris watched him go and thought how life had dealt a hard blow to the little family. She shivered despite the relative comfort of the room, shook her head in despair, then donned her coat and headed to do Elsie Connor's bidding.

*

Bertie Connor, a small insignificant man, slurred his speech as he tried to join in and follow the heated political argument. It was late 1913, and the threat of war had been the only topic of conversation for several weeks.

'We'll all end up in the workhouse if we can't feed our kids. What's to become of us?'

Bertie Connor spoke more to the contents of his beer tankard than to his workmates. He spent more time staring aimlessly into such containers, his face pitted and bloated with overindulgence in alcohol. The irony was lost to him that his family would have food on the table if he spent less time indulging his addiction to drink, and if indeed he had a table. His one pound in wages and the six shillings he paid for rent left very little for food and necessities for the Connor family. The more he drank, the more he slouched further over the counter, as he commiserated with the injustices of the world.

The door of the public house opened with a bang that made the men turn around. Ready to holler to have the door closed quietly, they noticed young Archie Connor searching for his father.

'Where's me da? Da?' the boy called.

'Over there, Archie,' replied one man, pointing to a corner of the bar where Bertie was slumped over, commiserating about the ills in society.

'Da, Da, come home now. Mam says it's time.'

Staring at his young son through bleary eyes, as if looking at a face that was both alien but somehow familiar, Bertie Connor slurred, 'Now, our Archie, what's the rush? Can a working man not finish his pint? I'll be home when me and me mates finish this serious discussion, now run off home and tell your mam I'll be along shortly.'

He turned back to his drink, only to hear the plaintive shout from his son.

'No, Da, no. You've to come right now. Mam's dying, and Mrs Young says to come and not dawdle, cos it's time.'

The overpowering stink that emanated from the beer-spilled room and unwashed bodies of the drinkers made Archie's eyes sting, and he rubbed them quickly.

Bertie Connor was frozen to the spot. Time seemed to stand still. He had been in denial about his wife's illness and sought solace in drink. He froze on the spot, unable to right himself to a standing position. Some of his mates who knew how things were with the Connor family, grabbed him by the arms and helped him out of the Frog and Pond.

'Come on, Bertie me lad, sober up and get home to Elsie,' said one. 'You run on, young Archie, me and the lads will get your da home.'

They struggled with the full weight of the blubbering man on their arms as they half-carried him along the short distance to his home. Steering him down two flights of dark, broken stairs to what passed as a basement dwelling was a monumental task, and they ended up carrying him by all four limbs before setting him down in the room where the dying woman looked on, sadness filling her soul and breaking her heart.

The men tipped their caps in respect as they took their leave of Elsie and returned to the beer house in silence, each lost in their own thoughts. Poverty was rife, but the Connor family had been handed a bad deal.

2

Assured that his da would be taken home safely, Archie ran like he had the devil chasing him to the home of Lizzie McCourt. For a nominal fee, she had taken the girls in for schooling for a few hours each day while their mam was ill. What she taught was questionable, though; neither Ruby nor Betsy could read or write, and were left to attempt to copy letters and numbers onto slate while Lizzie indulged her passion for gin and afternoon naps.

The only room in what passed as her home reeked of its unwashed, gin-fuelled inhabitant, who sat slouched in an armchair that she shared with a motley collection of stray cats. Her pupils sat on the dirty floor; their faces spoke of fear of their foul tutor.

Archie knocked loudly then barged in, shouting more in fear than anything else, 'Our Ruby, our Betsy, you've to come home right now. Our mam says it's time.'

The girls, subdued and afraid of the wrath of Lizzie McCourt, cowed around their brother as he took them by the hand and led them out of the dingy room for the last time. As they left, they heard screeching, 'You tell your da he owes me fourpence. I don't give no schoolin' for free, you tell 'im.'

Ignoring her, Archie ran with his sisters along the street to their home, hampered at times by little Betsy's slow pace and whimpering. They arrived in time to hear weeping coming from the open door of their hovel.

Archie ran in, dragging his sisters with him, only to be stopped by a red-eyed Doris Young. She wiped her tears with her apron and gathered the three children close to her.

'Oh, Archie, your mam's gone. She passed away after I got here. She's at peace now. Go in and give her a kiss, then you all come with me to my place.'

The children quietly entered the room where Elsie Connor lay dead – a peaceful look on her face as she held her latest baby. She looked younger than her thirty-four years. The lines on her face, once etched by pain, had given way to a more natural, youthful look – one that had won her many admirers and captured the heart of the once handsome Bertie Connor.

Ruby screamed. She looked at the solemn face of their neighbour, Mam's closest friend, then her eyes moved to the person on the bed. Her beloved mam was lying, as if asleep, with her newborn son attached to her. Mother and child were so close it was as though the cord had not been cut. Ruby wiped the hot tears that nipped her eyes as she clutched her little sister's grubby hand in hers.

Betsy, not quite understanding the enormity of what had happened, sobbed quietly. She was confused as to why everyone looked sad that Mam was sleeping.

Archie, holding them both, wept openly. Tears ran down his face onto the side of his nose, and he wiped them on his dirty sleeve before planting a kiss on the still warm lips of his mother, then fled from the scene into the arms of Doris Young.

Bertie Connor sat on the only piece of furniture that passed for an armchair, head in his hands, and cried like a baby. He was totally oblivious to his children's pain, or indeed to their existence at that moment. He drank from a bottle of cheap alcohol, as if in doing so his troubles would cease and his wife would be with him once more.

'Oh, me darling Elsie, what am I to do? There's so much I wanted to tell you.'

He mumbled incoherently into space, as his distraught children clung, not to him, but to a neighbour, such was the emotional distance between him and his offspring.

Bertie remained detached from reality. He did not move from the spot, but fell into a drunken stupor and remained in a comatose state, even when his wife's body was removed for burial in a pauper's grave. He lay where he fell, oblivious to life and death.

Such was the poverty in the area that undertakers were well used to such indifference, and carried out their task quickly and without pomp or ceremony. Elsie Connor was interred in what passed as a grave, surrounded by the poor of society. Interred without prayer, without witnesses, without ceremony. Dust to dust.

Unable to look after himself, let alone a young family, Bertie Connor spent more and more time in beer shops like the Frog and Pond, drowning his sorrows and making a nuisance of himself. He lost his job, became involved in several fights, assaulted a fellow drinker whose only crime was to offer condolences, and kicked another. He was eventually escorted off the premises by the police, banned from ever entering the establishment again, charged, and jailed. He was unaware of the needs of his children, who remained in the safe care of Stan and Doris Young.

The next few months were a blur for Archie and his siblings. They remained with Doris, who fussed over them, fed them well, bathed them in the tin bath by the fire until their hair and skin shone, and declared them bug-free. Her husband Stan brought a trunk from under the inset bed. It contained clothes belonging to their daughter Mabel. Now a married woman with children of her own, she had worked as a matchgirl in a busy Bryant and May workshop where she met Bill, a maintenance man. It was love at first sight for the besotted couple and, afraid of the impending war, like many others they married quickly before the men were called to serve King and country.

'We'll have a look through our Mabel's things and see if we can find something for you girls to wear,' Doris said, then laughed, 'Archie, I don't think any of our Mabel's frocks will fit you.'

The children laughed with her – it was a sound that had not been heard among them for a considerable time, if at all.

Stan Young, a man of authority who commanded respect from the men who worked with him in the dockyard, looked at young Archie.

'Don't you fret, me lad, I'm sure we'll find something among my clothes for Doris to adjust to fit you.'

A man of 40-something years, he wore his age well. He was tall, with a full head of jet-black hair that sported a widow's peak, and a heart full of compassion for the additional mouths to feed. His calm demeanour and that of his wife guided the youngsters through a maze of emotions and gave them a sense of security that had so far dodged their young lives.

Slowly, the fog lifted from Elsie's children.

3

Unknown to Archie, the dockworkers had collected money to help with the family's immediate needs until plans for the future were clearer. But the men insisted on handing the money to Stan, with the instruction that Bertie Connor was not to have any of it.

'It's not much, Stan, but the lads wanted to help the nippers,' explained the foreman.

Knowing how the workforce struggled to make ends meet within their own homes, Stan was almost overcome with emotion. Shaking hands with each of the men, he thanked them for the sacrifice they had made.

'Doris will put this to good use to feed and clothe the nippers,' he assured them. 'You can be sure nothing will be wasted.'

'We know that, Stan,' the foreman replied. 'You and Doris are the most honest people we know. You've a big heart taking on four kiddies; the lads admire you both.'

The family quickly settled into a routine that saw them safe and loved. Archie enjoyed talking man-to-man with Stan, who saw in the boy a lad wise beyond his age. Her two men, as Doris referred to them, had long chats about life and politics and the news of impending war. Stan became the father figure Archie had lacked in his young life.

As for Stan, although he loved his daughter Mabel, Archie felt like the son he never had.

'Will you be sent away to fight, Uncle Stan?' the wide-eyed boy enquired of his mentor. He copied many of the man's mannerisms, at times looking down at his feet, other times scratching his head, often tapping his foot to make a point – all to the silent amusement of Doris.

'No, young'un. I'm too old to fight, and I have an important job at the docks to see to the smooth running of things. There are different ways to serve King and country, not everyone will go off to fight. There will be lots of work here to keep me busy. We have to keep the country going and support our brave soldiers.'

The lad sighed. 'I wish I was old enough to join up and do me bit for the King and maybe get a medal.'

Stan shook his head. 'Archie, your job is here, looking after your sisters and the Nipper, like you promised your mam. That's a really important role for you. But you know, I think you'll be fine. You have a good head on your shoulders.'

Archie recalled his mother's words and agreed whole-heartedly with her sentiment, *The Youngs are good, God-fearing people, who you can turn to in time of trouble.* Although he missed his mother, he felt happier than he had been for as long as he could remember, and thrived under their care. He was a quick learner and soaked up everything he could from Stan.

Ruby and Betsy watched with fascination at the skilful way Doris adapted Mabel's clothes to fit them, and they danced around the kitchen showing off their new frocks.

'Look, Archie,' shouted an excited Betsy, lifting her frock. 'Bloomers, our Archie. I ain't never had drawers before in me life.'

'I'm going to learn to sew and make nice things to wear,' stated Ruby, as she carefully watched every move of the skilled seamstress.

Doris smiled. 'And I'm sure you will do just that. Here, come and watch, and I might just let you have a go at sewing.'

Both girls relished their new life and happily helped Doris with the household chores. They were unused to cleanliness, and revelled in the experience of feeling clean and loved.

What Doris Young lacked in stature, she had in love in abundance for the young waifs. They filled her home and heart, and satisfied the maternal void left when her only child had married and moved from the area. Scrupulously clean in herself and her home, she instilled in her charges the importance of cleanliness.

'Just because we are poor don't mean we need to be dirty,' she told them. 'Not when we can boil water and bathe in the tin bath and keep our clothes clean.'

When she had tenderly lifted the baby from the arms of his dead mother, Doris had feared for the baby's life. *This little 'un hasn't long for this world. He'll be joining his mam before the night is over.* She'd wept as she cradled him in her arms and carried him back to her home, fearing that his life was ebbing away.

She'd held him close to her warm body to generate heat, and, by some miracle, his almost lifeless frame had improved as the days wore on. Doris sent for a wet nurse who, for a half-penny a day, fed the hungry baby. Effie Gray, a young immature sixteen-year-old girl, was a product of the grim poverty and ignorance that was the life of many pre-war Londoners. She had given birth to a stillborn baby – a child she had been unaware she was having, and was bemused how it had got inside her pitiful body.

As the young girl sat by the fire, warming herself while she fed the baby, Doris prepared her bread and bacon dripping – the only meal the girl was likely to have.

'You have to keep your strength up to feed him,' Doris told her, 'and don't you be going frittering away those pennies. They're for you to buy bread and whatever you can get from the market. No drinking it away, or I'll have to look for another lass to feed the nipper.'

Terrified of losing the comforting warmth of Doris's home and the bowl of food each day, Effie was determined not to disappoint the formidable lady. As the days progressed, she became fond of the child who suckled her breast, and she sang to him and wrapped his little finger around hers. Effie's home was much like that of the Connor's, except that eleven people lived in the one-roomed hovel. She was glad to escape the mayhem for a few hours, and enjoyed the relative calm and cleanliness of the Youngs'.

Doris gave her a warm shawl to wrap around her shoulders, and when the girl arrived next day without it, she had an idea it had been taken from her by one of her callous siblings. Undaunted, and knowing the last thing Effie needed was a reprimand from her, Doris removed a shawl from the baby's crib with the instructions she wore it while feeding the baby, then used it to cover the nipper before she left.

For a few hours each day, poor Effie enjoyed living like a princess. With Stan and Archie out on an errand to fetch kindling for the fire, Doris took the opportunity to provide a warm bath in the tin tub by the fire for the girl, who had never experienced such luxury. She bathed her, washed her bug-filled hair, and helped her wash and dry her clothes, then gave her clean garments which Doris insisted she kept for herself and forbade her to share with her sisters.

Stan and Doris's home was similar in size and layout to that of Archie's former house, but there the similarity ended. The one-roomed house had two large inset beds – one held the three children, while Stan and Doris slept in the other, with the baby tucked into a makeshift crib nearby. A large wooden table – Doris's pride and joy – took up most of the remainder of the room and was used for cooking, eating, and as a work surface.

The woman kept her home as pristine as she could, scrubbing the large table regularly with a vigour that defied any speck of dust to escape her eyes. A roaring fire gave the room a cosiness the Connor children had never known. Iron pots of water bubbled on top of the stove, and were used for cooking and washing, while tempting smells often came from the large oven.

Doris, or Aunt Doris as she had become, gathered the children around her as she baked bread, made simple meals, and allowed them to take turns at scraping the bowl. A feature of the house unfamiliar to the children was linoleum which covered the floor. Doris scrubbed and polished it weekly, then tied rags to their feet and laughed with them as they slithered around the room, adding a shine to the floor. It was an idyllic time for them, and the youngsters felt secure and safe in the care of Stan and Doris. They were totally unaware of their impending change of fate.

4

Christmas as a celebration was something the children had never experienced. It had been just another day in their poverty-stricken home, with Bertie Connor taking up his usual place at the bar in the Frog and Pond, and Elsie unable to put much food on the table, let alone any extras.

One night, when the children were asleep, Stan approached the subject of Christmas.

'I was thinking we should spend some of the dockworkers' money on giving the nippers an experience to remember,' he suggested. 'We don't know what lies ahead for them.'

Doris sighed and nodded in agreement. 'It breaks my heart to have to part with them. Yes, let's do it. Let's make it a time to remember. What were you thinking?'

'I see there's a show on in Drury Lane, *Sleeping Beauty*. I was thinking we could take them there by motor omnibus,' said Stan. 'That would be a thrill for them, a day to remember forever.'

'It would be something different for me, too,' his wife replied. 'I've never ridden one of those new-fangled vehicles. Are you sure they are safe?'

Stan laughed. 'They're fine, Doris. I've ridden a few times. Mind you, they are open to the elements, especially if you ride on the open-top double deck, so we need to be well-wrapped up. And we'll have to walk a fair bit to catch the omnibus. Do you think they will cope?'

Doris smiled. 'Stan, I think they will be so excited they won't mind the walk. And with the baby almost weaned, we won't have to depend on Effie for milk. I'll get her to come in before we head off and let him drink his fill. It gives me a chance to feed her, poor girl. I dread to think what will happen to her when the Nipper is fully weaned. I'll need to see to warm clothes for us all. It sounds a good idea, and so kind of the dockworkers to help us give them a happy day. God knows, there may not be many ahead of them.'

The couple had often discussed the ominous threat of war and the implication for the youngsters. Stan knew how fond his wife had become of the young family, and couldn't bring himself to tell her that the authorities had already made a decision about the future of the Connor children. *She'll find out soon enough,* he told himself.

The following week, it was a very excited group that headed off to London town. The Nipper was wrapped warmly inside Doris's shawl, while Archie held Betsy firmly by the hand, and Stan led the way with Ruby. They joined a motley crew of revellers intent on celebrating in town. The wooden seats in the vehicle were uncomfortable, but it did not detract from the excitement as Stan pointed out places of interest as they rode along.

Alighting from the vehicle, Archie exclaimed, 'I ain't never seen as many people in me life.' He looked around in amazement at the hordes of Londoners going about their business.

'We need to stick close together,' Stan instructed the family, as he hoisted Ruby onto his shoulders. 'Archie, can you manage Betsy on your shoulders like this? If you get tired, let me know. Hold Doris's hand, and don't let anyone come between you. That way, we'll all be safe.'

They walked along together, taking in the excitement of stalls and sideshows ready to entice the Christmas revellers to part with their money. A cacophony of noise and merriment added to their excitement as they lapped up the sights, smells and sounds, lights and colours. Before they arrived at the theatre, Stan purchased hot chestnuts which they shared before joining a queue of merrymakers excited about the impending performance and the prospect of sheltering from the cold in the warmth of the theatre.

Inside, the venue was crowded, with people jostling for the best view. Betsy, overcome with fear, began to cry. Once seated, Doris held the little girl close on her lap to comfort her, while Archie took charge of the baby. The wooden seats were only slightly more comfortable than those of the omnibus.

Archie looked around in awe at the décor and glitter of the horseshoe-shaped theatre, and was fascinated at the side boxes so near the stage.

'Who are those people sitting in those seats?' he enquired, as he studied the men in frock suits and the ladies in colourful finery and hats.

'That's for posh folk, Archie,' Stan told him. 'Not for poor folks like us.'

'Someday I'll be rich and posh and sit in one of those boxes, and I'll wave to the crowd like I'm important.'

Stan and Doris laughed at the earnest young lad. 'And you may well do just that, me lad,' chuckled Stan. 'You may well do.'

Betsy soon forgot her fears as the show got underway and was as captivated as the rest of the audience. The hardness of the seats was forgotten as she clambered onto Stan's shoulders for a better view. Doris looked at her young charges and smiled at the joy on their faces and silently prayed, *God help these nippers if they have to leave us.*

When the curtain came down at the end of the performance, the chattering theatre-goers filed out into the cold
of the winter evening. Stan once more gathered the children
together for safety. They made their way through throngs of
raucous revellers to a stall where they purchased welcome
portions of hot peas and vinegar and had a sip of Stan's porter
before heading for the return journey. The vehicles leaving
the city were packed; people jostled for space, some hanging
dangerously from the platform.

'Room on top,' hollered a frustrated conductor, who was
fairly new to the job and unsure how to cope with boisterous
crowds.

Stan guided his group to the only available space on the
top deck, and they huddled together in the open, with the
biting cold wind gathering momentum as they drove along.
Darkness had fallen so there was nothing to take the children's
attention from the cold, and before long they had dozed off.
Doris closed her eyes briefly, while Stan remained alert for
their stop.

The walk home appeared longer and more tedious than
earlier; the rain had turned to sleet that lashed their faces
like icy cold snow pellets. Stan hoisted the girls onto his hips
where they clung to his neck and huddled in, while Archie
attached himself as close to Doris and the baby as he could.
Doris was glad she had given them all warm hats and gloves,
which provided a modicum of protection.

Exhausted from the journey, they were glad of the relative
warmth of the house. The small fire had burned steadily
during their absence, taking the chill off the room, and Stan
soon had it re-fuelled and roaring.

Doris settled the children to bed, after which she and Stan
sat by the fire with a hot drink.

'They're exhausted, poor lambs. Let's hope they sleep on in the morning while I organise our Christmas meal,' she commented wearily.

Earlier, Stan had helped the children make decorations from discarded newspapers he had found at the docks. He'd shown them how to cut paper into shapes on a chain.

'Mine look like Christmas angels,' announced an excited Ruby.

'Mine, too,' whispered Betsy, who adored her sister and agreed with everything she said.

'Mine are meant to be trees. I suppose they are kinda like trees,' replied a serious Archie, as he continued to cut.

When they'd finished, Stan had thrilled them by hanging their chains up around the room.

*

It was an excited family that sat together to sample Doris's Christmas fare. Despite shortage of some food, she had managed to serve oysters cooked in fish stock and potatoes. At that time, oysters were in plentiful supply and a staple diet of the poor, it was only in later years that they became a delicacy favoured by discerning diners.

By some sort of miracle, she had managed to make what passed as Christmas pudding, much to the delight of the children. They sat by the fireside with full bellies, and happy smiles. Stan had made the girls tiny wooden dolls, while Doris had sewn little outfits for them. For Archie, he had constructed a cart with moving wheels. And the baby had not been forgotten; Doris had fashioned a warm shawl for him.

Stan, with his strong tenor voice, and accompanied by Doris's contralto voice, sang to the wide-eyed children and taught them to sing, *God Rest Ye Merry Gentlemen* and *I Saw*

Three Ships, that they belted out with gusto. They listened enthralled at the story of Tiny Tim and, with Stan's prompting, chorused, 'God Bless us, one and all.'

It was with a heavy heart that Doris settled the children for the night, fearful for what lay ahead for them.

'That's the best Christmas ever,' whispered Archie to no-one in particular, as he nodded off to sleep.

'We've done our best for Elsie's brood,' Stan consoled a tearful Doris, as she wiped her eyes. 'Everything is out of our hands now. I just wish it could be different.'

5

The year 1913 turned into an ominously unsettled 1914, with talk of war dominating the life of the citizens as they waited anxiously for news. Events in the far-off Balkans and the name Archduke Franz Ferdinand had meant little to the masses, and it was left to politicians like the incumbent of 10 Downing Street, Herbert Asquith, to understand the repercussions and to make decisions.

But in the summer of 1914, talk finally became reality when war was declared. It was to affect the lives of many thousands of people across the world, and brought a devastating change to the life and security of the Connor children.

Despite the care and love lavished on them, Archie was worried about the future.

'Aunt Doris,' he ventured to say, 'what's to happen to us, to me and the girls and our Nipper?'

It was a question Doris had been dreading. Her shoulders sagged and her heart raced as she tried to control her emotions. This was not going to be an easy conversation. She licked her lips, took a deep breath, and wished Stan was there to help her.

'Archie, lad. Now that war has been declared, our Mabel is coming back to live with us. Her man has joined the army and is away to fight for King and country. She has two kiddies and another on the way. I'm sorry, lad...' her voice cracked with emotion, 'but there won't be room for you all to stay here. You'll all be going to the workhouse... Now don't cry, lad, it's for the best, and you'll be fed and educated. Keep your head down and do what you're told, and all will be well.'

Archie hugged the woman he had come to see as a substitute mother, his small body shaking as she bit back her own sobs. They clung to each other and she let the young boy cry his eyes out. He held on as tightly as he could, as if doing so would prevent them having to leave.

Ruby and Betsy, who had been quietly playing with toys, looked up at the sound of weeping. Ruby stood up.

'What's wrong, our Archie?'

Her brother, too overcome with sadness to reply, looked at his sisters and at the baby who was cooing happily in his crib, before freeing himself from Doris's comforting arms. Then he stood up and ran from the house, tears streaming down his face and nipping his eyes.

Archie ran without caring where he was going. Tears stung his eyes and temporarily blinded him. The cold air penetrated his body and echoed the cold pain in his heart. But he ran on, oblivious to his surroundings. Only when he passed the Frog and Pond did he realise he had been running in circles and was now a stone's throw from his former, derelict hovel of a home.

Exhausted physically and emotionally, he climbed down into the basement of the building, where he curled up on the doorstep and wept. He wept for his mam, for the only life he had known, and vowed he would keep his promise to keep the family together. He was totally oblivious to the dark, dingy building that smelt of decay and death. The door was closed and barricaded by wooden planks, a sign the authorities had taken back the house that he had once called home.

He sat on the broken step for a long time. *We ain't going to no workhouse,* played over and over in his thoughts. Noticing a tiny opening in the barricade, enough for a small boy to tug and widen enough to squeeze through, he crawled into the stinking hovel. He wept as he looked around the room at the meagre pieces of wooden crates that had served as their furniture. The authorities hadn't seen them worthy of salvaging, leaving them to the mercy of the rodents who had once shared the house with the family.

Beleaguered, Archie sat on the cold floor for hours, the only sound coming from his rapid breathing and the scratching of mice as they searched for food. The light from the one window in the room began to fade and he shivered from cold and damp, his stomach rumbling with hunger as he fought to stay awake.

Suddenly, he remembered his mam's instructions, and prised open the loose floorboard where she had squirreled away a meagre amount of money. *It's for a rainy day*, she had told Archie when she knew she was not long for this world. *Your da knows nought about it. I want you to use it, son, when I'm gone. It ain't much, but it will tide you over for a bit.*

Archie counted the money his mother had wrapped in a rag. Four shillings and threepence halfpenny. *A fortune*, he thought. He wrapped it carefully, put it in his pocket, and with a last look around his home and a vicious kick at a rat that ran across the room, he set off to collect his sisters and baby brother, unsure how he would protect them from the fate of the workhouse or where they were to live. He'd heard horror stories of such places; of cruelty, hard work, and beatings, that filled him with dread, and he was determined to keep them safe from a place where people were punished for being poor. Archie was resolute in his vow to keep his siblings together, as his mam had wanted.

With renewed purpose, he ran to fetch them from the Young's home, with no idea of where they would go from there.

The rain was relentless as Archie ran back to the house, stopping only briefly at the door to catch his breath and plan what he was going to do without hurting the feelings of the Youngs.

Back in the warm room, he looked around and noticed both Doris and Stan's demeanour, and stopped in his tracks. They looked distraught. Stan's shoulders sagged as he hugged Doris, whose eyes were red with weeping.

'Where's our Ruby and Betsy, and our Nipper?' he yelled, as he glanced around the room. It was silent, free from the carefree laughter that had filled the home for several months.

Stan Young stood and placed his hand gently on the shoulders of the young lad he had grown to love as a son. With a deep sigh, he explained, 'Sorry, Archie. The authorities came for them while you were away. I just got in from work when they arrived. They're coming back for you later this evening. It's for the best, lad. You will have a roof over your heads and food.'

'No!' screamed Archie, as he thumped angrily at Stan's chest.

Stan remained silent and allowed the boy to vent his anger; he, too, felt helpless in the face of such a traumatic turn of events.

After a few minutes, Archie freed himself from the man's clutches, then turned and once more fled from the house.

6

Archie's heart pounded in his body; he felt as if it was going to burst. He had no idea where he was going. He had to find his family and quickly. Not knowing where the workhouse was, and determined to avoid being spotted by the authorities, he moved carefully through the unfamiliar streets, tripping over debris and fighting off a pack of dogs intent on making a meal of him. He hurried on, occasionally looking back to make sure the hungry canines were no longer in pursuit, and relieved to see they had turned their attention to a bird carcass.

He looked at various buildings where his family might have been taken. Eventually, he came to a large brick building. Struggling to read the notice on the gatepost, he suddenly became aware of someone nearby.

'You don't want to go in there, son. That's where they put the loonies, the folks wot's lost their minds. You lookin' for sumat?'

Archie looked in the direction from where the voice had come, and in the dim lighting, made out an unkempt, creepy-looking man, grinning at him. The stranger emerged from the darkness and approached him menacingly.

'Me sisters have been took away to the workhouse and I'm trying to find them,' answered Archie. He was terrified, but determined to find his family, even if it meant talking to the downtrodden man.

'You won't find them there, that's for men,' the sinister man replied. 'The women's place is across the river. Want me to show you, for a shilling?'

He strutted nearer to the wary boy, and Archie tried hard not to react to the stench as the man approached. His torn overcoat was tied at the waist with cord, and his toothless sneer made shivers run down the boy's spine.

Archie was momentarily tempted to part with a shilling, but had an innate sense of who to trust that held him in check. He didn't want to part with his mam's precious money.

'No thanks,' he shouted, and immediately ran off.

As he fled, he heard the ragged man laughing as he called out, 'Ye'll never find it. I've sent you the wrong way.'

Archie did not care. His mind was focused on one thing. *Other side of the river? I'll head there.* Unsure of his bearings, his senses told him to smell the water, look for ships, and find a bridge over the mighty River Thames.

It took longer than expected, and he had to dodge hordes of idle men sitting around on street corners, chewing tobacco and sharing beer from various types of containers. The smell from them was obnoxious. *Did I smell like that before Aunt Doris cleaned me?* he wondered. With his scrubbed face, shining hair, and clean clothes, he felt quite presentable. It gave him an air of confidence that wearing dirty rags could never have done. *Poor mam, she did her best for us.*

The smell of food emanating from a nearby stall reminded him how hungry he was, and he was drawn towards the tempting aroma. Seeing a potential customer, the stallholder called out, 'Hot pie and peas, tuppence a go. Best mutton pies in town. Jug of porter, two pence.'

Archie pondered about parting with four pence from his precious store of cash, but hunger and the tempting allure of food won him over. He moved out of sight to extract some money, carefully returning the cash to his pocket, and purchased his supper.

'You look hungry, me lad. When did you last eat?' asked the stallholder as he watched Archie scoff his food and drink.

'Can't remember,' replied Archie, wiping his mouth on his sleeve.

'You're not from this side of the river, are you, boy? I've been watching you moving back and forward. You lookin' for sumat?'

Archie explained that he was looking for the workhouse to find his sisters and brother. 'They were took away this morning, 'cos our mam died.'

'Sorry about that, me lad. Here, have some more pie, it's on me. Now, the only workhouse around here is Holborn – the red building over there where the ships are. Can you see it from here? It's further away than it looks.'

'Yes sir, I see it. I'd best be getting along,' Archie replied. 'Thanks for the pie.'

'A polite fellow like you shouldn't be around these parts, not when night is falling,' the stallholder warned. 'It can get rough when the ships dock and the sailors take to the streets. The weather's going to get worse, look at those dark clouds. It won't be long before there's a deluge. Best take shelter and keep yourself safe, there's some shady characters around these parts.' The man added, 'Oh, and the workhouse over there is only for women and girls. Men and boys are in one upriver, so you won't find your brother and sisters under the same roof. No, they separate them they do. No fraternising allowed.'

'Fraternising?' questioned Archie.

'Hey, don't you mind me. Now, run off before darkness falls, and mind what I said, keep hidden and keep safe. Best keep your search till the morn. Have you somewhere to stay tonight?'

'I'll be fine. I can go back to me aunt.'

Archie moved off, his eyes darting from one place to another as he headed towards the area where he hoped to find the workhouse. Knowing that the workhouse guardians would be searching for him, he had no intention of returning home even if he could find his way back in the heavy rain that blinded and disorientated him.

He ran on until he reached the heart of the docks, and was fascinated at the sight in front of him. He stopped briefly to gaze at the hustle and bustle of sailors offloading and loading bales and sacks and all kinds of packages, hoping to finish the task before the light faded. The noise from the workers shouting instructions to each other as they lowered the sails carried in the wind; it sounded frightening and threatening.

Wearily, Archie hid among a bundle of bales and sacks that sheltered him from prying eyes and from the chill of the night, and listened to the cacophony of dock life until the effects of the porter and sheer emotional exhaustion lulled him into a deep sleep.

7

Archie awoke to a rocking movement, like that of the rope swing he and some friends had tied to a tree. He knew he was somewhere different, but it took him some time before he became alert enough to sit up and rub sleep from his eyes. He tried to figure out where he was.

The memory of the previous day suddenly jolted him into life, and he struggled out from the piles of sacks where he had unwittingly spent the night.

In the semi-darkness, he could make out that he was surrounded by bales and crates and other containers, in some kind of warehouse or storage centre that seemed to sway to and fro. Focusing his eyes and listening for familiar sounds, he heard water lapping on the walls of the cellar, and thought the previous night's rain had worsened.

Stunned into reality, he realised he was on a moving ship. Finding it difficult to walk without stumbling, Archie headed towards the shaft of light coming from a trapdoor above him. He was too short to reach it, and struggled to climb onto piles of bales until he had a foothold to scale towards the gleam of light. With some difficulty, he opened the trapdoor just enough to wriggle out and roll onto a wooden floor... and found himself on the deck of a ship, well out at sea.

As Archie's eyes quickly adjusted to the light, the salt spray from the cold waves hit him in the face. His eyes nipping, he looked around, confused and frightened.

'Hoy!' called a voice. 'Hoy, you! Stowaway found over here, Captain,' the sailor hollered as he grabbed Archie by the collar and marched him unceremoniously to the wheel room.

Captain John Keller was a formidable man. Tall, unkempt and menacing, he was bare-shirted despite the cold, and a huge scar ran across his face, from one side to the other. His tattooed chest of a naked lady moved like a series of pictures as the giant man came towards the young boy.

'Stowing away on my ship, boy? That earns you a good whipping.'

Archie, terrified for his life, tried to explain about the events of the previous day that had led him to unintentionally board the ship. 'Please, sir, let me go,' he pleaded. 'I've got to find me sisters and brother. They're in the workhouse. Please turn the ship back. I've got to get off—'

He never finished the sentence. He felt a crack of a whip on his back. The pain was unbearable, but he was determined not to cry. Then he was thrown to the ground like one of the sacks he had slept on.

Biting back tears, Archie struggled to his feet. The swaying of the ship made it difficult for him to stand, much to the enjoyment of the crew who had gathered to watch the antics of a landlubber.

'Let you go?' laughed the Captain. 'You ain't getting off this ship 'til we dock in the Americas.'

'America?' screamed Archie as he attempted to stand.

'Aye, aye, we're heading to the great America. You're in for a long sail, boy.'

Archie sobbed inwardly, *Mam, I promise I'll get home and find them.*

With the entertainment over, the crew headed back to their duties. Dan, the First Mate, was instructed to set the stowaway to work for his passage. Less scary than the Captain and more approachable, the sailor felt some sympathy for the boy who looked reasonably clean and cared for, unlike the regular urchins who attempted to stow away.

'Follow me, young sailor,' he said kindly. 'Don't worry about the Captain. He won't bother you if you keep your 'ead down and work your passage. Right, first things first, let's find you a place to sleep… Over here, under those tarpaulins, it should be warm and dry and away from the worse of the spray. Now you've got to find your sea legs.' He smiled at Archie. 'Let's get you walking around the deck and set you to work your passage to the great America.'

'I can't go to America. Please,' Archie begged, 'ask the Captain to turn the ship around and let me get home to find me family. I've got to find me sisters and brother.'

Dan shook his head. 'Aw, lad, that ain't going to happen. We're on course for the great America. Content yersel, you can't change anything.'

Archie gave vent to his emotions and cried like he had never done before. Dan, not impervious to the young boy's plight, felt his heart go out to him. This was not one of the typical stowaways who looked for adventure by hiding among the cargo.

'Aw lad, there's naught to be done, so make the most of it,' he soothed. 'Don't upset yersel, it will only draw the Captain's attention and yer don't want that. Keep yer 'ead down and time will pass for ye.'

For the remainder of the voyage, Archie scrubbed the decks, followed Dan's instructions, and kept out of the Captain's sight. He tried to ignore his calloused hands that bled painfully as the journey progressed. Dan wrapped them in cloth that served only as a temporary relief, and brought food which Archie took to his den and devoured as only a growing boy could. His clothes, once spotless from Doris's handiwork were now ripped and filthy, his knees covered in cuts and bruises.

Dan had taken a liking to the young lad, and listened to his tale of sorrow, and his determination to get back to find his family. He was impressed by the boy's hard work around the ship.

After weeks of misery and what had felt like no end in sight to his miserable existence, Dan took him to watch as land appeared on the horizon.

'That, me lad, is the great America – the greatest country in the world from what I've seen in me travels around the globe. The land is further away than it looks, so we're on board for a few more days.'

'Have you been to faraway places, Dan?'

'All over the civilised world, near enough.'

Dan spent the remainder of the voyage regaling Archie with tales – some perhaps a figment of his imagination, but all hungrily absorbed by the inquisitive boy. The remaining days passed quickly, with Archie watching anxiously as they sailed nearer to land.

Eventually, the ship docked at New York. After helping to unload the cargo, Dan instructed Archie to stick close by him when they disembarked.

'It's a jungle out there at the docks. A lad like you could be trampled on or pushed about, or worse.'

Archie had no desire to know the 'worse'. He was unsteady on his feet, but laughed with Dan at his own clumsiness.

'You'll soon get your land legs back, young'un.'

'Can't I find me a ship that's going back to England and creep onboard?' Archie asked. 'I'd put up with a whipping to get home.'

'You won't get a ship going to England for months now. And if you get caught, you could be thrown overboard,' said Dan, hoping to prevent the boy from attempting anything foolish.

He sighed. 'Meantime, come with me to the lodgings, wot I use when I'm in America. Granny Peggy will see you're alright 'til we figure out what to do with you. I can't leave you to fend for yourself.'

8

Archie had no choice but to trust and follow Dan. The hustle and bustle of the docks had less attraction for him now that he had enough of ships and docks.

Dan held his arm and guided him through the horde of sailors who were anxious to reach town and taverns. The noise from the docks reminded the boy of what he'd witnessed in London, and he longed to be back home. The activity and speed of loading and unloading cargo no longer enthralled him, and he was confused by the workers' strange language.

'What are they saying, Dan? All that shouting seems to be a different language. Ain't they English?'

Dan laughed. 'There are sailors here from all over the world, young 'un, and what you're hearing most of is the American accent. They're speaking English but with a different accent.'

Archie frowned. 'Sounds kinda strange.'

Once free of the docklands, Dan pointed out various places to the awe-struck boy who had never heard of, or imagined, a skyscraper, let alone a city filled with the towering buildings that reached high towards the clouds. His neck was sore with craning to see the tops of the buildings, and he felt small, like a tiny insect. Had Dan not had a firm grip on him, he would have tripped over obstacles that lay scattered and abandoned on the ground.

The two walked for some time through busy crowded streets where people sat around on doorsteps conversing with neighbours. As they turned into one street, Dan pointed out the house where they were to stay.

'Over there, Archie, where the blue door is lives the cheeriest person in the world. Nothing upsets Granny Peggy. Come on, let's go.'

He opened the door with a clatter, dropped his bag noisily onto the floor and called out in a jolly voice, 'Granny Peggy, where are you? Your lovable rogue is home.'

They heard scurrying from the back of the house, and a few minutes later a tiny, smiling, rosy-cheeked woman – a mop of grey hair held in place with clips – came into view. She threw her arms around Dan, who lifted her off her feet and swirled her around.

The giggling woman was breathless as she called out, 'Put me down, you scoundrel, or I won't say I'm pleased to see you.'

Dan did as she asked. 'Granny Peggy, meet young Archie. Archie say how de do to Granny Peggy.'

Archie held out his hand to shake the woman's hand, but she drew him to her and gave him the biggest hug he'd had in a long time.

'Welcome, Archie, welcome to Granny Peggy's.' She looked at Dan. 'I guess this young man is gonna be a guest? Come on in and we'll get you guys fed. Looks like you haven't eaten a decent meal in weeks, and a good scrub in the tub won't do you any harm. Remember what I always say, Dan, cleanliness is next to godliness. We'll get those grubby clothes washed. You two would frighten the life outta the kids in this street.'

'And you sure do tell me that often, you old witch,' Dan laughed.

Archie stood where he was for a brief moment, taking in the warmth of the welcome. He felt a strange contentment as he gazed around the cosy house that seemed to stretch as far back as he could see. Any fears he'd had regarding the latest stage of his weird adventure were soon dismissed by the warmth and kindness of Granny Peggy and Dan.

Archie relaxed in the hot tub – a real luxury for him after weeks at sea. He'd almost fallen asleep when Dan hollered, 'Hey, water-boy, time up. Here's clean togs for you. They'll do until Peggy has your gear washed. It's time to eat.'

Aware of the rumbling in his belly, he dried off and dressed, then sat at the kitchen table to enjoy some welcome chowder and homemade bread. Over their food, the adults listened to Archie's story in his own words, without interrupting the boy's flow.

Peggy's soul ached with sorrow for the young lad, and she and Dan assured him that something would be worked out for his future return to England. She made up a bed for him in the back of the house near the kitchen, where the heat from the oven kept him warm. She fussed over him, mended his clothes, tended his cuts and bruises, and gave him a roof over his head.

Archie was enthralled with her accent, and remarked to Dan that Granny's voice sounded funny.

'We're in America now, lad, they all speak different from you and me,' Dan told him. 'You'll soon get used to it. Who knows, we might make an American out of you yet.'

'I don't want to be an American. I want to stay English and get home to me family,' Archie sobbed. The emotion and trauma of the past weeks overwhelmed him, and he gave into deep sorrow and heartache.

'Oh, poor kid.' Peggy hurried from the kitchen and hugged the boy whose sobs were now uncontrollable. 'Get it out your system,' she told him. 'You'll feel better after a good old cry.'

The young boy snuggled into her warm body and wept until he had no more tears to shed.

The following day, recovered from the voyage and feeling settled with Granny and Dan, Archie was shown around the city. Dan wanted to be sure the bemused boy knew how to get back to Peggy's house should they become separated. The pair seemed to walk for miles, but both relished the freedom to do so after their long sea voyage.

'This part of New York that we've come to,' explained Dan as they entered a rather salubrious area, 'is where the rich folk live and work.'

Archie's gaze took in the magnificence of the shops, houses, and hotels, his eyes widening in amazement. The two walked out most days to explore the vast city and to give Peggy a chance to rest.

'Get outta my sight, you rascals, and give a body peace to get on with my chores,' she laughed as she shooed them off with her broom.

Several weeks later, Dan left for a short voyage to the Hudson River, leaving Archie in the capable hands of Peggy. But he assured the boy he would make enquiries about finding a way of getting him back to England.

'I'll keep me ears and eyes open for news of sailings to England. Don't fret, we'll get you back as soon as we can.'

With a final warning to stay safe and to look after Peggy, Dan tousled the lad's hair and backslapped him heartily. Dan said little about his past, but Archie felt he had a story to tell.

While his friend was away, Archie's days were busy. He helped Peggy around the house, fetching and carrying things that were becoming too heavy for her. And he felt happy and secure in the care of an adult who seemed to take all the worries from his young shoulders.

'I ain't getting any younger and my old legs are slowing me down,' Peggy told the boy she had taken into her home and into her heart. 'You're a great help to me, Archie. Your mom, God rest her soul, would be proud of you.'

'Thank you,' Archie said with a smile. 'Yeah, my mam did her best for us.'

The image of his dying mother seldom left him; she was in his thoughts last thing at night when he prayed to whoever was listening. He wasn't sure if there was a God but thought it best to pray, just in case. *I'll find them, Mam. I will, and we'll be together again.*

'How did you and Dan get to know each other?' he asked Peggy one afternoon, as he helped her fold the laundry.

'It were a long time ago,' she began. 'My husband Alexander was a dock worker, and one day he fell into the water when he lost his footing and tripped over a rope that tied the ship up. His foot caught in the rope and he couldn't get free. The water was lapping around him and pushing the ship nearer and nearer to where he struggled to free himself. He thought he would be crushed to death.' Archie noticed a tear in the corner of her eye that ran into the crevice of her wrinkled face, as she continued, 'No-one could hear his screams over the noise going on around him but Dan, working nearby, spotted him. And with no fear for his own safety, he jumped in and saved Alexander then carried him on his own shoulders all the way here. He called around a few days later to enquire about him, and we kinda got to know about him and his travels. Alexander insisted that he base himself with us whenever he was in New York, and that's how it all started.'

'And your husband?' queried Archie, tentatively sensing that there was a sad ending to the story.

'His foot never healed right. It was almost severed by the rope. Gradually gangrene set in, and he didn't recover from the infection. He died almost a year to the day that Dan fished him out of the water. If it weren't for Dan, I wouldn't have had those last few months with my Alexander.'

Archie hugged the emotional lady and shared her pain at the loss of a loved one.

'Look at me, an old fool crying over spilt milk. Young Archie, you have a good heart and a good head on your shoulders. You're wise beyond your years.' She smiled through her tears. 'Come on, let's get going with this laundry then we'll have a cool drink and a cookie.'

9

Over the following months, Peggy gave him the confidence and freedom to come and go as he pleased, with a proviso that he returned home before dark. 'Otherwise,' she told him, 'I'll be outta my mind with worry.'

On one of his long walks and relishing the freedom to wander, Archie found himself once more in the salubrious part of the city Dan had shown him in his first few days. As he sauntered along, admiring shop windows that held goods he had never seen in his young life, and ignoring the steady rain, a limousine stopped nearby. Archie looked in awe at the vehicle; he could see his reflection in the shine.

A chauffeur stepped out and, with a flourish, opened the door to allow the passenger to exit the car. A tall, distinguished man with an air of confidence and authority walked to the door of a large hotel. He was well dressed, and his long coat had a fur collar that was buttoned high to keep out the winter chill. Archie ran after him.

'Sir, sir. Excuse me, sir,' he called out.

The chauffeur tried to push Archie away, but he continued shouting to the man, 'Sir. Sir!'

Pausing on the steps of the hotel, the smartly-dressed man turned to see what was happening.

'Leave the kid alone, Jackson,' he instructed. 'Bring him here.'

Archie, unfazed by the commotion, slowly approached the man. 'Sir, you dropped your wallet when you got out of the car.'

He handed the wallet over then turned to carry on with his walk, stopping suddenly when the gentleman called him back.

'Come here, kid. I want to thank you for that.'

When the man opened his wallet to take out some dollars, Archie's eyes widened. He had never seen as much cash in his life.

He shook his head. 'No, sir. No thanks are needed.'

Once more he went to walk on, but the man insisted he stop. By this time, the rain was started to fall more heavily.

'Come inside, before we are all soaked,' the man urged. 'I want to thank you properly.'

Archie hesitated, unsure of what to do. The man seemed friendly enough, and Archie's instinct told him he could trust him. The heavy downpour made the decision for him.

The man opened the door and led Archie into a palatial building – the entrance hall of the hotel would have filled Archie's street at home. The boy hesitated, unsure whether or not to proceed as he stood in awe and took in the scene before him. The foyer was bright and airy; chandeliers hanging from a high ceiling seemed to twinkle and dance and throw a kaleidoscopic display of light across the area.

Archie was mesmerised by the beauty of the statuettes raised on plinths that circled the lobby and enhanced the exquisite arena. There was a bustle of to-ing and fro-ing of staff and guests, and the boy watched in awe, his mouth wide open as he soaked in the atmosphere. He felt as if he had walked into an alternative world, one that would fold up and vanish before his eyes.

The gentleman smiled at his reaction and pointed to a seat in an alcove.

'Sit here a moment and let me say a proper thank you.'

A waiter arrived, as if from nowhere. 'What can I get you, sir.'

'My usual, Clint, and a soda for this young man here.' Turning to Archie, he said, 'Now then, tell me why you handed me my wallet instead of running off with it?'

Archie looked stunned at the question.

'But, sir, it wasn't mine to keep. It belonged to you. I saw you drop it when you got out of the car.'

The man looked at the lad in front of him and saw an honest boy; he read people well, and knew the young lad sitting there with eyes wide open was genuinely shocked at the suggestion that he would do anything other than return the wallet.

'You're an honest young man, and I like that in people. Tell me about yourself. But, firstly, let's get introduced.' He held his hand out. 'I am C.J. Croft and you are in my hotel.'

'Archie Connor, sir,' he replied as he stood to shake hands. 'This is *your* hotel? Gosh.'

The man smiled broadly. 'It is indeed. It's one of many that I have the honour of owning.' He was amused to find someone who had no idea of who he was. His photograph adorned posters promoting his empire, and few people had not heard of the entrepreneur, C.J. Croft.

'You're not from these parts, are you?' he asked. 'I detect an English accent, if I'm not mistaken. What brings you to Manhattan?'

'Manhattan?' questioned Archie. 'I thought I was in New York.'

C.J. Croft roared with laughter. 'You are a breath of fresh air. You must be new to the city. Where are your parents? Your mom? Your dad?'

At the mention of his mother, Archie choked back tears, determined not to weep in front of a stranger. He took a deep breath and quietly replied, 'Me mam died, sir; she were poorly and didn't get better. Me dad's a useless lout, me mam says. He got put in jail and died, and me family got put in the workhouse – well, all except me.'

While Archie continued with his tale, C.J. Croft remained silent, allowing the lad to speak uninterrupted. But he laughed out loud on hearing how Archie found himself at sea.

'You are a tonic, young man. Imagine waking up on the high seas!'

Archie shook his head. 'I was scared for my life, sir. I begged the captain to turn the ship back and get me home, but all I got was a whipping for stowing away and sailors making fun of me.'

C.J. Croft gently probed the lad to find out as much as he could about him. Oblivious to the man's greatness, Archie felt comfortable in his presence. He sat on the sofa, swinging his legs as he spoke, totally relaxed and unfazed by his surroundings.

'What do you plan to do, Archie Connor, now that you're here?'

'I'm going to get some work, maybe shine shoes or something, and save until I can get home to find me family. As soon as I've enough money, I'll get on a ship back to England. Dan says if I try to stow away they'll throw me overboard. I promised me mam that I'd keep the family together. I've got to get back soon.'

'Who is Dan?'

Archie explained about Dan and Granny Peggy. 'Dan looked after me on the ship and made sure I worked me passage, and he brought me food. He lodges with Granny

Peggy when he's in America, and she's looking after me 'til I've got enough money to get home to find me family.'

C.J. Croft send for food and watched as young Archie devoured the plate of sandwiches. He detected a confidence that belied the boy's age and experience of a life of poverty.

'I could use a smart lad like you,' he said. 'Would you like to work here in my hotel? If you work hard and save your wages it would help you buy a ticket home to England.'

Archie's eyes glowed as he looked around the grand foyer, taking in the exquisite furnishings, the walls adorned with paintings set in gold frames, the chandeliers that lit the room like a thousand stars. For a few moments he was stunned into silence.

'Well, young Archie Connor? What's it to be?' prompted the entrepreneur.

'Yes please, sir, I'd like to work here... if I'm any good. I'm only twelve, what could I work at?'

'I think you'll do well here. I will employ you and restrict your working hours. Now, finish your snack and we'll fetch this Granny Peggy of yours here to show her where you'll be living and working, and reassure her that you'll be well cared for with us. It won't all be work; we have education classes on Thursdays, and you'll have time off to go visit her. I want my staff to be as well educated as possible. I'll arrange for Jackson my driver to take you home and return with your belongings and Granny Peggy.' He smiled. 'I'm looking forward to meeting this woman. Will we give it a go, Archie Connor?'

The boy's eyes lit up as he looked around and almost reverently whispered, 'Oh yes, sir.'

10

The next few hours were a whirlwind for the young boy. Only a few months ago, he had slept on dirty, rough sacks on a ship's deck; now he snuggled into shiny leather seats, cocooned in a spacious car he could only dream of looking at from a distance. He smelt the leather upholstery and patted it reverently.

The chauffeur, Jackson, turned out to be a kind family man who took his job as CJ's bodyguard extremely seriously. He was impressed at Archie's honesty, and chatted to him throughout the journey, pointing out places of interest. The lad sat in awe, as he stretched his neck to get a better view; he felt he was dreaming and would soon wake up.

The arrival of the luxurious car caused quite a stir in Granny Peggy's street, with neighbours coming out of their homes to see who would emerge from the fancy vehicle.

'It must be a film star or someone real important,' remarked a neighbour.

'Or the President?' suggested another.

'I don't think the President would visit us, but it sure is someone important.'

Jackson climbed out, opened the door with a flourish and saluted his young passenger before following him to Granny's door. The onlookers gasped in amazement when they realised that it was Peggy's young lodger who had climbed from the sparkling limo.

Peggy, alerted by the commotion in the street, was stunned to see Archie beaming from ear to ear as he introduced his new friend.

'Granny Peggy, this is Jackson.'

'May we come in for a moment?' the chauffeur asked politely. 'I have a letter here for you from C.J. Croft.'

It took Peggy a few minutes to take in what was happening on her own doorstep. More and more people had gathered as rumours had spread that a celebrity was visiting.

The stunned woman invited them into her sitting room and searched frantically for her glasses. Her cheeks were red, not only from the heat from her stove where she had been preparing dinner, but from the excitement of seeing young Archie arrive home in such a posh car. Had it not been for the boy's beaming smile, she would have feared he had gotten himself into trouble.

She donned her glasses and, hand shaking, read the letter from the richest man in New York. She fingered the embossed writing paper with its hotel stamp and logo as if it were a sacred document, and read the arrangements. Should she approve, Archie was to live and work at the hotel.

'My, my, what a turn up. Oh my. C.J. Croft?' She said his name almost reverently, like God had visited. 'And I've to go meet him! Oh, my sainted aunt! Me, Peggy O'Mara, getting to meet the greatest man in New York. My heart's all a-flutter. I best go and wash my face and put my best frock on.'

Jackson and Archie laughed together at the flustered lady who insisted on serving them her home-made beef stew before heading off to make herself presentable. By the time the trio emerged from her house, the entire street – or so it seemed – had gathered to watch as Jackson opened the car door to allow his passengers to settle into the plush seats.

'Oh, my!' stuttered Granny Peggy as she inspected her new surroundings. 'Oh, my!'

It was as if she were incapable of saying anything else. She snuggled with Archie into the leather seats as Jackson drove off, pointing out, as he had done with Archie, the places of interest.

'Oh, my!' was all that was heard from the back seat.

When they arrived at the hotel after what Peggy later told Dan was a dream ride, Jackson indicated where they should wait while he summoned his boss. Like Archie, she was bemused and in shock as to what had transpired over the past few hours.

'Oh Archie, what's happened to bring you here?'

Before he could reply, the imposing figure of C.J. Croft approached, smiled at the mystified lady and introduced himself.

'C.J. Croft, ma'am, it's a pleasure to meet you. You must be Granny Peggy.'

Overcome with emotion, she shook hands and whispered, 'Peggy O'Mara, milord. Pleased to make your acquaintance, I'm sure.'

'Let's sit here and get to know each other.' He indicated a quiet area of the hotel lounge. 'That's a fine young man you have with you. I'm very impressed with him.'

Seated in the luxurious surroundings, sipping the best cup of coffee she declared she had ever had, the excited woman sat in awe as C.J. Croft, one of the world's richest men, requested her permission for Archie to live and work at the hotel.

'I'm aware that Archie is only a lodger in your establishment, but you appear to be the only adult in his life at the moment to give permission for him to work here. He is young and won't work long hours or be taken advantage of. I have an excellent housekeeper who will relish having Archie to fuss over.'

Peggy, somehow found her tongue, and relaxed as she and C.J. Croft discussed Archie's immediate future.

CJ warmed to the caring woman, as he had with her young charge. Satisfied that all was above board and that her newest lodger was keen to begin a new phase in his life, the entrepreneur took his leave of her, assuring her that she was welcome to visit the hotel at any time.

Greta, the housekeeper, was summoned and introduced to them both. Taking them on a tour of the establishment, she explained she would oversee Archie's welfare and immediately put Peggy at her ease. The pair were shown the accommodation area and introduced to some of Archie's work colleagues.

'He's a good, honest lad is Archie,' Peggy assured Greta. 'He won't give you any trouble.'

The housekeeper smiled. 'CJ took a shine to him because of his honesty. He'll be well looked after with us. We will send the limo for him a week from now.'

Still somewhat shocked at the whole experience, Peggy, with Archie, departed with Jackson to be driven home. *What a tale I have to tell Dan when he comes home,* she thought. The smooth ride home almost lulled her to sleep but, not wishing to miss a second of it, she fought fatigue.

Once more, her neighbours were out in force at the arrival of the limousine, and they watched as Jackson ushered them out of the car and graciously escorted them to her door, where he kissed Peggy's hand before departing.

'Oh my,' she said, as she settled in her armchair to relive the dream.

Archie, still stunned by events, managed to make coffee, which they both sat and drank in near silence until fatigue took over.

'It's like a dream, Archie,' she told him. 'Let's get you off to bed. We've a lot to discuss tomorrow.'

Archie headed for his snug bed and chuckled as he heard Peggy pottering around the kitchen, muttering again and again, 'Oh my.'

11

When Archie arrived to take up his new position, he was introduced to Jim, the head bell boy, who would help him settle in. They would share a room at the top of the building, and Archie was to learn to be a junior bell boy.

Although there was a few years' age difference, there was an instant rapport between them. Jim Belmont, or Jimbel as he was known because of his job, was to become a lifelong friend of the young boy and help with his learning. Tall and lanky with the potential of more growth to come, the older boy had a charming grin that endeared him to the guests.

That morning, they rode the elevator as far it would go, then walked two flights of stairs to their attic bedroom.

'This is where the live-in staff like us live,' Jimbel explained. 'Some folk travel in daily, but me and loads of others live on the premises. I don't have family now, so the arrangement suits me just fine. I used to live with my grandpa, but he died and I was sent here by the authorities who got me a job. It's my home now and I love it.' He grinned. 'I wouldn't want to be anywhere else. Every day is different, and there are lots of guests to attend to.'

A long corridor stretched the length of the entire hotel, with numerous rooms and bathrooms leading from it. Jimbel stopped at number seven and showed Archie where he was to sleep. After his voyage when he'd slept on the rough deck, Granny Peggy's corner bed had seemed like luxury, but now, looking around the boys' room, Archie felt as though he was in paradise. Three well-spaced beds looked inviting, a long cupboard served as a wardrobe, and a table and some chairs sat in the window area with a view over the roof. The entire room looked welcoming to the young boy whose life had been totally turned on its head within a period of a few months.

'Gosh,' he said. 'This is nice. Who has the third bed?'

'No-one now. People come and go. The guy who had that bed was dismissed for stealing from a guest, something CJ does not tolerate. The other bed was Timmy's – a lad from the country who couldn't cope with city life and had to leave. He was afraid of his own shadow, and when any of the guests spoke to him he stammered and stuttered and generally fled in tears,' explained Jimbel.

'Mr Croft is keen for all his staff to be educated, especially in reading and counting. He says education is for everyone in society, not only for the rich. He's a good man is CJ, as we call him. If you work hard and keep out of trouble, you'll do just fine here.'

Archie considered what had been said about education.

'I'd like to be able to read and write and send a letter home to England, to let Doris and Stan know where I am. I learnt to read and write in the poor school, but not enough to write a proper letter.'

'Hey, I can help you with that,' offered Jimbel. 'I'm good at my ABCs. Right, we've to go to Greta for your uniform, and you can tell me later about this Doris and Stan.'

They made their way down two flights of stairs and rode the elevator to the basement, where Archie had a quick tour of the area before heading to the sewing room where several girls and ladies were busy with various tasks of sewing and mending. They located Greta in an office where she was working on some alterations to a uniform to fit the latest diminutive employee.

'Ah, perfect timing. I've finished altering this uniform. Looks like it might be a perfect fit. We don't usually have such small guys to cater for.' She laughed. 'CJ must have taken a shine to you. Go behind that door there and try this on.'

Archie fumbled with the unfamiliar style and fabric but eventually emerged, to the delight of Greta and Jimbel.

'Wow, you sure look the part. The guests will love you,' gasped Greta, as she helped with some tricky buttons. 'You look just swell. The guests will adore you. Right, slip it off again, I need to sort these buttonholes then off you go with Jimbel. You shadow him, follow him, and copy his way of working. You'll soon learn the trade. My only worry is, will you be tall enough to reach the elevator buttons?'

They laughed at the image of Archie jumping to press the buttons.

'We'll get a box for him,' declared Jimbel, then led his young charge through a maze of kitchens, laundry, storerooms, and other areas essential for the smooth running of the hotel. As they passed through each area, the older boy introduced him to various staff. They all seemed delighted to welcome the tiny bellboy into the hotel family.

'He's cute,' remarked one.

'He's adorable,' said another.

It looked as though there were several of the female staff keen to mother the youngster already.

'I'll never remember all those names,' sighed Archie. 'There's hundreds of them.'

Jimbel laughed. 'You'll soon catch on. Some you won't see very often, as we'll be in a different part of the building. But you'll get to know the ones we see every day.'

That night, Archie lay on his comfortable bed, mulling over the events in his life that had brought him to this new adventure. As he nodded off, his nightly prayer once again ran through his thoughts: *Mam, someday I'll find our Ruby and Betsy and our Nipper, and we'll be together again. I promise.*

*

Months turned to years. Six years had passed since Archie first set foot in America. During that time, Dan came and went from his various sea voyages, and captivated Peggy and Archie with his adventures.

'Did you come across any more stowaway ragamuffins?' enquired Peggy as she roared with laughter at Archie's guilty face. The three were gathered in her cosy kitchen on one of Archie's free days.

'None of the calibre of this tough guy,' chuckled Dan. 'There was one lad who got scared and tried to jump into the sea once or twice. He had to be confined for the entire journey.'

'I'm sure glad you didn't bring him home with you,' said Peggy. 'I've enough excitement from this lovable rogue to last me a lifetime. Come on, Archie, tell Dan about your work and the guest with all that jewellery.'

Granny Peggy continued to fuss over her charges while she and Dan listened to Archie's tales of life in the luxurious hotel.

'Who would have thought that a stowaway from all those years ago would end up working in such an imposing building,' said Dan, and he hugged his young friend, amazed at how much he had sprouted in height. 'I'm so proud of you, Archie.'

'Thanks, Dan. If it wasn't for you, I don't know where I'd be.'

'Probably at the bottom of the sea,' added Granny Peggy, smiling warmly at the two young men who had brought her so much joy.

At times, Archie looked deep in thought, and his friends knew to leave him with his memories. The young man was remembering the Christmas of 1914, when Doris and Stan had given them a memorable experience, and renewed his vow to find his family.

'You thinking of your folks, Archie?' Peggy ventured after a while.

Archie nodded. 'Yeah, I guess I should be thinking of going back to look for them now that the war in Europe is over. I'd love to bring them here and give them a good life.' He sighed as he stood to help Peggy clear the table.

'Honey, if that ever happens, you all have a home here with me until you get them settled.'

Overcome, Archie hugged the kind woman who had taken him under her wing, and whom he looked upon as another substitute mother.

12

The days and evenings passed quickly with them catching up on each other's lives, before both had to return to work – Dan to faraway shores, and Archie to C.J.'s hotel. He had settled to a life of good food, a warm bed, friends, and plenty of dollars, which he stored away for the intended passage to England.

A spurt of growth drew much tut-tutting from Greta as she regularly adjusted his uniform.

'At this rate, Archie, I'll be running out of material,' she teased as she made yet another alteration.

Regular guests adored the young English boy and asked especially for him on their return visits. In his early days, they were amused to watch him stand on a tiny step to reach the elevator buttons, and impressed by his ability to handle the luggage trolley.

His smile earned him many friends and a considerable amount of dollars to add to what he called his 'going home fund'. With very little expenditure, he had amassed a considerable amount; enough, he reckoned, to buy a passage home and provide for his siblings until he found work.

Over the years his cockney dialect had modified slightly as he picked up American words. And he relished learning. His first attempt at letter writing, with help from Jimbel, was to

Stan and Doris. He related his adventures, ensuring them he was safe and would be returning to collect his family and find a safe home for them. He had no idea of the devastation of his homeland, nor the destruction and hardship caused by war. Every hour he worked helped him to save generous tips that rich guests insisted on giving to 'the sweet English boy'.

C.J. Croft, on one of his regular visits to the establishment, made a point of seeking Archie out for a chat. Many of the great man's employees found themselves dumbstruck when he approached them, but Archie was comfortable in his presence.

'I have some news for you,' CJ told him. 'I told you I would investigate what happened to your family, didn't I? The manager of my London hotel, Oscar Nash, is making enquiries on my behalf and hopes to find out where your siblings are living. He will contact me as soon as he has information.'

'Thank you, sir. I wouldn't know where to start.'

Months passed before Archie was called to CJ's office one day to be given the latest update from his London colleague.

'Archie, it appears your sisters have been in the same area all these years,' his employer revealed. 'It wasn't Holborn as you thought, but Poplar.'

Archie shook his head in amazement. 'But that's near where we lived!'

He beamed with delight as CJ handed him an address where Ruby and Betsy had been since the day they were removed from the home of Doris and Stan Young. He was unaware then that, due to war damage, they had been relocated several miles further away.

'Unfortunately, there is no word yet as to the whereabouts of your brother, but don't be downcast,' said CJ, as he noticed the look of sadness cross the young lad's face. 'Don't despair, young man, my colleague is still making enquiries. You must understand that life has been difficult in England during the war years, as I'm sure you are aware. It's not easy to locate a six-year-old orphan with only a surname. London is full of children like your brother.

'As soon as I have more news, I will contact you immediately,' he assured his popular young employee. 'Keep saving your dollars and I'm sure we will be waving you off to England before long.'

'Thank you, sir. I'm saving every dollar. I want to travel comfortably, not like the way I arrived.' He laughed at the memory of that journey. 'And I need to have enough money to return here with my family. Granny Peggy has offered to look after them until I find a place for us to stay.'

CJ admired the youngster's resolve, which had never wavered since their first meeting. 'That's an ambitious plan, Archie Connor, and I wish you every success. Never let go of your dreams, my boy, and I'm sure we will see you back here. Remember, your job will always be open for you, but until then,' he smiled, 'get off with you and look after my guests.'

It was several more months before Archie was called to the office to accept a telephone call.

'It's from CJ,' said an excited Greta. 'He is in Washington on business but wishes to speak with you. He has something to tell you.'

Archie was in awe of the telephone machine; he'd observed it from a distance but never had cause to use it, although he'd watched guests use the ones placed around the hotel lobby. He was puzzled how someone could speak into the mouthpiece and at the same time listen to someone talking at the other end.

Yet here he was, holding such an instrument to his ear and hearing CJ's voice as clearly as if he were in the room with him. The handset was heavy, and he used both hands to steady it as he listened.

'Archie, I have an address of an establishment in London where an orphan boy by the name of Herbert Connor lived during the early part of the war, but no longer resides there,' his boss told him. 'We may be clutching at straws, so don't get your hopes up. It will be a starting point in your search for your brother. Now, my secretary has written down details for you, and also information of a ship leaving for England in two weeks. Once there, you've to go to the address on the paperwork and make yourself known to Oscar Nash, who will guide your quest as much as he can.' He paused briefly before adding, 'But be prepared for it to be a long search in difficult times.'

The young man, startled at hearing his voice appear to echo throughout the room, could only reply, 'Thank you, sir. Thank you.'

Archie was elated at the thought of returning home and being reunited with his sisters. And he was determined to remain in England until he had news of the now six-year-old Nipper.

The next few weeks were a frenzy of activity for him, with Greta sewing and mending clothes and generally fussing over him.

'You don't want to arrive in bell boy outfit, now do you?' She wiped a tear from the corner of her eye as she put together suitable attire for the lad whom she had taken to her heart. *I'm gonna miss that guy,* she admitted to herself.

Jimbel produced a valise left over by a guest who had instructed him to dispose of it as it no longer served any purpose.

'This will do just fine for the man about town that you're gonna be,' he told Archie. He, too, had a heavy heart at the impending parting.

Before long, and with mixed feelings, Archie said goodbye to Jimbel and the hotel staff who had been his family for the past six years.

Struggling to keep his emotions in check, Jimbel said, 'Now, you remember to write to me, buddy. I taught you your ABCs, so use them well and write me as soon as you have news.'

Archie hugged him and, through blurred vision, replied, 'I sure will. I sure will.'

'Come back soon to us,' chorused some of the staff who had gathered in the foyer to see him off.

With a last glance at the imposing building that had become so familiar to him, Archie headed off to say goodbye to Granny Peggy. While happy at his news, she wondered if she would ever see him again.

'Now, you be sure to come back here with your family,' she told him in no uncertain terms. 'There will always be a home for you all.'

Overcome by his own emotions, and a little anxious of what lay ahead, he nestled into her shaking body and wept with her.

'Say 'bye from me to Dan,' he said, choking back his sobs. 'I was hoping he'd be back before I left.'

With a last wave to Peggy, and filled with trepidation, he left for the port where he was to board a ship to England. It felt strange to be leaving the country he had grown to love, and he wondered if he would ever see these shores again.

13

He presented his ticket at the booking desk and had his paperwork duly stamped. As the clerk handed back Archie's passage ticket, he whistled in surprise as he remarked, 'You must be mighty important. You've been upgraded from steerage to a four-berth, paid for by none other than the million-dollar man, C.J. Croft himself. He gave instructions that you were to be given all meals during your passage to England. You related or something?'

'Yeah, a close friend,' replied the smiling Archie. He collected his paperwork and luggage and headed to the waiting ship, determined to write to his mentor as soon as he landed in England. He was in awe of the great man's generosity.

The Archie Connor who boarded the ship as a confident, determined young man who knew what he wanted in life and would stop at nothing to fulfil his dreams, was very different from the sleepy, bedraggled boy who had found himself unwittingly sailing to America.

He located his cabin and found he was to share with another passenger – a rather rotund man of about fifty, with receding hair. A merchant salesman, well used to sailing between New York and England on business, he introduced himself as Rooney O'Hara. 'Known to all as Roon,' he said, as he shook hands with Archie.

'The steward tells me we are to have this cabin to ourselves, with plenty room to spread out,' he continued, barely stopping for breath. 'I often had to share with three others. It gets a bit cramped, and not all travelling companions are the best of roommates, what with, snoring and filthy habits. It can be quite nauseating at times, which is why I spent more time on deck—'

'Archie Connor, sir, delighted to make your acquaintance,' interrupted the young lad, hoping to stop the flow of chat. 'I'm sure we'll do just fine. Which bunk would you recommend that I take?'

'Ah, a polite gent, that's delightful. I'm sure we'll have a pleasant journey. Here, why don't you inhabit the top, my aging bones find it difficult to climb... I remember one voyage—'

His story was interrupted by a knock at the cabin door, and there to Archie's delight stood a grinning Dan.

'Oh Dan, what a surprise to see you here,' the youngster said, grinning. 'You didn't tell me you were sailing on this ship.'

'I wanted to see your face. I swore Granny Peggy to secrecy, and she managed to keep quiet, surprisingly enough. We'll be sailing together once again,' laughed Dan, remembering the memory of the voyage when Archie Connor entered his life.

'Great to see you, Dan, I'm over the moon.' Archie paused. 'Hey, where are my manners? Let me introduce you to my cabin mate.'

Dan shook his head. 'No need, Archie. Roon and I have met several times; he crosses the Atlantic more often than most. I was able to secure a cabin for you both, knowing that you will be excellent company for each other. It will make the journey go quicker.'

The three chatted for some time before Dan excused himself to attend to his duties.

'We'll be sailing in ten minutes. I'll catch you later. Good to see you, Archie, and you too, Roon.'

The six-week voyage passed quickly for Archie, who spent most of his time on deck savouring the sea air and tasting the salt from the spray. He kept himself fit by walking around the deck, increasing his speed and building stamina as the days went by.

His cabin mate turned out to be a very knowledgeable man who listened without interruption to Archie's life story and his search for his siblings. Showing him the paper with the information as to their whereabouts, Archie was delighted that Roon was familiar with the area in question.

'Be prepared to see lots of wreckage and devastation in the capital,' the older man warned. 'The war took its toll on poor old London town, and it won't be the same London you once knew. This part here,' he pointed to the address where Archie hoped his brother might be found, 'this here area was almost totally wiped out, so brace yourself for a shock. Have you anyone to help your search?'

Archie explained the assistance he expected to have from Oscar Nash, and that he had been instructed to go directly to him when he arrived in London.

'Oscar Nash and C.J. Croft?' Roon's eyes widened in surprise. 'My, my, you sure mix in high places. Oscar Nash runs the biggest, most expensive store and hotel in London. I can only afford to look in the window of that store.'

Archie saw little of Dan on the voyage, but on the rare occasions when they met, he enjoyed conversing with him. He was sad to realise that he would more than likely not see his friend again once the ship docked at Tilbury.

'Now, you know how to get into London, don't you?' Dan asked. 'It's a long way from where we dock – over twenty miles and many hours of travelling – and I'd be happier knowing you were safe.'

'I'll be fine, Dan. Roon has promised to travel with me, and once in the city he'll set me on the right road to Oscar Nash, where CJ says I've to go directly. I'm anxious to get the girls from the workhouse, but Oscar Nash is expecting me, so I'll do as requested. You know, when I first met Roon, I thought I was in for a boring time, but he's been great to talk to.'

Dan laughed. 'That's why I arranged for you two to share a cabin. I didn't want you squashed in with some of the other passengers and not have room to move.'

'You're a good friend, Dan. I'll miss you.' Archie unashamedly hugged the man who had looked out for him ever since his strange encounter on board a ship to the unknown. 'I've been blessed to know you. I'll write to you, Dan, when I have news to tell.'

'I ain't much of a reader, but Granny Peggy will help me out if you keep it simple. No big words, mind,' he laughed as he helped Archie pack his luggage. 'You've got nice clothes here. Look after them.'

'I will. Greta made them for me.'

Knowing it was almost time to part company, they made small talk to spare the pain of separation.

The ship docked in a foggy, damp Tilbury in the early hours of a dull English day. Archie's stomach was full of butterflies as he disembarked into the gloomy port.

'We won't get transport to London for a few hours,' explained Roon, 'so let's go get ourselves some food and get out of the dampness. Oh, I've forgotten how dismal and smoky England is, and I need to find my land legs again after those weeks at sea.'

Archie remained quiet, his thoughts taking him deep into his memories of home, his dying mum, his useless, now-deceased da, his sisters and the Nipper. *I'm home, Mam,* he thought to himself. *I'll find them and keep us together forever.*

Roon led him to a tavern where they drank porter and ate a hearty, if somewhat greasy breakfast, before travelling on to the capital.

The journey from Tilbury was long and uncomfortable, at times on foot, and by various other means – at one point, the affable Roon managed to persuade a travelling farmer to allow them to ride with him. On arrival in London, Archie was sad to be parting company with his travel companion, who pointed him in the right direction to the West End where he was to locate Oscar Nash.

'You can ride on the omnibus and save yourself a trek,' explained Roon. 'It's quite a distance to the posh end of the town.'

'Thanks, Roon, but I think I'll walk a bit and stretch my legs after the sea voyage.'

With a firm handshake, the two parted company.

14

Archie had other plans. Before he searched for Oscar Nash, he wanted to find his former street and discover the fate of his neighbours, the Youngs. Roon had prepared him for what lay ahead, describing the bomb damage and destruction in the area, but it had only made him more determined to know how Stan and Doris had fared during the war years.

He trundled on, stepping over bricks and debris that had once been homes to many Eastend residents. The destruction disorientated and saddened him, and he had to stop to consider which direction he should be walking. There were no noticeable landmarks that touched on the memory of the twelve-year-old boy who had fled in terror six years ago.

The sky was gloomy, darker than he remembered, and he shivered, unsure whether it was from the cold or the emotional thoughts and memories rampaging around his head. A vagrant, or so it seemed to Archie, was sitting by a pile of debris, lost in a world of his own. On seeing the well-dressed youth, the man asked politely if he could help.

'You looking for something, lad? Don't think I'm being nosy, but I've been watching you walk up and down. You searching for somewhere or someone?'

Archie warily approached the man, but up close he appeared less frightening than at first, and seemed genuinely trying to help.

'Thanks, sir. Yes, I've been abroad – just docked a few hours ago – and I'm trying to find the street where I once lived. I was only a kid when I left and haven't seen anything that reminds me of it.'

'You don't need to call me, sir. I'm Jake. Pleased to make your acquaintance, young fella.'

'And you, too. Archie Connor,' he said, as he shook hands.

Jake stood, dusted himself and exclaimed, 'Archie Connor? Not Elsie and Bertie's boy?'

Archie felt his heart skip a beat. 'Yeah.'

'Good God, man. Everyone thought you had drowned or summat when you ran away. Don't you remember me? Jake Border. I was one of the chaps who helped your da home from the Frog and Pond the night your dear mam passed away.' A weary smile broke across the man's face. 'I recognise you now, you look like Elsie. Where've you been? You seem to have done well, going by the clothes you're wearing.'

'I remember you, yeah,' Archie nodded. 'You and some others got my da home in time for Mam to say goodbye. I've been in America, Jake. It's a long story. Can we go somewhere, and I'll buy us something to eat and catch up on things?'

Archie realised that there must be a reason for Jake to look so dishevelled.

The older man shook his head. 'I'm not one for taking charity, thanks all the same. But it does my heart good to see you.'

'Look on it as thanks for getting me da home,' Archie offered again, 'and I'm kinda hungry. Wouldn't mind a bite to eat.'

'In that case, okay. There's not much around here, but if you don't mind a bit of a walk, there's a place where they serve good grub and let the likes of me in.'

It was obvious that Jake lived from hand-to-mouth, and as he ate uninterrupted, Archie told of his adventures from running off to look for his family to landing in America and returning home to London.

'I've got to find our Ruby and Betsy,' he explained, 'and our Nipper.'

Jake finished his meal and told Archie of events during the war that had devastated so many lives.

'Our street took a direct hit. Many of the tenements, like your mam's, were already closed and unoccupied, but others like the Youngs were not so lucky. The house was destroyed, but thankfully they were in the safety of the shelter of the underground where most people had gone when the wretched sirens that we all dreaded went off. Sadly, their daughter Mabel's wee nipper, a girl of about four, was buried in the rubble.' He paused briefly before adding, 'They dug her tiny body out with bare hands.'

'Oh Jake, that's so awful. What about Stan and Doris, did they survive?'

'They did, lad, but they took the wee one's death hard. We all had to suffer in those awful days. They were rehoused in a terraced street not far from here. I'll show you when we've finished here.'

'And you, Jake, what happened to you and why are you living on the streets?'

'Ah, Archie lad, I'm not living on the street. I've got a bed in a men's hostel along the road from here, but I can't stand being indoors among broken and scared people. So I come out each day and sit where you saw me, where my house used to be. I sit with my memories then I go back to the hostel in the evening.' The man's voice cracked with emotion, 'I lost everything when a bomb fell on my house. My wife Nellie, and our two sons, our Bobby and our Timmy, died together in the blast. I've never forgiven myself for not being there to protect them. I was out searching for work when the siren went off and I took shelter. I'll never get over losing my family, and as a single homeless person I don't qualify yet for a house. It's families first.'

Archie was genuinely shocked to hear the man's heart-breaking story. 'Oh Jake, I'm sorry.'

Jake finished his drink and stood up. 'Thanks for the food, lad. Let's not sit here getting more morose. Come on and I'll show you where to find Stan and Doris.'

As they made their way through the ruined streets, Jake pointed out places known to Archie but which were now simply piles of rubble. 'Over there was the Frog and Pond,' he explained. 'All gone now.'

They parted company after Jake pointed out the building where the Youngs now lived, and Archie thanked him and promised to look him up.

'You'll find me where you saw me today,' the older man told him. 'Good luck, lad, with your search for your family.'

He did not hold out much hope for Archie's chance of finding his siblings, and was pretty sure the search would be in vain, but he did not want to deflate the young lad's dreams.

Archie watched the man shuffle off back to the rubble where he felt close to his lost family. Jake was broken and trodden, but Archie recognised a steeliness of character that he himself possessed, and felt sure the older man would rise like a phoenix to rebuild some sort of life for himself.

15

Archie turned his attention to his surroundings. He was in a long street of dark, dismal, terraced, Victorian-style flats, where it seemed several families displaced by the bombing had been rehoused. At number 5, where Jake told him he would find the Youngs, he hesitated before climbing into the semi-darkness of the building. It looked grim. Paint peeled from the walls that ran with dampness; any attempt by the twelve families housed there to keep the area clean, was having little effect.

He climbed to the third floor as instructed, and was faced with four doors, with no indication of which one housed the Youngs. He hesitated. Something in the recess of his mind triggered a memory of his time with them when Doris, despite poverty, cleaned her house until it shone. Archie smiled as he noticed that one door, the one on the right, was cleaner than the others. Someone had made an effort.

He knocked loudly with a clear purpose in mind and waited, shifting from one foot to the other with excitement. After a few minutes, the door opened to reveal Stan Young, older looking than Archie had expected. Behind him, looking from a door off the hallway, was Doris.

Archie smiled at the couple, who looked bemused at the well-dressed youth standing at their door.

Stan eventually spoke. 'Can I help you?'

Archie smiled, and before he could reply, a scream emanated from Doris, who rushed towards the door.

'Archie? Is it really you? Our Archie?'

Stan, as if emerging from a dream, whispered, 'Archie? Archie Connor?'

He nodded. 'Yes, here I am, safe and sound.'

Before he could utter another word, Doris hugged him as she pulled him indoors.

Stan, now more alert to what was going on, held him close and exclaimed, 'Oh Archie! We thought you were dead.'

Doris burst into tears as she studied the youth who was grinning from ear to ear.

The next few hours proved to be a whirlwind of hugs, tears, and a little laughter as they renewed acquaintances and listened to how life had changed for each of them over the past few years. Stan and Doris listened in awe as Archie regaled them of his American adventures.

As the young lad spoke, Stan saw a confident, assured man, a far cry from the twelve-year-old waif who had run from their home in terror such a long time ago.

'Archie, it's so good to see you alive and well, and looking prosperous,' he told the lad. 'We searched everywhere for you. Some of the dockworkers teamed up and divided the area into who would search where. It went on for days, until they called it off, thinking you had drowned, but we never believed that. A pieman near the docks remembered seeing you heading for the water. Oh, Archie, I can't believe you are here. Your mam would have been so proud of how you've turned out.'

'I don't think so.' Archie held his head in his hands as memories came flooding back. 'Mam asked only one thing of me, to keep the family together. And what did I do? I've let her down.'

Doris wiped her tears at the sadness she saw in the eyes of the lad who looked so like his mam that it almost took her breath away.

'Don't think like that,' she scolded kindly. 'You did what you thought was right by trying to find them; you didn't run away. But what an adventure you've had, and what a tale you have to tell your family! America! Oh, Archie, it does my heart good to see you. Here you are safe and well, and the image of your mam. I presume you will be looking for the others?'

'That's why I'm here, Doris. It took me a long time to gather enough money to afford a ticket back to England. Now I need to find our Ruby and Betsy and our Nipper, and I need to find a job and a place to keep them safe.'

'There will always be a home with us, Archie, for all of you, until you get yourself organised,' commented Stan as he stood and hugged the youngster.

Archie was overcome with emotion, and sobbed as memories came flooding back, memories mixed with sadness and joy.

'Don't worry about where to stay, but finding work might be tricky,' Stan told him. 'So many men have returned from the war, and jobs are in short supply. It's a miracle to see you sitting here, and what an adventure you've had. America!'

Archie saw the strain on both their faces from the experience that war had inflicted. Doris's once fair hair was now tinged with grey, her flawless skin showed signs of aging and stress, her eyes depicted a deep sadness. Stan appeared to have lost height; he stooped as if in pain, and his face, like Doris's, was etched with sorrow. As Doris fussed over Archie in her usual way and prepared a meal, the couple spoke of the horrors of war.

Stan began, 'We lived in fear of bombs and dreaded the loud wailing sound of the sirens, as they shattered the little peace that we had. We lived on our nerves, never knowing when we would have to run to the nearest shelter – in our case, the underground across the road. We had to run like the devil was after us – and in a way, he was – to get under cover before the bombs fell.'

Doris added, 'We had a basket by the door with supplies and blankets ready to pick up and run. You had to be prepared; there was no time to gather things together. Preparation was essential for survival, as you never knew how many hours you would be in the shelter. Our Mabel and her three nippers lived with us, but you knew that when we had to let you go.' She paused briefly, before adding, 'It always grieved us that we couldn't keep you all and find space on the floor. But it wasn't possible. It almost broke my heart.'

Doris stopped speaking and, overcome with emotion, wept into the tea towel that she held in her hand. Stan took up the story.

'Archie, we lost our four-year-old Beryl, Mabel's youngest, when the house took a direct hit. It was 1916. She had her third birthday on September 1st, and we gave her a doll. The siren sounded, and we gathered everyone together and ran downstairs. Outside in the street, Beryl yelled that she'd left her dolly. She pulled her hand free from Mabel's grasp and ran back to the house… just… as the building collapsed around her.'

Stan could not continue. Tears filled his eyes as he recalled the horror of that night. Doris took over.

'Stan told us to run for shelter while he ran back and pulled boulders and rubble away in an effort to find the babe. A rock fell onto him and almost broke his back. He's not been able to stand properly and is in constant pain.'

'Oh Stan, how awful. And the little girl?' asked Archie. 'What happened?'

'It was three days before they could get her broken body out of the rubble. The neighbours and complete strangers helped move stones, but we knew she wouldn't survive. It broke our Mabel's heart, and she was never the same again. Bill, her man, was away fighting the very people who had killed his child. When the war ended, he came home to hear the news of the baby – as she was when he left. I'll never forget his face when he realised that he would never see her again. What with the horrors of what he saw at the front and the tragedy of little Beryl, as well as trying to cope with Mabel who had withdrawn into herself, it was enough to send him loopy. And he ended up in an army hospital at the coast.

'Our Mabel gave herself a shake and moved there with their other two nippers. She won't ever come back here; there's too many memories. So we don't see them very often, due to the difficulties of travelling, and Stan can't sit for any length of time on the omnibus seats.' She smiled sadly. 'We write to each other regularly, though. We think we've made our last trip; it was too uncomfortable for Stan.'

At the mention of writing, Archie asked, 'So you didn't get my letter? I learned to read and write, and the first letter I penned was to you to let you know what had happened to me.'

She shook her head. 'Oh, Archie love, we never got any letter. Times were difficult, and letters seldom arrived. The only thing that did get through were telegrams telling people bad news. When we hadn't heard anything of you, we feared you were dead. Some of the neighbours helped Stan search the streets for you. It's a miracle that you're here now.'

Archie told them of his instructions to locate Oscar Nash, who had information for him about his family.

'I need to get there soon, then start looking for our Ruby and Betsy and our Nipper.'

The couple insisted he stay with them and base himself there.

'Archie, I don't want to discourage you,' Stan told him, 'but you need to prepare yourself for a long search. Things are different now. People have been displaced, families torn apart by war. It may be a harder task than you think. I want to warn you not to build your hopes up too much. I hope God will lead you to your family, I really do.' He bowed his head to hide the hot tears that filled his eyes as he thought of what might lie ahead for the young man.

Doris, looking at the two desolate males, attempted to lighten the despair that hung like a veil of depression in the room.

'Don't be too disheartened until you know what's what,' she said. 'We have a spare room now, with two big beds that our Mabel used. They are there for you, and when you find the others there's a bed here for them all. God bless you, Archie. You look exhausted. Off to bed with you, and you can carry on with your business tomorrow after you've recovered from your travels. We'll talk some more in the morning.'

Archie smiled and got up to hug Doris. 'That's a kind offer to take us all in again like you did when Mam died. I'd like to say yes please until I find somewhere for us to be together as a family. You are so kind.' He reached into his pocket and drew out some money. 'Please take this for food and whatever you need for my family.'

Stan looked shocked, 'Oh lad, we can't take your money. You'll need it for the future.'

Archie pleaded, 'I saved most of my wages. Please, let me pay my way.'

Stan realised that the lad was determined, and did not want to rob him of his pride.

'Okay, you win, Archie,' he said. 'We'll only use what we need and return the rest. Agreed?'

'Agreed.'

He hugged them both and followed Doris to his room.

*

Next morning, over breakfast Stan explained that despite his injuries he had been retained by the shipping company as a part-time office clerk.

'It's not quite what I was used to, but it's work, and it brings in money,' he said. 'Between that and Doris taking in some sewing and mending, we get by.'

With clear instructions from Stan as to how to get to the area of London that he was unfamiliar with, Archie set off with mixed feelings. He was relieved to have found his friends but sad at their loss of a grandchild. Jake's fate also preyed on his mind, and he thanked his lucky stars that he had not been in the country during the war years.

But Stan's words of warning lay heavy in his heart as he walked tentatively through the destruction of the city. He knew now it wasn't going to be easy to find his family, but his thoughts kept returning to his mother's dying wish. *Mam, I'll find them, I promise.*

16

O scar Nash, manager and director of one of the largest hotels and department stores in the country, stood by the bay window of his office and looked out at the London gloom. There were signs of war damage everywhere, with some establishments even in such a salubrious area closed and boarded. Nowhere seemed to have escaped the devastation of war.

He shook his head at the wanton destruction, and asked himself: *For what?* Some said it was the war to end all wars. A war where millions lost their lives in god-forsaken lands they had never heard of, and for what? Maimed and broken men wandered around the city searching for work. Many had lost their homes; wives had moved on, some with other men when they feared their men were never to return, or simply grasped an opportunity to pick up life with a wage-earner and be secure once more.

Oscar Nash did his best to help where he could, but there was a limit to how many people he could employ. He instructed kitchen staff not to throw out food waste, but to make it available to those in need. There was always a steady stream of grateful men seen at the side door of the hotel.

Emitting a deep sigh, borne of frustration and anger, he returned to his desk and the task in hand. He was a kindly man who appreciated his privileged life and wished to help those less fortunate than himself.

Outside, Archie stood on the pavement and looked at the building where he was to report. He could see it too had not escaped the ravages of war. In the window was a large notice proclaiming business as usual during repairs, and pieces of masonry lay where they fell.

Once inside, he made enquiries as to where he would find Oscar Nash. He was respectably dressed, carried himself well, walked with confidence, was polite and articulate, and determined not to deviate from his objective.

'Mr Nash doesn't see people without an appointment,' replied a rather severe-looking receptionist in answer to Archie's request. 'May I ask the nature of your business?'

She was ready to dismiss him as yet another hopeful looking for employment until Archie introduced himself.

'Archie Connor, ma'am. I have a letter of introduction for Oscar Nash from my former employer, C.J. Croft of New York.'

The receptionist studied the youth and held out her hand to take the envelope from him.

'It's marked private, ma'am.'

The woman who prided herself in protecting her boss from unannounced visitors, reddened as she pressed a button that connected her directly to Oscar Nash.

'Yes, Irene?'

'Sir, I have a young man here by the name of Archie Connor with a letter of recommendation from Mr Croft.'

'Ah, I've been expecting him. Bring him in right away and order tea and biscuits. I don't want to be interrupted while my visitor is here.'

She escorted Archie up the main staircase to a carpeted area that spoke of prosperity. The corridor walls were decked with paintings of country scenes that gave a warmth to the area. Reaching a door marked with the name of the occupant, the receptionist knocked and announced the visitor.

Oscar Nash stood to greet his guest.

'Thank you, Irene.'

An imposing figure in his well-tailored suit, Nash had neat reddish hair that showed only a slight sign of grey at the edges, and his neatly trimmed moustache enhanced his image. He stood tall and straight, giving the appearance of a successful businessman. He puffed on a cigar that blew smoke around the room and occasionally concealed his features.

'Welcome, Mr Connor. I've heard so much about you from my business counterpart in New York. Pleased to make your acquaintance. CJ speaks very highly of you and has instructed me to do all I can to assist you in your search for your siblings. Please, take a seat and we'll get started. I trust you have seen something of the devastation of the city?'

'Yes, sir, I have been shielded from the reality of what went on here during the war. It must have been a dreadful time.'

'It was indeed. I lost several staff members – young lads about your age who went off to fight and never returned. The workforce is slowly being replenished with returning soldiers. Of course, the women who took over during their absence and did an outstanding job to keep the hotel and shop functioning, had to leave. Sadly, I've had to let some of them go to give priority to the men. It's not a pleasant task to inform someone that they are no longer required.' He shook his head sadly. 'War has many casualties.'

Archie thought how unjust it seemed for the women to lose their employment but kept his opinion to himself. He had immediately warmed to the company director, who reminded him of his New York mentor.

Tea arrived and after pouring it for his guest, Oscar Nash retrieved a folder from a drawer and handed a sheet of paper to his visitor.

'This is what my people have discovered so far. Your two sisters, Ruby and Betsy Connor, were taken on the demise of your mother, to a workhouse not many miles from where you and your family once lived. The building suffered the fate of many others in the area and, although it did not take any direct hits, it was damaged from wreckage from nearby unstable structures. However, it continued to function for some time as an establishment for women and girls. Some inmates, including your sisters, were moved to other similar establishments when airship bombings began in earnest and the authorities feared that London would be attacked.

'It took some time to track the whereabouts of your sisters,' he went on. 'As you can imagine, things were chaotic, and records of inmates in such establishments were not up to date. However, we now have definite proof of their whereabouts and I myself contacted the guardian of the establishment where they are presently relocated, again not many miles from the original workhouse. I have established that eleven-year-old Ruby Connor and ten-year-old Betsy Connor reside there, and I have arranged for you to visit your sisters. There is some discrepancy over their actual dates of birth, but the two girls are indeed your siblings.'

Oscar Nash handed the young man an envelope containing details of the findings.

'Visit?' questioned Archie. 'Sir, I've come to collect them and take them out of there. I'm not just here on a visit.'

Oscar Nash looked Archie in the eye and saw a determined, perhaps headstrong, youth who was perfectly capable of fighting his corner should a dispute arise.

He sat back in his chair before continuing, 'Ah, that throws up problems. The establishment require assurance that you are of good character, have a place of safety where the girls will reside, and that you have financial means to support them. Also, the children have to agree to willingly leave the security of the place they have known and lived in for six years. It's best that you know this to avoid a setback. Unfortunately, my people have yet to find the location of your brother.'

Archie sighed, disappointment etched on his face as he hunched his shoulders in despair. One moment he felt elated at the news of the girls, then saddened at the setback regarding the Nipper.

Recovering his composure, he quickly assured Oscar Nash that two of the three requirements were already endorsed.

'Sir, CJ has vouched for my character and I have a letter to that effect. I have also procured safe accommodation with friends who are only too happy to share their home with us until such times as I can obtain accommodation elsewhere. My main difficulty is in securing employment, as I know that soldiers who have returned from the war require employment and surely have priority over someone like me who has only recently arrived back in the country. Until I find employment, though, I have savings to tide us over for some time.'

Oscar Nash quizzed Archie on the characters of Stan and Doris Young, and listened as Archie told him of the care and attention given to them on the death of their mother. He recognised that the youth had a good head on his shoulders, and was a planner, an organiser, and a person determined to complete his search for his siblings. Unknown to Archie, Oscar Nash already knew much of his history from his dealings with CJ, but had wanted to assess the lad for himself. He was an outstanding judge of character and prided himself on choosing his workforce with utmost care. He studied the young man in front of him and liked what he saw.

'Mr Connor… Archie, you don't mind me calling you that, do you? You seem to have things well thought out and I'm impressed by that. CJ thinks very highly of you, and that is enough for me to be in the position to offer you employment here, if you would be interested.'

Archie smiled. 'Interested? Of course, I would, sir. I can turn my hand to anything, and I'll work hard.'

'And I'm sure you will. We can discuss this at a later date. Now, off you go and continue your search. Be assured that if there is any word of your brother, I will be in immediate touch with you by wire telegram at the address where you currently reside. Leave the details with Irene. Return here one month to the day and we'll discuss your employment. Good luck, Archie Connor.' He stood and shook Archie's hand. 'I'll ring for my chauffeur to take you back to your lodgings.'

Archie smiled and shook his head. 'Thank you, sir, but I prefer to walk to clear my head and familiarise myself with this part of the city. I've been at sea for six weeks, and still can't walk in a straight line. I need to recover my land legs.'

They both laughed and Archie made his way back out of the building.

As Oscar Nash settled back behind his desk, he shook his head as he thought of the uphill struggle that lay ahead of the young man in rehabilitating his siblings, and how the search for his brother could well prove to be futile.

17

With a lighter heart, Archie walked for miles, carefully avoiding rubble and wreckage while planning the future with his family. Eventually, he returned to Stan and Doris's home and over their evening meal he related his findings, showing them the address where he had been instructed to go.

He sighed, 'If I hadn't fallen asleep and ended on the high seas, we would never have been apart.'

Despite his air of maturity and confidence, Stan could sense the heart-breaking guilt and vulnerability of the waif who had run from their home all those years before.

'Archie, the authorities would not have released the others into the care of a twelve-year-old boy, and they would have taken you into care, too.' He told him, 'There was nothing you could have done.'

Archie shrugged. 'I guess I hadn't thought of that. Now, I need to go to a place called Holborn where our Ruby and our Betsy live.'

'Oh Archie, that's not far from here,' Doris said. 'Who would have thought they lived so near? There's a Poor House in the area, perhaps that's where they have been living.'

'Mr Nash told me that a bomb fell on a school in Poplar, killing several children, and after that some of the workhouse kids who lived nearby were sent to other workhouses or Poor Houses that hadn't been damaged. First thing tomorrow I'm going to fetch them out of there, and we'll be a family again… that is, once I find our Nipper.'

'It's late Archie,' sighed Doris, with concern in her voice, 'and it's getting dark. Best lad if you settle for the night. Sleep on it and we'll help you work something out. Go on, off to bed, you look as if you can't keep your eyes open another minute.'

'Yeah, you're right. I am tired,' he replied, slipping into his American use of the affirmative. 'I think I'm suffering from travel fatigue. I'll say goodnight, and thanks again for taking me under your roof.'

'Off with you,' replied Doris, smiling. 'You're our Archie, and always will be.' She hugged the exhausted youth. 'It's only a couple of days since you set foot in England. You still need to rest.'

*

Archie slept late the next morning. The strain of the long sea voyage and the emotions that had surfaced from his return to his homeland had taken their toll on his body.

Doris let him sleep. She and Stan moved quietly around the apartment, and it was almost midday when he awoke and rubbed his eyes in an attempt to focus on his surroundings. He lay for a moment, savouring the warm bed, before his thoughts turned to the events of the previous day, with its promises and disappointment.

He washed, dressed, and after a hearty breakfast, left to begin his hunt for his sisters. With Stan's directions firmly implanted in his head, he set off.

He spotted Jake sitting by the rubble of his former home.

'Hi Jake. Do you mind if I sit here with you for a while?'

'Well, if it isn't Archie Connor. I was beginning to think you had been a figment of my imagination, but here you are as large as life. Sit here with me and tell me how things are progressing.'

The two chatted for some time, with Archie giving him an update on his search.

'Oh, and while I remember,' he said, 'Stan and Doris say you have to call over to them for a meal and a chat. They didn't know of your tragedy and want to speak to you. I suppose sharing your loss with them will help you all.'

Jake smiled sadly. 'Thanks, lad. I'll give a thought to their kind invite, but I'm not one for mixing much with folks at the moment. It's too emotional to talk or even think about what happened.'

'Yeah, I understand, or I think I do. When Mam died, I didn't have anyone to talk to until I met Dan and Granny Peggy. They helped me come to terms with my loss and the loss of the family.'

Archie told a bemused Jake about his life with them in New York.

'Sounds like they are nice people,' the older man said.

Archie nodded. 'The best, Jake, the best.' He stood up. 'I'd better be getting along to find this place.' He showed Jake the makeshift map that Stan had drawn on a scrap of paper. 'This is where I have to go.'

'I know the area, Archie. Would you like me to go part of the way with you and put you on the right road?' Jake offered. 'With the devastation in the area, it might be difficult to find. Some streets are unrecognisable.'

Smiling broadly, Archie helped Jake to his feet. 'I'd like that,' he said. 'Thank you.'

The two walked for a while, climbing over debris and masonry left in the street and, under Jake's guidance, taking a diversion to avoid an area where the entire street had been reduced to rubble.

Eventually, Jake pointed out the road that Archie was looking for.

'There is the place you're searching for. Look for a large brick building. Good luck, lad.'

Archie shook the man's hand. 'Jake, you've been a great help. I'll let you know how it goes. Remember to call in at the Youngs; they would like to see you.'

As he watched the young man head off on his mission, Jake turned to make his way back to the place where memories lingered. He appreciated the Youngs' offer but knew he wouldn't impose on them looking as he did, like a homeless and downtrodden man. *I have my pride,* he thought.

Archie walked slowly along the road, looking carefully for the address that he had been given. He was so engrossed in his purpose that he stumbled over rubble that had been left where it had fallen from a damaged building. He cried out in pain, righted himself, dusted his clothes, and noticed what looked like the building he had been searching for.

His first thought was, *This place looks grim.* The windows were dark and dirty with little evidence of curtains or blinds, and the rusty iron gate creaked as he walked up the grimy steps to a paint-peeled door. What passed as a garden was overgrown and neglected. *Surely no-one lives here,* he told himself.

Taking a deep breath, Archie pulled on the rope bell that hung precariously from somewhere on high, and waited.

18

As a five-year-old child, Ruby Connor was a resilient, happy-go-lucky girl with an endearing smile. Her flimsy dress barely covered her bare backside, and shoes were unheard of. She once saw a well-dressed girl with red shoes that fastened with a buckle, and Ruby longed for a similar pair. As she sat on her father's knee, on a rare occasion when Bertie Connor had time for his children, she asked for a pair of red shoes with a buckle.

'Yes, my princess,' he replied through a haze of alcohol. 'Nothing is too good for my girl. I'll buy you a pair, just you wait and see.'

Ruby waited in vain for the promise to be honoured. She was poor, but knew nothing else. People in the area lived a stark, deprived life, but it was the norm and no-one questioned why they should be any different from their neighbours.

She had a mass of naturally curly chestnut hair that had never seen a comb. Her mam would run her fingers through it in an attempt to unravel the tresses and remove the lice and hair bugs that lived deep in her child's head. Such was life for Ruby and her little sister.

They both adored their brother. Archie was something of a hero to them and, despite his young age, was the father figure they craved, since their biological parent spent little or no time with them. The arrival of the Nipper completed the little family, but their security was shattered within days.

Ruby was bereft at the death of her mam. No amount of consoling from Doris or Stan could remove the image from her mind of her dead mother lying on the bed holding the Nipper in her arms. At first, she had thought the baby was dead, until Doris gently lifted the whimpering baby and handed him to Stan to take to their warm home.

Doris had gently carried the distressed girl, while Archie held four-year-old Betsy's hand as the sad procession moved from their hovel of a home for the last time, tears streaming down their faces. Betsy had sobbed more from confusion and fear than from a realisation that she would never see her mam again.

The next few days had been clouded in grief while Stan and Doris did their best to console, bathe, and feed the children, while attending to the poorly baby. All four were badly malnourished and neglected.

Days turned into weeks, and the bereaved youngsters settled into a calm routine of sleeping and eating. Slowly the children emerged from a foggy existence and, with love and attention, thrived under the care of their surrogate parents. The girls clung to Archie who took to heart the responsibility of being the eldest.

Ruby loved helping around the house, following Doris's instructions on how to sew and mend and make simple meals. With Betsy in tow, she accompanied Doris to the market and listened as the wise woman haggled for cheaper prices. The stallholders, well aware of the situation she found herself in, often threw in extra portions of basic foodstuff that Doris miraculously turned into nourishing meals.

Weeks turned into months. And Christmas was the most wonderful time that Ruby had experienced in her short life. Her eyes had lit up in wonder at the theatre experience; the omnibus ride, albeit cold and wintery in the evening darkness; eating hot chestnuts, hot peas, and sips of porter. It had been a magical time for the child and continued into Christmas Day with a gift of a wooden doll wrapped in paper and tied with a blue ribbon. She had sung with gusto as they all sat around the fire learning festive songs from Stan, then she'd helped Doris stir the special pudding and felt that life could not get much better.

Unknown to her, life was about to plummet to a depth she could neither understand nor envisage.

The day that Doris and Stan explained to the children about their move to the workhouse was the most traumatic of Ruby's young life. In an instant, her security had been whipped from under her feet. Tears that hadn't been shed for months resurfaced, and she looked in disbelief at Archie, her dependable, loving brother, and saw only despair.

This was real. They were to move from the protective custody of Stan and Doris to an unknown place which, even at a tender age, filled her with fear. Little Betsy, unaware of the enormity of the unfolding trauma, sucked her thumb as she held Ruby's hand in hers.

A scream from Archie stunned them momentarily.

'No! No! We ain't going to no workhouse.'

No amount of reassurance from Stan could calm the boy. His whole body shook in anger – fury that life could be so cruel, robbing them of their beloved mam and now removing them from a happy home life.

Wiping his eyes on his sleeve, they watched him run out of the house, banging the door behind him as if protesting to the building that had housed him for many months.

Stan had turned to run after Archie, but Doris implored him, 'Let him be, love. He needs to cry it out, he'll be back in a few hours.'

'Where's our Archie?' screamed Ruby, as she headed towards the door, only to be restrained by Stan.

'He'll be back soon, lovey. He needs to be on his own for a minute or two.'

'I want our Archie,' wailed Betsy, as sadness enveloped her.

With a heavy heart, Doris had wiped their tear-stained faces, brushed their hair for the last time, and hugged them as tightly as she could. She'd sat with them both on her lap and let them cry until they fell asleep in her arms, their dreams and hopes crushed and replaced again with sorrow.

A wagon drawn by a worn-out horse stopped at the tenement, and a man and woman alighted, knocked loudly on the door, then came into the room. The noise woke the girls, who looked at the strangers and whimpered.

'Here to collect four Connor children: Archie, Ruby, Betsy, and an unnamed baby boy,' announced the fierce-looking man, whose appearance did nothing to console the girls.

'Give me a minute to collect their spare clothes,' pleaded Doris, wiping tears on her apron.

'No need for that,' responded an equally frightening-looking woman. 'We've got plenty of clothes, they won't need anything. Come now, don't dawdle,' she said, and she roughly pushed the children towards the door, after relieving Stan of the Nipper.

'Where's the older lad? He is to come with us.' enquired the woman.

'He was upset and ran out for some fresh air, 'replied Stan. 'He'll be back soon, I'm sure.'

'And we'll be back later,' she replied. 'Have him ready.'

'At least give us time to say goodbye,' wept Doris, struggling to control her tears.

'Best to let them go,' replied the man, softening his voice slightly. 'We find in these situations it's best not to linger.'

Ruby's last sight of the couple who had shown them so much care and love was of Doris weeping in Stan's arms, 'Oh, what have we done, Stan? What have we done to those poor mites?'

19

The wooden wagon that collected the Connor children was similar to that in which prisoners were escorted. There were bars across the side and rough wooden benches to sit on.

'Stop that sniffling. I can't be doing with brats like you.' The woman terrified the already scared children, but thankfully the baby slept throughout the journey.

Clutching her wooden doll that she had grabbed from the table as they left the house, Ruby stroked its woollen hair and sobbed as quietly as she could. As the wagon jostled them along a mud-splattered track, she dropped her doll and bent to retrieve it.

'What's that thing?' questioned the woman.

'It's my doll. Uncle Stan made it for me, and Aunt Doris sewed—' Ruby never finished her sentence. A sharp smack on the side of her face silenced her.

'Give it here. We don't allow toys,' the woman yelled, and she tossed the doll through the bars and onto the street.

Ruby held her face in her hands and rocked back and forward holding back silent tears. Betsy clutched her and, sensing the atmosphere, remained quiet.

Eventually, the wagon came to an abrupt halt, throwing them forward onto the floor.

'Ger up, stay here, and don't move or you'll get more of the same.'

Holding the baby under her arm, the woman climbed from the wagon and spoke to the man.

'Won't be a minute, Sid. Got to get rid of this sodden baby then we can get these other brats delivered.'

Ruby looked through the wooden bars in horror.

'Our Nipper! Where is she taking our Nipper?'

Turning around, the man answered, 'It's okay, my lovey, he's gone to be with the boys. We don't have boys and girls under the same roof. Oh no, we don't allow that. Best you keep quiet. Aggie don't like kids sniffling and crying. Shush, here she comes.'

'Right, Sid, drive on.'

Some fifteen minutes later, the vehicle came to a shuddering halt, throwing Betsy onto the floor.

'Ger up, you, off the floor. Welcome to your new life.' The woman roughly prodded and pushed the girls from the cart.

Ruby stood in horror at the brick building in front of her. Despite her young age, the dark and menacing façade created an ominous fear in her heart. She looked at her little sister, who cowed beside her, and realised that Betsy had not uttered a word since they had left the Youngs' house.

She gripped her hand and whispered, 'Don't worry, our Betsy, I'll look after you. Our Archie will come for us soon.'

Sid went off to stable the horse, leaving the girls to the mercy of the intolerable Aggie, who pushed open the heavy oak door and nudged the girls none too gently into a dark, dismal hall.

'Sit here and don't move. Someone will come for you.'

Ruby, too scared to move, held onto Betsy and stroked her hair in a soothing rhythm. She could feel her little sister's heart racing. All around them was a deathly silence, as if the building was empty. Slowly adjusting her eyes to the dimness in the hallway, Ruby saw how stark it was. Apart from the chair she and Betsy shared, there was no other furniture, pictures, or wall-hangings. It was bleak.

Ruby dreaded the return of the fearful woman. After what seemed an eternity, footsteps were heard coming from the opposite side of the hallway.

'Wake up, our Betsy, wake up,' she whispered as the footsteps got nearer.

She braced herself for another encounter with the nasty woman and was relieved to find that the footsteps belonged to an older girl wearing a servant's rough woollen dress. She smiled at the children.

'Come on, I've to take you to Matron. My name is Daphne. You must be the Connor children.'

Ruby could only nod in agreement.

'Don't be shy. Keep your mouths shut and do what you're told, and you'll be fine around here. Right, in you go. Matron is waiting.'

'I need to pee,' whispered Betsy.

'Over here. I'll show you the bucket room, but be quick. Matron doesn't like to be kept waiting.'

The girls had no idea what a matron was but were soon to find out.

'Miss Roache, the Connor girls, ma'am.'

'Thank you, Daphne. You are dismissed.'

Ruby and Betsy held hands as they stood in front of a formidable lady. Not as friendly as Daphne, but thankfully not as frightening as Aggie, Matron was tall, erect, and unsmiling. She wore a full-length, long-sleeved dress made of rough material, with a high collar and a grubby lace covering at the neck. She loomed over the two trembling children.

Augusta Roche was a law unto herself; her word was law, as these shivering waifs were about to find out. There was no room for maternal feelings or outspoken inmates in her establishment. The only daughter of elderly parents, she had ministered to them until their deaths then, as an impoverished woman unlikely to marry, she was offered a position in the workhouse where her formidable, authoritarian presence saw her rise to the position of Matron. It was a post she relished.

The board of guardians gave her free reign to run the establishment as she saw fit, thus wiping their hands of much of the responsibility. And she ruled it with a rod of iron. She invented a fiancé, Thomas Gilson, and concocted a story of his death during the war, wearing her mother's ring to indicate her engagement to the non-existent Thomas.

'Girls, due to your family circumstances, you have been placed here in the care of this establishment, and here you will remain until a responsible relative can be found to care for you, or until you reach the age of sixteen – whichever comes first. The board of guardians are now your legal guardians. You will learn to clean and cook and read, count, and write. You will learn too about the wrath of God and the evils of wrongdoings. Do what you are bid, obey your elders and betters, and do not find yourself in my office for any misdemeanours.'

Ruby had no idea what a misdemeanour was but was determined not to encounter whatever it was. Matron opened the door and showed them back into the dark hallway.

'Sit outside and wait for someone to come for you.'

After an uncomfortable wait, Ruby's heart sank with the reappearance of Aggie.

'Get a move on, you two,' she snarled. 'We don't have time to dawdle.'

20

The two girls were rushed across the hall and down a flight of dark concrete stairs. As they negotiated the steep steps, Betsy fell twice, whimpered, and was pulled to her feet by the impatient servant.

When they arrived at the bottom, they found themselves in a cold basement room that held several bathtubs. A young girl was screaming as she was immersed in cold water by another servant-girl.

'Shut up, Molly Grimsson. You know what happens when you pee the bed,' the girl shouted. 'Stop struggling, you're splashing me.'

'I can't help it, sorry, I can't help it,' the child sobbed.

'Stop sniffling. I've got these two brats to see to. I haven't all day. Aggie, get started on stripping and head shaving.'

Aggie, who seemed to be below the servant in the pecking order, replied, 'Right away, Florrie, right away.'

She looked at the two sisters. 'We'll start with the kiddie. You,' she pointed to Ruby, 'get your dirty clothes off ready for a bath.'

Ruby found her voice, enraged at being told that she wore dirty clothes.

'These ain't dirty. They were clean on this morning. Aunt Doris makes sure we're clean. I don't need a bath, nor does our Betsy. We ain't dirty.'

There was a momentary hush then a deep intake of breath from the two adults and the girl in the bath, followed by a crack across the face.

'That'll learn you to do wot you're told,' Aggie snarled. 'We don't take cheek from brats like you.' And she grabbed Ruby by the hair, removed her clothes, and sat her naked on the cold floor. 'Sit there 'til I finish with your sister. At least she has the wit to keep her mouth shut.'

Aggie removed Betsy's clothes and threw them on top of Ruby's discarded garments. She proceeded to roughly shave Betsy's hair, and kicked the tresses away from her as they fell to the floor, like wool shorn from a sheep. Betsy remained silent throughout.

'No. Stop! Leave her hair alone!' screamed Ruby, as she rubbed the stinging weal that formed on her face. But before she could recover from the shock of watching Betsy's lovely hair being cut, Florrie had left the screaming Molly in the bath and cornered Ruby.

'So, we have a fiery one here? We'll soon knock that out of yer. We don't allow lice and dirty heads here. Cleanliness is next to godliness and you'd better learn that quickly, madam.' She finished her tirade with a slap on Ruby's bare buttocks.

Thirty minutes later, two weeping children emerged from the washroom, heads shorn and bleeding, and dressed in coarse, itchy, grey dresses, to join the other dozens of inmates in a room that served as a dining area. They were pushed onto a hard bench, and sat in silence with their heads bowed.

Not a sound was heard in the room until the shrill voice that Ruby recognised as that of Matron, called out to the assembled group, 'Bow your heads in prayer.'

She intoned a lengthy plea to the almighty to rid the evil from the souls of these ungrateful girls and such like requests. As if on cue, the children intoned, 'Amen.'

A clatter of metal bowls announced the arrival of the meal – a dish of watery gruel. Ruby stared at the contents and made no attempt to eat. A pretty girl seated next to her whispered, 'Best eat. We get nothing more until tomorrow. Shush, don't talk, eat.'

Ruby forced the lukewarm gruel down her throat and whispered to Betsy to eat.

'No talking over there,' shouted Matron as she looked around for the offending child. All heads were bent towards the gruel; no-one dared to look for fear of being targeted and punished.

At the sound of a bell, the children rose as one and stood in line to leave the dining area. As they reached the door, Daphne returned and took charge of Ruby and Betsy.

'I'll show you where you'll be sleeping. Come with me.'

They followed her down a long staircase to a large dormitory in the basement area, their progress hampered by Betsy's faltering steps.

Daphne spoke quietly to the terrified girls. 'We've all been moved down here now because of the bombs and the war and things. What you need to know is, if you hear bombs overhead, you get under your bed, lie on your front with your arms over your head. That way, Jerry won't get you.'

Poor, confused Ruby had no idea who Jerry was. Twenty girls were discarding their day clothes for rough nightwear and, when ready, they knelt by their beds. No-one spoke.

Daphne escorted the children to a bed where the pretty girl who had spoken to them earlier, knelt by the side.

'You're to share a bed with Pearl. Get undressed, fold your clothes neatly, and leave them on the floor by your bed. Put these nightdresses on and kneel beside Pearl.'

Seeing Betsy struggle with her coarse grey dress, Ruby turned to help her but was stopped by Daphne. 'She has to learn to do it for herself,' the older girl whispered.

With difficulty, and with not a few tears, Betsy managed to change into her nightclothes and, following Ruby's example, folded her day dress and laid it on the floor.

'Now kneel,' instructed Daphne as she left the room.

The click of heels announced the arrival of Matron who intoned a night prayer in a loud voice, 'Now, I lay me down to sleep...' to which the entire group of girls joined in.

'Bed, no talking. Sleep. Good night, girls.'

'Good night, Matron,' they replied. 'God bless you, Matron.'

With Betsy in between them, Pearl and Ruby struggled to find space in the bed. Pearl whispered, 'Don't talk or cry, and whatever you do, don't pee the bed or you'll suffer the consequences. Shush. Try to sleep.'

Ruby spent a restless few hours adapting to the coarse blanket that barely covered her and eventually, emotionally exhausted, fell asleep dreaming of bombs and Jerry and cold baths. It seemed no time at all until she was roused from sleep by Pearl.

She rubbed her eyes and looked around her. *Where am I?* Reality hit hard when she saw the other children hurrying to change into day clothes.

'Quick,' whispered Pearl. 'Get up and get dressed before someone comes.'

Ruby shook the sleeping Betsy and lifted her from the bed and began to dress her. *Oh no, the bed is wet.* Observing the other girls, she knelt by the bed, having first wiped Betsy as well as she could with her own nightdress.

Matron arrived and intoned the morning prayer. 'Bed inspection,' roared the formidable woman.

Ruby followed Pearl's example and turned down the bedding for inspection. Aggie arrived to assist in the check; it was clearly beneath Matron's role to touch such items.

Aggie went from bed to bed, occasionally calling, 'Wet.' Reaching Ruby's bed, she called out, 'Wet', then lifted the nightdresses from the floor and inspected them. 'Two here, Matron. The new girls.'

Those unfortunate enough to have committed such an affront were frogmarched to the bathroom where cold baths awaited.

Ruby tried to protect her sister by calling out, 'It weren't her, miss, it were me,' but to no avail. Her effort resulted in another slap from Aggie and both girls being dunked in cold water.

'That'll learn you to keep your mouth shut and your bed dry.'

Such was life for the Connor girls for the next six years.

21

The fate of the Connor baby was less traumatic. He was given into the care of Violet Holden, a motherly thirty-something widow whose husband Jimmy was killed in the early days of the fighting. She had twelve babies under four years of age in her care, all abandoned by their families or detained by the workhouse guardians when orphaned or had parents who were unfit to look after them. Violet thrived on caring for her baby brood, as she often referred to them. The work was constant as she tended to the needs of each one in a separate part of the men's workhouse.

'Another one without a name, poor little mite,' commented the guardian in charge of the age group as he handed over the Connor baby. 'We have a date of birth and a surname, but no first name. Seems like his mam died just after giving birth to this little chap.'

'Poor mite. Right,' said Violet, 'we'll call this little fellow after the Prime Minister.' And so the name of Herbert Connor was added to the records.

'He's tiny,' she remarked, 'but he's been well looked after. There's not a rash to be seen and he's clean, not like some of the others.'

Young Herbert spent his early years shielded from the horrors of war and with no knowledge of his humble beginnings. It was the happiest time he was to experience. He gurgled and smiled a toothless grin until his baby teeth appeared, and Violet helped him to crawl and steadied him as he took his first faltering steps. With the other tots, he lived an almost idyllic life until it was deemed time for him to move from the security of Violet's nursery into the main workhouse and school.

Like all institutionalised children of the time, he lacked stimulation and limited companionship, and quickly learned to submit to the harsher regime. He was a quick learner who soaked up like a sponge everything the masters, with their own limited knowledge, taught him. Knowing no other life, he accepted as norm the routine of frugality, poor nutrition, and lack of motivation.

His best and only friend was Nobbs, who joined him in the poorhouse as a four-year-old waif. The two spent as much time together as was permitted, and rarely left the confines of the workhouse unless to tend to the garden for short periods of time. Herbert Connor was totally unaware that he had siblings – one of whom was anxiously searching for him.

For Betsy, the incarceration in the workhouse took a toll on her already fragile health. She had been a sickly baby and slow to develop. But the strict regime and constant punishment of cold baths left her frequently frightened and, as a result, she became a selective mute. She spoke only to Ruby, in whispers, and no amount of shouting, prodding, or smacking from staff, especially Aggie, could produce speech from the scared child. She lived a miserable existence in fear of Zeppelin raids that she did not understand, and the horror of falling bombs that she overheard staff talk about.

On one of the rare occasions when the children were allowed to work in the garden 'to do their bit for the King', an air raid warning sounded; the wailing sound pierced their ears and the children were terrified.

'Take cover, head for the basement shelter!' came the shrill instruction.

Despite an attempt at an orderly line heading to safety, several children were pushed to the ground. Betsy, who had not yet mastered stairs, was one of them.

'Ger up! Get a move on or Jerry will get you,' roared Aggie, as she pulled Betsy unceremoniously along with her, kicking her as she went.

Young Betsy fell onto the concrete stair, blood pouring from a gash on her head. She was grabbed by the arm and yanked into the darkness of the basement shelter. Unknown to the woman, Betsy had broken her arm. The pain was excruciating but the child refused to call out or cry. It was much later before anyone noticed that she was unconscious.

Daphne, who was attending to some others, saw the child slumped in a heap on the floor. She gently touched her.

'Come on, little one, wake up,' she urged, before noticing the limp arm hanging loosely by Betsy's side and blood pouring from the side of her head. 'Oh no!'

She lifted her carefully and, when the all-clear signal was given, carried her upstairs to where Matron and other guardians were settling the frightened children in the dining room with an unusual treat of cocoa.

'What have we here?' questioned Matron, who did not approve of children being carried.

'Matron, ma'am, this little one has broken her arm. She's been going in and out of faints and there's blood pouring from her head.'

'Give her here. Fetch a doctor while I put her on the chaise longue in my office.'

Augusta Roache was not without feeling at the plight of the tiny child, and attended to her in her limited way until Doctor Fletcher arrived.

'Fetch her sister here,' she instructed Daphne, who had returned to offer assistance.

Afraid that the weak child might die in her presence, the Matron wanted Ruby to witness how well she had cared for the child. She did not want any blame apportioned to her should Betsy Connor die.

Ruby stood beside her poorly sister, softly calling her name and holding a cloth as directed at her head, while the doctor examined her.

After giving her a thorough check over, Doctor Fletcher declared that there were severe breaks in the girl's right arm. 'I have to sedate her and try to set this arm,' he said. 'It's out of shape.'

He turned towards Ruby. 'Are you strong enough, child, to hold your sister as still as you can while I perform a procedure?'

Through tears, Ruby replied, 'Yes, sir. I want to help our Betsy.'

The doctor used barbiturates – the only tranquiliser available to him – to sedate Betsy, and proceeded to pull on the arm to set it in place. An involuntary shudder went through the child's tiny frame, and a whimper was heard before she succumbed to the full effect of the sedation.

Ruby screamed, 'Is she dead?'

'No, my dear,' explained the kindly medic. 'She is sleeping now. The longer she sleeps, the better it will be for her healing. The flow of blood has stopped now that I dabbed iodine on the wound, but I'll bandage it as a precaution. We need to keep an eye on it should the wound reopen.'

Turning to the white-faced Matron, he instructed that the child be allowed to rest and to be given nourishment.

'She is rather small for her age and looks under-nourished,' he said. 'Feed her as well as you can with all the rationing we have to contend with. And might I suggest this brave girl here be allowed to stay with her night and day until the child is healed. I shall return in a week's time to check on her progress.' He frowned. 'It is a rather severe break, and the child may have serious after-effects and limited use of the limb.'

Doctor Fletcher strapped Betsy's arm, collected his fee, and took his leave of them.

Augusta Roache realised how close she had come to losing an inmate and the trouble that would have caused her with the board of guardians.

'Daphne, take the child to the little room along from the dining area,' she instructed. 'I want you to take full charge of her. Sleep in the room with her and carry out Doctor's instruction regarding her care.'

Hesitating, the girl replied, 'Yes, Matron. And what about Ruby?'

Matron looked at Ruby, whose eyes had never left her sister's face, and felt an unusual surge of pity and respect.

'She can stay with her sister.'

22

Life for the sisters during Betsy's recuperation improved greatly under the constant care of Daphne, who tended to the sick child with sympathy and love. She enjoyed mothering the two little waifs and chatted freely to them, knowing that they would not be interrupted. No-one cared enough to check on them, and the sisters had the opportunity to learn something of the older girl's life story.

'I never knew my parents,' she told them. 'My mam died giving birth to me, so my granny reared me and when she died, I was eight years old and was placed in the care of the workhouse guardians and ended up in here. I learned quickly to keep my head down and my mouth shut. Last year, Matron gave me responsibility over the younger children, which got me out of the adult wards. It was horrible there.'

Ruby asked wistfully, 'Will me and Betsy be here forever?'

Daphne hesitated before asking, 'Have you any relatives out there?'

'Our Archie. We ain't seen him since the day they took us away. He ran off. But our Archie will come for us someday, that's my dream. Our Archie will find us,' she said confidently, 'I know he will.'

Daphne hadn't the heart to disillusion the child by telling her that every child in the workhouse dreamed of being rescued.

Apart from her chores and lesson times, Ruby was allowed to be with Betsy, who suffered greatly from air raid shock, which resulted in night terrors. Thankfully, only Ruby and Daphne heard her plaintive cry, so no other staff member had their sleep disturbed. And between them, Daphne and Ruby calmed the distressed child.

Following the bombing of a nearby school, which resulted in the death of several children, the board of guardians took the decision to move as many children as possible from the area to another workhouse that had lain empty and dilapidated for several years.

'We cannot accommodate all the inmates there,' the chairman of the board informed Matron. 'The establishment is small by comparison and has lain empty for some time. I am sure you in your efficient way will have it up to standard before long. The board have decided that the younger children up to the age of ten years will move with you. Arrangements will be made to effect this within the next few days.' He handed her a sheet of paper. 'I have here a list of servants who will accompany you.'

A frenzy of activity began in earnest with beds, bedding, and other pieces of furniture being loaded onto wagons for transportation. A squad of servants and older inmates had been sent ahead to clean and scrub the building ready for the intake of younger children.

'I want this establishment to be thoroughly cleaned before I set foot in it,' demanded Matron, who despised dirt.

And so, for the first time in several years, the sisters had their first sight of life outside the walls of the workhouse. They rode with others in a cart pulled by two horses, and stared in awe at the sights around them: buildings reduced to rubble; gaps where family homes had once stood; boarded-up premises that would never function again. Devastation was all around.

Despite this, Ruby soaked in the delights of breathing fresh air and was mesmerised by the sky and floating clouds that looked to her like moving pictures that changed shape and position, in a show of majestic power. Betsy, afraid of the unusual cacophony of street noise, clung to Ruby who tried to soothe her fear by pointing out the pretty pictures in the sky.

Having cleaned the premises to Matron's satisfaction, the dreaded Aggie returned to the original establishment to care for the older children, much to the relief of those who had suffered under her regime of abuse. From then on, life for Ruby and Betsy was less fraught.

The first few months in their new home were calmer, with Daphne and Pearl befriending the sisters. Augusta Roache relished her new role in the smaller, more compact building, and appeared to have mellowed slightly in her attitude and handling of the children. But an unexpected visit from one of the board officers alarmed her, and she feared that she might be moved just when she had settled into a comfortable routine.

However, the official assured her that all was well and that the board were satisfied with the smooth relocation.

'I am here on another matter altogether,' said the man. 'I have here a letter from a distinguished businessman with news that concerns two of your inmates. It appears that a relative of the Connor girls – an older brother who has been searching for them – will call here to remove them from the premises. You are to afford him every assistance and have the girls ready for collection at 12 noon tomorrow.'

He handed the letter to Matron who adjusted her eyeglasses and read the instructions from the board of guardians and the enclosed letter from none other than London's best-known hotelier, Oscar Nash. Mr Nash was acting as guarantor, and vouched for the upstanding character of one Archie Connor, Esquire.

'Oh!' exclaimed Matron. 'We never have relatives turning up to claim their family. This is a first during my time. I shall of course see to the children myself and have them ready for tomorrow.'

When the official left, Augusta Roache sat back on her chair and contemplated the news. *Thank goodness, the little one survived her fall,* she thought. *How dreadful would it have been if she had died before being reunited with her brother? That would have reflected badly on me.*

Regaining her composure, she rang for Daphne – the one person she relied on. Matron admired the girl's competence and attitude, and trusted her to see to the routine running of the establishment.

'Daphne, I need your assistance in a matter that has come to my attention,' she told her. 'It appears that an older brother of the Connor sisters has materialised from I know not where, and will call tomorrow to remove them from our care. I will inform the girls myself, but not until morning. We must keep to our night routine at all cost, so I do not want any excitement or upset to disturb this establishment.

'I want you to look out the best shifts and dresses that you can find; launder and mend them, and have them in pristine condition for tomorrow. After breakfast, bathe the children in clean, warm water, and dress their unruly hair as best you can. I swear I've never seen such a mass of curls. The more we trim it, the wilder it seems to get.' She looked intently at Daphne. 'Do not mention this to anyone,' she warned. 'Now, I shall allow you to read this correspondence. I know you read well, thanks to excellent teaching in this establishment. Please sit.'

Never in her entire time in the workhouse had the girl been allowed to sit in the presence of Augusta Roache. Daphne perched nervously on the edge of the chair as straight as she could, much to the approval of Matron, and carefully read the correspondence. When she reached the end of the letters, she struggled to hold back her tears, but knew that a show of emotion would be frowned upon by her formidable superior as a sign of weakness.

Handing the letters back, she said, 'I will have them ready as instructed, Matron.'

When she left the Matron's office, Daphne went to a quiet part of the house, where she curled on the floor and succumbed to floods of tears. *Oh, how I'll miss those darling children,* she sobbed to herself.

Later, as she settled the Connor girls for the night, Ruby whispered, 'Have you been crying? Your eyes are all red.'

'No, Ruby, it's only a cold. I'm fine.' And she quickly removed herself from the room to keep her emotions in check.

The next morning, the girls were stunned to be bathed in warm, soapy water and have their hair carefully tended to, rather than the usual tug of brushing that left their eyes watering. Daphne, who never normally bathed them, was gentle in contrast to some other staff who had little concern or time to appreciate how rough they were treating such frail bodies.

Dressed in freshly laundered dresses, Ruby realised that something was amiss with their friend.

'Daphne, what's going on?' she asked. 'Why are you sad?'

'Ruby darling, I can't tell you anything.' She smiled to reassure the youngster. 'I want you to know I love you both and will think of you often. Now, come along quietly, we don't want to be caught chatting.'

Still none the wiser, Ruby and Betsy were summoned to the Matron's hallowed office to hear news that would impact on their young lives.

'It appears, my dear children, that you will shortly be leaving our establishment,' the Matron announced. 'Your brother, Archie Connor, has been searching for you for several years and will arrive shortly to remove you from our care. I trust your time with us has been fruitful and that you will speak highly of the care given to you, should anyone ask. Now, go off with Pearl who will give you something to eat. Remain with her until summoned.'

Two rather bemused children followed Pearl to the kitchen – an area never visited by inmates. There they were given nourishing food, the likes of which had never been served to them as workhouse children.

Being conditioned to obey, they ate as instructed, but Ruby's mind was in turmoil at what she had heard from Matron. *Was it true? Were they to leave this place of horror forever… and with our Archie?*

Sensing something of a change in her sister's demeanour, Betsy ate as much as she could despite her limited control with her spoon.

Ruby whispered, 'Our Archie's coming for us, Betsy.' She smiled. 'We're leaving this place.'

With little memory of 'our Archie', the child nodded, accepting that whatever was about to happen must be good since Ruby was grinning from ear to ear. *But why were Pearl and Daphne looking sad?* she wondered. It was all very confusing.

23

Archie was shown to the Matron's office, where she warmly welcomed him. He was pleased to see that the interior of the building was much cleaner than the outer part appeared to be.

He was excited and nervous at the prospect of setting eyes on his sisters whom he had never stopped thinking about, he had slept badly, and woke to the realisation that he would soon see his sisters. But it was obvious that he was to be questioned, albeit discreetly, by Matron before the long-awaited reunion. He satisfied her curiosity by relating a little of his life in America, omitting to tell her how he had initially arrived there.

Augusta Roache had once harboured a notion to travel, and was intrigued by the young man's description of the new world.

After some pleasant conversation, she said, 'You must be anxious to be reunited with your dear sisters. I myself informed them this morning, with a mixed reaction from them. Ruby was at first stunned, then on realising the implication, attempted to relate the news to Betsy, who I have to tell you has some health troubles.' She paused briefly before choosing her words carefully. 'Betsy has become what we call a selective mute; she speaks only to her sister, and then only in private. She had a dreadful fall during one of the disastrous air raids, and unfortunately her mind has been disturbed by the horror of war. She endured the pain of a broken arm with great courage. The limb healed somewhat but she has lost a great amount of movement. We gave her our best care and attention.' She smiled at Archie. 'Such a sweet child, I'll miss her terribly. Without much ado, Mr Connor, I shall fetch your dear sisters.'

Archie rubbed the sweat from his hands; his heart was racing so fast that he was sure it could be heard by everyone in the building. Excited at the prospect of the reunion, he rubbed his eyes nervously and with some trepidation speculated as to how he would be received by his siblings. He closed his eyes and tried to remember how they looked when he had last seen them, but in his anxiety and panic he could not conjure up their features.

Suddenly his thoughts were interrupted when the door opened to reveal two anxious looking girls being led in by Augusta Roache.

Archie stood and walked towards them, then smiled. 'Our Betsy. Our Ruby!'

The girls looked at each other, then Betsy cowered behind her sister, unsure of the well-dressed man with such a strange accent.

'It's me. Archie,' he said softly. 'I've come to take you home.'

Silence lasted a long minute until Ruby freed herself from Betsy's grip and ran to her brother.

'Our Archie! Oh, it *is* you, our Archie. Look, Betsy,' she looked briefly towards her little sister. 'It's our Archie, all posh-like.' Then she threw herself into his outstretched arms and hugged him tightly. 'I always knew you would be the one to come for us. Where've you been?'

He laughed. 'It's a long, long story, our Ruby. Let's get out of here, and home.'

Still holding onto Ruby with one hand, he crouched and knelt before little Betsy and looked right into her eyes.

'Hello, our Betsy, how are you? Remember me, your big brother? Archie.'

He moved slowly forward and hugged her gently, aware of the limp arm by her side.

'Let's go home,' he whispered.

There was no reaction from Betsy.

Archie took both girls by the hand and, nodding to Matron, led his sisters from the workhouse for the last time.

Augusta Roache, unused to seeing such a display of emotion, locked her office door and sat weeping for a long time. *I must be getting soft in the head to let those children move me so,* she thought to herself.

Had the little group looked back, they would have spotted Daphne and Pearl sadly watching the little procession cross the road.

A new chapter was about to begin for the Connor children.

*

Archie studied his sisters; they were pale as if they had been deprived of sunlight. They looked under-nourished, and although their dresses were clean, the material was rough and looked uncomfortable.

'Don't you have shoes?' he asked.

'Never had no shoes, our Archie.'

Ruth did all the talking while Betsy clung to her sister and looked furtively from her to this person who had suddenly appeared in their lives. She consoled herself that Ruth seemed happy, so it must be alright.

They crossed to a park and sat together on a bench, where the girls looked in awe at the sight in front of them: a pond where ducks swam around, while people fed them pieces of bread; blue skies with fluffy white clouds that intrigued them; and coloured leaves that fell gently from the trees. Several smiling people were walking around, children running among the falling leaves, laughing and shouting at the crunching noises from their footsteps.

The trio sat in silence as Archie watched their reaction to their surroundings and planned what he had to do. After a time, he asked, 'Do you remember Aunt Doris and Uncle Stan?' He let the question sink in.

'Yes!' exclaimed Ruby. 'We stayed with them, didn't we? And Uncle Stan made me a doll.'

A whisper came from Betsy, 'Me too, dolly.'

Archie fought back tears as he looked at his damaged little sister – a tiny ten-year-old waif – and vowed to do everything in his power to keep her safe.

'Well,' he continued gently, 'we're going to live with them again. Would you like that?'

Questions tumbled from Ruth in an unstoppable flow of excitement. 'What about Daphne and Pearl, will we live with them no more? Where have you been, our Archie? How did you find us? Why have you got a funny voice?'

'So many questions, our Ruth,' he laughed, as he cuddled her. 'We have a lot to catch up on, but first we need to ride the omnibus to where Aunt Doris and Uncle Stan live. They are waiting for us. Betsy,' he offered gently, 'would you like me to carry you?'

She nodded and allowed Archie to hoist her into his arms. He gently tucked her limp arm by his side and set off to walk until they heard the rumble of traffic. He felt the child tense in his arms.

'Don't fret, poppet, you're safe now.' He realised something of the extent of their incarceration. 'Didn't you ever go out?'

'Never,' replied Ruby. 'We were indoors all the time. It got scary at night cos we didn't have lights on, cos Jerry might see us and drop a bomb on our heads. We had to lie under the bed. Once we got out to the garden at the back to dig potatoes for the King. Didn't the King have his own potatoes?' she questioned, hardly stopping for breath.

As the questions continued to tumble from her lips, Archie had a brief insight into the regime that they had endured for so many years.

A whisper came from Betsy. Her mouth was almost level with Archie's ear as she said, 'Bad Aggie pulled me down the stairs cos Jerry was coming, and I fell and broke my arm.'

It was the longest sentence she had ever spoken.

Archie was loath to question the girls any further; he was sure more tales would come from them once they were settled with the Youngs.

'Look, here comes the omnibus.'

Betsy cuddled into him as the noise and bustle increased in volume. But Ruby took in everything about the journey, and it was a joy to see her face light up at this new experience.

After some time, they arrived at their destination and alighted carefully. Betsy, more composed now, stroked the face of the strong man who held her. In a glimmer of recognition, she whispered, 'Archie? Our Archie?'

He was overcome with emotion, as he had feared she would not remember him.

'I am, poppet. I'm your very own Archie, all grown now and happy to be with you again.'

She stroked his face and played with his nose as she had often done as an infant, and they laughed together, with Ruby joining in the fun.

'We have to walk a little through the marketplace,' Archie explained. 'Hold on tight to me, Ruby, it can get very busy.'

The marketplace was a cacophony of noise, with stall holders and barrow boys calling out to potential customers to stop and buy. Ruby put her hands over her ears to cut out the unaccustomed noise.

The smell from a food stall was tempting. 'Are you hungry?' Archie asked them. 'Would you like a hot potato?'

'We're always hungry, our Archie,' said Ruby.

Archie carefully sat Betsy down and instructed Ruby to keep hold of her while he made his purchase, then he led his sisters to a corner where they sat on a wall and devoured the sweet vegetable in total silence.

'We best be moving on,' he urged. 'It's getting colder.'

Hoisting Betsy once more onto his hip, they set off for the last trek, with Ruby holding his hand as she skipped along beside him.

24

'Careful where you place your feet, Ruby, there's lots of sharp masonry around,' Archie warned as the terraced row of houses came into view. 'Here we are, girls, up here. We have a lot of steps to climb.'

Betsy's arms tightened around his neck as she whimpered, 'Don't like steps.'

'Don't fret,' he soothed. 'I'll carry you safely to the top. Just hold on to me.'

Hearing voices on the stairway, Stan opened the door to see the motley procession arrive. Doris wiped her eyes as she joined him.

'My babies, come in, come in.'

Ruby held back, a little unsure if the elderly people were in fact Aunt Doris and Uncle Stan. They looked different from what she remembered.

Archie carefully put Betsy down and shook his shoulders to get life back into them after the burden of carrying the fraught child for so long.

'Here we are, Aunt Doris and Uncle Stan. Our Ruby and our Betsy, all grown up from when you last saw them,' he announced.

Doris hugged the young man and turned to the girls, 'Well, girls, are you hungry? I've got a very special pie for tea.'

She wanted to hug them both but hesitated, as she could see the bewilderment in their faces. 'Oh, Ruby and Betsy, it does my heart good to see you again.'

Ruby looked around her. 'This is different. Are we in a different house?'

Stan realised the cause of the confusion in the child's face.

'This is a bigger house, Ruby,' he explained. 'The old one was too small and was pulled down during the war. We have plenty room for you all. Would you like to see your bedroom?'

Ruby nodded and took Betsy's hand while they followed Stan, who seemed to walk very slowly.

As they left the room, Archie quickly filled Doris in on Betsy's health problems.

'They've had a dreadful time,' he told her. 'I want to get more information from them about the past seven years. Betsy's like a little damaged bird with a broken wing. But now she is free from the nest, I intend to care for her with every ounce of my being.'

'Don't push for information,' Doris advised. 'Let it come gradually when they feel more secure. They look dreadfully under-nourished, but I can fix that with good, wholesome food. And we need to get them outside into the fresh air while there's still warmth in the autumn sun. Their skin is far too pale and unhealthy looking. Poor mites. First thing tomorrow, I'm heading to the market for clothes for them, anything that I can adjust to fit them. And shoes, of course,' she added. 'They need shoes.'

They were interrupted by an excited shout from Ruby.

'Archie, come and see. Look, big beds with covers on them, and look at the walls, they are full of flower pictures.'

The house had two large bedrooms. One had been used by Mabel and her family, and was bright and airy. On top of the beds were colourful quilts, and a wardrobe with a built-in mirror reflected even more light into the room. Two little chairs, with a knitted teddy bear on each, sat by the beds.

Colour had been absent from the sisters' grey, drab lives for so long that they both laughed excitedly as they gazed around the room they were to share with Archie. A folding privacy screen, adorned with flowers, completed the décor of the room.

The second bedroom that led off the hallway was decorated in much the same way with a less flowery show.

'Stan was adamant that he didn't want to sleep with flowers everywhere,' Doris explained, 'that's why the room is slightly plainer. We were able to bring most of our furniture from the old house, including the big kitchen table. What a day that was when we brought as much as we could down those broken stairs. Neighbours were helping each other, as people do in dire circumstances,' she told them. 'We all had to be out within two days of notification that the building, or what was left of it, was to be demolished. I was glad to see the back of it.'

Leading off from the main room was a tiny scullery with a sink large enough to wash in. And after a light supper for their delicate stomachs, the girls sat quietly while Doris washed their filthy feet in the sink, trimmed their toenails, and applied soothing balm before wrapping each foot in cloth.

'That should help heal those nasty scratches and bruises,' she told them. 'Right, little ones. Let's get you off to bed and I'll come in and tell you a nice story like I used to do when you lived with us. Do you remember?'

'Oh, yes,' replied Ruby.

'Tomorrow, we'll have a cosy chat with Archie, and he'll tell you all about his adventures. Now, jump into bed and I'll be back to tuck you in for the night.'

Doris left the girls' bedroom, only to be stopped in her tracks by their voices chanting prayers.

She signalled to Archie to listen at the door. Ruby and Betsy were kneeling by the bed, heads bowed, saying, '*Now I lay me down to sleep…*' finishing with, '*Good night, Matron. God bless you, Matron.*'

It was a snapshot of the institutional life the two youngsters had led for so long.

*

Over the coming days, the girls enjoyed spending time outdoors, with Stan and Archie helping Betsy to manage the stairs. Daily visits to the nearby park and market were favourite haunts for the little family, and the girls' skin gradually took on a more natural colour. They relished time together as they listened eagerly to Archie's tales of America, and roared with laughter at his sea adventure.

'Wish I could go to America,' Ruby remarked wistfully.

'Me too,' uttered young Betsy, whose speech was improving with each passing day.

'Mm, maybe someday. Maybe someday,' responded their brother. He was reluctant at this stage to reveal his long-term plan to take his siblings to New York.

Within a few weeks, Ruby, who had lost none of the strong personality that she had held in check to avoid punishment from the wicked Aggie, gradually became more content and secure. She regaled the adults with tales of the regime of fear and evil, with Betsy adding little snippets of information that Archie stored in his head. He was incensed at the stories of cold baths and cruelty meted out by the servant Aggie, and vowed to avenge his sisters' treatment.

'They were held like prisoners,' he told Stan, when the others were out of earshot. 'I had heard horror stories of the workhouse, but to treat little girls like that, was criminal.'

25

Now employed as a trusted front-of-hotel doorman, Archie welcomed guests with genuine professionalism, and made many friends among staff and returning guests. His experience working for C.J. Croft had given him the confidence to deal with even the most awkward of guests.

Oscar Nash had no concerns about his newest staff member, and kept a careful eye on the young man whose demeanour gave nothing away of his heartache at not finding his brother. All avenues had been explored in the search for the Connor baby, but had so far produced one disappointment after another.

Stan and Doris felt helpless as they watched the despair etched on his face after each fruitless search.

'Don't give up hope,' they told him. 'He's out there somewhere.'

'I'll never give up on finding him, Stan, not while there's still breath left in my body.' Archie's resolve had never wavered. 'The war has wiped out several buildings where I'd been told they might have housed our Nipper. I spoke to someone in authority who told me several of the kids contacted the dreadful influenza that spread rapidly in some of the establishments, and some of the boys were moved to a sanatorium in the country.

'He gave me an address, but didn't hold out much hope for success. I'll ask my boss for a few days leave of absence and head out to the country. I'm so grateful the girls avoided the influenza that appears to have taken many lives.'

'It did indeed,' Stan replied. 'It wiped out entire families. Do you remember young Effie who came each day to see to the Nipper? Her entire family were taken by the illness, as were many of the neighbours. Why we never caught it remains a mystery to me.'

Doris interrupted their discussion. 'I'm convinced our survival had a lot to do with the fact I keep a clean house. That's my theory. Maybe someday I'll be proved right.'

Although he was delighted to see his sisters thriving under Doris and Stan's care, Betsy's plight was never far from Archie's thoughts. The more he learned of her treatment at the hands of one particular servant, the angrier he became. He was not an angry young man by nature, but such cruelty triggered a side of him that surprised even himself, and he sought revenge.

Relishing the freedom to roam, he often excused himself when everyone was settled after supper, and went for a walk.

That brisk autumn evening, he walked for a while until he located the establishment where the cruel Aggie now worked. Identifying her from her brash colleague's shouts, he concealed himself and observed the evening routine, where the workers had the task of climbing from the basement by outside stairs to dispose of the bathroom waste in a cesspit. It was common practice for slops and other unimaginable items to be tossed into the gutter, adding to the already putrid stench and raging illness that blighted the city.

In the semi-darkness, Aggie was unaware of the dark-clothed man concealed at the head of the stairway, until a voice whispered, 'Aggie? Are you Aggie?'

Startled at seeing a man lurking there, she peered into the darkness to identify the stranger who had called her name.

'Aye. Who wants to know?'

The reply came in the form of a rough push. The woman fell backwards down the broken steps, with the contents of the bucket covering both her and the servant behind her, as she tumbled and rolled downwards.

'Ya clumsy oaf!' hollered the servant who was following Aggie, and was now drenched with the stinking contents. 'Ger up, and clean this mess.'

By the time she realised Aggie was unresponsive, the assailant had long gone.

I hope it will be a very long time before that woman hits another child, Archie thought as he made his way home.

No-one ever knew the truth of the incident. After months of recovery from broken limbs, Aggie had little memory of the mysterious man, and of much else. It was presumed that she had lost her footing that night.

Her assailant kept the incident to himself. His wish that no child would be harmed by her again, was sealed forever.

*

Oscar Nash regularly sought out Archie and enquired as to the well-being of his sisters. Appalled on hearing of the damage done to little Betsy, he arranged for her to be seen by one of London's top physicians, Mr James Bowen-Grant – an expert in children's health.

On a crisp autumn morning, the family set off by underground to Regent's Park station. The musky smell and erratic movement from the tube initially alarmed the girls, who had unhappy memories of basements. And Betsy, still unsure of stairs, was even more afraid of the moving escalator. The adults, thinking the ride would be a new exciting experience, were oblivious to the girls' silent fears.

Once back above ground, Ruby breathed deeply and whispered reassuring words to her sister who was shaking and unsteady, as if evil memories had resurfaced to haunt her. The little girls walked on, holding each other's hands, heedless of the chatter of the adults, as Stan pointed out places of interest while Doris remarked on the fashions in shop windows.

It was only when Archie spotted some squirrels in the park that the girls showed any interest, and they gazed in awe as they watched the rodents race up and down trees, pausing at times to use their sharp teeth to nibble nuts that had fallen to the ground.

Archie purchased peas and vinegar from a stall before the group split up – Stan and Ruby to explore the park, while Archie, Doris, and Betsy headed to the clinic which was set in a prestigious area of London, and entered by a series of several outside stairs. Betsy hesitated.

'Come on, poppet. You can do it if I hold your hand,' encouraged Archie.

Betsy had almost mastered the stairs to the Youngs' flat and was slowly gaining confidence in the familiar building. But faced now with the unaccustomed stairway, she tensed her frail body and fought back tears.

'Can't. Can't.'

Reluctantly, Archie carried her into the building, where they were met by a pleasant receptionist who introduced herself as Jane, and shown into the room where the eminent Mr James Bowen-Grant stood to welcome them. Doris, her feet sinking into the plush carpet, was unused to such opulence, and held back as introductions were made.

Archie, well-used to dealing with people from different divisions of society, was unfazed as he shook hands with the man he hoped could help Betsy.

Bowen-Grant, a jolly character, put them at ease with his firm handshake and gracious smile. He was small and slim with very little hair, a few strands of which appeared to have a life of their own as he moved his head.

'Well, little lady,' he quietly addressed the child. 'Do you like puppies?'

Betsy nodded shyly, and he pressed the intercom to request his receptionist to bring a tiny puppy to meet his little client.

'Meet Misty, my little canine friend. Would you like to hold him? He's very friendly?'

He observed Betsy as she stroked and played with the puppy, his sharp eyes watching how she coped with one arm hanging by her side. The doctor stood beside her, lifted the limp arm and held it gently as he guided it across the pup's back. Then the astute physician carefully ran his hand along the arm while Betsy was distracted by Misty. After a while, he turned from the engrossed child and spoke quietly to the adults.

'At some point there has been an attempt to realign the arm, rather crudely I must admit, resulting in loss of power. However, if you are willing to allow her to undergo a procedure, I can straighten the deformed limb and, with a series of gentle massage exercises over a period of time, restore some movement. It will not heal the damaged limb, but will give a little more flexibility than she has at present.'

Doris and Archie looked quizzically at each other, searching for the right response.

It was Archie who spoke. 'How much will this cost, sir? I have some savings,' he frowned, 'but fear it may not be enough to cover what you are suggesting.'

The doctor smiled broadly. 'Ah, young man, I expected to be asked that and I have good news for you. A substantial sum of money has been wired from a benefactor in New York – a gentleman well known to you, a Mr C.J. Croft – who, on hearing the plight of this little girl from his London colleague, Mr Oscar Nash, has generously funded whatever treatment is necessary.'

Archie's mouth fell open in surprise at the revelation. Doris dabbed her eyes and looked across to Betsy who, totally oblivious to the conversation about her future, played happily on the floor with the puppy.

'For once, I find myself speechless,' Archie said eventually. 'That is an amazing gesture. I must write immediately to thank my former employer. If you can help my sister, please go ahead and proceed with your plan.'

Doris held her shaking hand in Archie's as they listened to arrangements being made for the child. They left the clinic bemused, elated, and almost flying as they took in the enormity of the result of the consultation.

As they left the building, Doris grinned at Archie. 'I've never known you to be so quiet,' she told him. 'Let's find the others and tell them the good news.'

26

During his free time from hotel work, and with the girls being cared for by the Youngs, Archie familiarised himself with his home city, and came across the London Library where, for a small fee, members were allowed to use the writing room.

He enrolled as a member, and relished the opportunity to read from the large selection of books and to spend time in the writing room where, on buff coloured paper, he penned some letters to America. The first was to his benefactor, C.J. Croft.

London. October 1920

C.J. Croft, Esquire

   Sir,

   Your generosity in funding medical care for my sister has overwhelmed me. Thank you for your kindness. Betsy's surgery and gentle therapy resulted in an increase in mobility, to the delight of all concerned. She may never have full use of the limb, nevertheless progress has been made. I can never repay you for the considerable contribution to my family's welfare. Thankfully they did not succumb to the dreadful influenza that swept the country.

   On another matter, while I successfully rescued my sisters from the dire workhouse, I have been as yet unable to locate my brother. Several establishments were suggested to me, alas,

*my search proved futile. I intend to continue until my task is
accomplished and my family are together.*

    Yours respectfully,

    Archie Connor

He also corresponded with his friend Jimbel, updating
him with reports on his search for his family, the weather in
England, his employment, and his reunion with the Youngs,
concluding with:

*My dream to bring my family to New York is still alive in my
heart. Someday, my dear friend, we will meet again.*

    Sincerely, your friend,

    Archie Connor

Letters were slow to arrive from America, but he wrote
regularly to Dan and Peggy and read their replies to the
enjoyment of the family as they sat around the kitchen table.
Stan and Doris were enthralled to learn of the young man's
adventures during the years they had believed him to be dead.

His search for his brother, however, was relentless and
exhausting. Archie trailed from one end of the city to another,
only to be met with either partly demolished buildings or
closed doors, as his request fell on deaf ears.

'Wrong place, lad,' he was told at one address. 'This is a
home for women.'

But hope came from one such establishment when a senior
servant invited him in.

'I can't help you, sir, but there is a meeting in progress of our
board of guardians,' the servant explained. 'Please wait here
until they finish, and someone may be able to advise you.'

He sat in a dark hallway, void of colour, of pictures, and of
anything remotely welcoming or homely. Silence was broken

only by distant clattering of dishes and whispering voices from the kitchen area. Before long, a putrid smell of what seemed like rotten cabbage filled the area.

A bell rang somewhere in the distance, and a pitiful line of women shuffled towards the source of the reek. Most were old and infirm and held onto fellow inmates. Wanting to escape from the depressing scene, Archie stood to leave when a strong authoritative voice called him into a room.

'I hear you are enquiring about a lost relative. Allow me to introduce myself. I am Cyril Bruce, head guardian of this organisation. How may I be of assistance?'

'Archie Connor, sir. Thank you for taking time to see me.'

He was shown into an office where he proceeded to relate the fate of his family and his frustration at not locating his brother. He showed the letter of introduction from Oscar Nash to Cyril Bruce, who took notes as he listened, impressed by the manners and deportment of the confident young man.

'Ah, you are a well thought of employee of my associate Oscar Nash. We serve on various committees. Hmm, give me a few days to make enquiries. If your brother is not on our records, he may be registered in another district,' said Bruce. 'I shall enquire from my colleagues, but I have to warn you that war took its toll on inmates, as did the influenza that our returning fighters brought back with them from their hellhole of existence.' He stood and shook Archie's hand. 'Return at the end of the week when I may have news for you, but please don't build up your hopes.'

Archie found himself outside in the autumn sunshine, glad of the opportunity to breathe fresh air away from the stench that he was sure had saturated his clothes.

As he walked, he recalled his sisters' stories of their detention in the workhouse and questioned how the powers that be, like the gentleman he had just met, allowed such grim establishments to exist without providing some modicum of comfort and respect for the inmates. Society, he mused, was remiss in its care for people who, due to circumstances over which they had no control, found themselves in establishments that were nothing short of prisons. They were made to suffer for being poor. *Why are people allowed to live like this?* he wondered.

He pulled himself out of his brooding and mulled over his meeting with Cyril Bruce. Then, with a spring in his step and hope in his heart that all was not yet lost in his search for the Nipper, headed back to report to the family.

Archie kept himself busy over the next few days, both at work and at home, but he could hardly contain his nervousness, to the annoyance of Doris.

'Archie lad, you'll wear away the lino or the soles of your shoes if you don't stop parading around the room,' she scolded kindly. 'You're making me dizzy.'

'Are you going to find our Nipper?' enquired Ruby, who had vague memories of the baby.

'I hope so, poppet, I sure hope so. I can hardly contain myself.'

The following days passed slowly for Archie, who was distracted to the point of being reprimanded at work for giving a guest the wrong key and for forgetting to pick up bread for Doris.

At the end of the week, he left early to travel back to the home where he hoped and prayed he would be given some answers. He arrived on time to be met by the head of the women's establishment, who apologised for the absence of Cyril Bruce; he was attending to business in another institute.

'Mr Bruce has asked me to give you this information. It appears that several children from the last known establishment where your brother was housed, succumbed to the influenza. Those who survived were sent to a country institute many miles from here. No-one knows what happened to them, as contact was lost in the confusion of war, what with people searching for families and workhouses filling up with displaced people, it has been impossible to keep track of the whereabouts of every inmate. Mr Bruce wishes you well.' She handed him a piece of paper. 'This is the only address he could find, after extensive enquiries. It may well be a waste of a journey for you. It is referred to as Moorland Mansion in the parish of Lincoln, that's almost two hundred miles from here.'

Archie took the paper from her, thanked her, and left feeling hopeful despite the thought of a long journey. Returning home, he discussed his plans with Stan, who was wary of the lad venturing on such a journey and the travel it would entail.

In the library that had almost become a second home for him, Archie studied a map of the area that the librarian had located, and made a rough copy of the route he planned to take. It would take several days and was peppered with danger for a lone traveller. Stan, apprehensive about the impending trek, wished he was fit and able to accompany him.

Doris packed food and saw that his clothes were suitable for the journey, despite misgivings about the dangers for Archie. Although the lad was mature, she was concerned that he was in many ways emotional and vulnerable when it came to his family.

'I'll take rail transport as far as I can out of London,' he assured them, 'and stay a night at a tavern. It should be easy enough to hitch a ride into the country. Don't fret, Doris, I'll be just fine.'

Our Nipper

If he thought his journey was going to be pleasant, Archie was soon disillusioned by the reality of what a two hundred miles journey entailed.

27

Travelling out of the capital was, despite some discomfort, the easiest part of his journey. He remained alert, his mind buzzing with what lay ahead. His travelling companions in third class slept for most of the journey, which prevented him having to converse with an overweight woman who reeked of alcohol and lack of washing. Since experiencing both dirt and cleanliness during his young life, he was somewhat intolerant of people who made little or no effort to keep their bodies clean.

The railway guard announced their arrival and, as the train came to a shuddering halt, Archie was thrown forward almost on top of the snoring woman. She woke with a start and fumbled in her bag for some alcoholic beverage that she offered to her fellow travellers. Archie thanked her politely and alighted from the train, glad to have his feet on firm ground.

His bones ached and he shook himself to improve his circulation before making his way to a tavern pointed out to him by a fellow traveller.

'Keep your belongings with you, and don't let anyone see where your money is stored,' he was warned. 'There are some shady characters around these parts ready to pounce on a weary traveller. Keep your wits about you and you'll be fine.'

Archie thanked the gentleman for his advice and entered the tavern – a dark and dingy building with a low roof that added to the dimness. Smells of rotten food, stale alcohol, and unwashed bodies almost turned his stomach, and had he been less weary, he might have left the premises to seek shelter elsewhere. Approaching the counter, he asked the server for a room for the night.

'That'll be ninepence halfpenny, and sixpence extra if you want breakfast,' replied the rather unkempt barman, whose filthy apron was covered in beer stains and food particles. He scratched his chin, flicked a few spots from it, and held out his hand for money.

Hoping he had not been observed, Archie withdrew some coins and put them into the grubby outstretched hand.

'Room four, top of the stairs,' said the barman. 'This is a respectable establishment. No noise, and no women allowed.'

Guffawing was heard from a corner table where drinkers watched as the traveller made his way upstairs.

Archie's hopes of a quiet night's sleep were dashed when he discovered the walls were so thin that he heard the occupants of the next room snoring heavily as if in competition with each other. Exhausted, he lay on top of a filthy mattress, covered himself with a similarly grimy cloth and, clutching his precious money pouch, tried to sleep. He slept fitfully and awoke to see one of the tavern's guests hovering over him, eyes bulging, black teeth showing from his foul-smelling mouth as he attempted to remove the cover.

'What have we 'ere then? You want company under them covers to keep the cold out? Move over.'

Archie sat bolt upright. Through weary eyes, he judged the dangerous situation and ran from the room with the echo of raucous laughter ringing in his ears.

As he headed out of the tavern, the grinning owner called out, 'No breakfast then, lad? Oh well, that's sixpence profit for me.'

Archie did not stop running until he came across a clear brook, where he hurriedly drank, then washed the grime from his face. He longed to strip off and wash the lingering stench of the tavern from his body, but feared he would be spotted and robbed of his possessions. He ate some berries from nearby bushes, picked a turnip from a field, and felt his stomach churning from the after-effects.

With no idea of where he was, he walked for miles. Somewhere along the way he dropped his makeshift map and walked on without knowing if he was heading in the right direction, until he came across a small town where a market was in progress. There, he ate his first hot food, purchased from a stallholder whose customers gathered around warming themselves as they ate. The jovial crowd were known to each other and shared their stories and adventures.

Someone spotted Archie and drew him into the gathering. Soon they elicited his story, and one cheery farmer's wife plied him with bread and cheese and took him under her wing.

'A young lad like you shouldn't be alone in these parts,' she said. 'Where are you heading to?

'Moorland Mansion?'

'Yeh, I know of it. Belonged to Sir Clive Moorland. Been in his family for centuries,' informed a knowledgeable merchant.

Another stallholder who had joined the happy group added his version.

'Sir Clive never married, there was no heir to the estate, so it fell into the hands of the local authorities who let it lie empty for several years before opening it as a sanatorium at the height of the deadly influenza. I heard from a groundsman who worked there that many of the inmates were young boys from the city workhouse, all victims of the sickness. He told me the children had no chance of survival as the disease had taken a grip.' The man shook his head. 'The place has lain empty for a while. No-one in their right mind would go there, too many ghosts for my liking. They closed it down after about three years.'

Disheartened at hearing this, Archie frowned and said almost to himself, 'I've got to go there. I've got to know what happened to my brother.'

'Stick with us, lad, and when the market is over you can ride with Vin and me to our place. There's a nice warm barn where you can spend the night, then Vin will see you on the right road. A young lad like you shouldn't be making that journey on your own, it ain't safe,' consoled the farmer's wife, who was moved by Archie's tale.

Archie held back tears at the hospitality offered to him. His life experience had given him an innate feeling of who to trust, and Lottie, as she was called, was one such person. It was a rather jolly ride from the market to their farm; the twelve miles seemed to pass quickly as the couple, aided by good food and porter, sang and laughed as they travelled along. Sandy, the trusted steed needed little guidance; he knew instinctively where to go.

The couple welcomed Archie into the warmth of their home, showed him the pump where he could wash without being interrupted and, after a supper of delicious rabbit stew, took him to a warm barn where he slept soundly.

A noisy rooster, clearing its throat for its dutiful morning session, brought him out of his sleep. He lay for a time taking in the sights and smells of the farm, the sweetness of the hay, and the guttural grunting from the family pig who he was to learn was called Trotter and who was to be his travelling companion for several hours.

He listened to the morning dawn chorus of bird song, stretched his long limbs, brushed off straw from his clothes, then headed to the farmhouse. After a hearty breakfast and laden with bread and cheese, Vin loaded up the cart and declared it time to go. He and Archie took off to sell Trotter to a relative.

Waving a towel, Lottie called out, 'Take care, young man. God go with you on your quest.'

28

The travellers settled into a rhythm as they jogged along, moving from side to side with the movement of the cart. Vin was an interesting character with tales to tell that Archie surmised were more from his imagination than from real life.

'We breed pigs, me and Lottie. Have done so for years. My relative buys them and gets on with the job of slaughtering. I can't do that at my place as Lottie has no stomach for it,' he explained. 'She lets herself get too attached to them, especially Trotter. I tell her it's only a beast and we need to live. We need to eat.'

Archie did not wish to know any more details as Trotter, riding behind and unaware of his impending doom, nuzzled his neck as if to make friends. The beast's hot breath comforted him as if it knew what lay ahead for his travelling companion. From time to time Vin burst into song and encouraged his passenger to join in.

'I ain't much of a singer but it helps pass the time, and Sandy here doesn't seem to mind. I swear that animal trots in time to my singing.'

The journey took most of the day as they rode deeper into the countryside, the occasional silence broken only by the clip clop of hooves and steady breathing from Trotter. They stopped once or twice to eat and to give Sandy a rest.

'It won't be long afore darkness creeps in. I have to hurry on a bit now, so I can't take you right to the Moorland estate. I'll drop you off as near as possible,' said Vin. 'You mind out, young fellow, there's mischief about in these places. I'll be returning this way in two days, so if you need a hitch up, listen out for Sandy here.'

Archie jumped down when the cart stopped at a rough patch, patted Trotter and Sandy, and thanked Vin for looking after him.

'Keep to the left,' the man said, pointing to where the weary traveller was to head. 'It's about a two-mile hike from here, and you should see the house through the trees as you go around the corner. Not somewhere I'd want to be. I haven't set eyes on it for a few years now, not since we heard the folks in there were ill with influenza. Good luck, lad, in finding your brother. God speed.'

He waved and moved off. 'Gee up, Sandy,' he called to his horse, 'we got to get ourselves to Lester's farm afore dark. Don't envy that lad's reception when he gets to that creepy place.'

His trusted stead nodded as if in agreement, and headed for where a warm stable of sorts awaited him.

Archie soldiered on, trampling through rough grass and bushes as he increased his pace. The path was at times difficult to find, but he followed what he thought was the right road. Darkness was beginning to fall, and tiredness took hold, dashing his hopes of completing his mission while there was still light. He was sensible enough to know when he was beaten.

He tripped a few times, resulting in a gash on his head that bled profusely, but he managed to stem the flow and prevent blood from ruining his now rather crumpled jacket.

Eventually, Archie lay under a thick bush on a dry grassy section that provided a bed for the night. He looked in wonder at the stars and began to count them until, overcome with sleep, he closed his eyes for the night. The only sound to be heard was the hooting of an owl as it laid claim to its nocturnal domain.

He woke to the ominous silence of the countryside, broken only by the wind blowing through the trees, as if warning the traveller to escape from whatever lay ahead. He dusted himself down, smoothed his hair with his hand and wished he had access to water to wash the congealed blood from this face.

His stomach rumbled and he regretted not having kept some bread from the previous day. *I'm sure they'll give me something to eat and drink before I take our Nipper home, and let me freshen up*, he thought, still trying to convince himself that his trip would have a happy outcome.

But any hope he had of completing his task was soon replaced by despair as the house came into view. It was clearly abandoned. The depressing brick building stood like a deserted sentinel guarding an abyss where once a monument to civilisation had proudly stood, but was now an eerily, empty relic of past days. Using a stick to clear a path in front of him, Archie trudged on through knee-length foliage until he was in full view of the house. He stood in awe as he took in the horror in front of him, fear taking hold of his once confident persona as he studied the building.

He felt a shiver go through his body that reached his pounding heart. *Surely no-one has lived here for many years, if ever*, he thought. *It's an evil-looking place.* Archie had been in denial at the stories told to him at the marketplace, and had painted a picture in his head of a happy home where a smiling Nipper awaited.

He rummaged in his pocket for the paper that Vin had given him with the instructions as to where he would find Moorland Mansion. He was sure he was in the right place, but confused at what faced him. *This can't be right, can it?*

He approached the house and climbed several broken steps to the main entrance, avoiding water that gushed from a broken gutter. There, carved on a moss-covered stone, he saw a faded inscription that confirmed he was indeed at the correct establishment. Moorland Mansion. *Mansion? Perhaps it was once worthy of the name, but now?* He hesitated before trying the wooden doorknob, as if turning it would release dispossessed souls, such was his assessment of the place. His hand shook as he pushed on the rotting wood, and it creaked as he gently nudged the filthy door that opened into a dark hallway that smelled of damp, death, and decay.

'Hello!' he called out. He didn't expect a reply, but felt he had to be polite should anyone be lurking there. 'Hi there.' His voice stuck in his throat and echoed as if he were in a cave.

Venturing further into the hallway, the light from the doorway casting an ominous shadow and adding to his dread of what might lie beyond, Archie screamed as something ran across his feet. He was well used to rodents, but the suddenness of its appearance made him jump. Composing himself and, sure that no humans inhabited the dwelling, he ventured on from the hall, holding a stick firmly in his hand to ward off unwanted vermin that might come his way.

A large room on the right had some light emanating from its dirty sash windowpanes that once would have been the source of sunlight. Archie imagined the room being full of light and laughter, but was now sadly neglected and left to rot. A few sticks of broken furniture did not equate with his idea of a mansion, reminding him more of the poverty-stricken home he had shared with his parents a lifetime away.

He moved on across the hall, where a similar sized room showed the same signs of abandonment. He went deeper into the house, checking each door as he went. Unsure of the safety of the staircase and, lacking any source of light other than that from the doors that he had deliberately left open, he carefully checked each step with his stick before stepping on. Parts of the handrail were missing and only added to his cautious climb.

The upstairs rooms were bleak and as depressing as the others. Satisfied that no one, not even a vagrant, inhabited the desolate mansion, he made his way out into the light and fresh air. Glad to leave the building, he walked around the grounds that seemed to stretch as far as the eye could see, and tripped on a boulder of sorts that turned out to be a neglected gravestone.

Looking around, he realised he was in an overgrown grave-yard. Several stones were legible. To his horror, they contained names and ages of inmates from Moorland Mansion who had succumbed to the Spanish influenza, a relatively short time ago. The neglected and abandoned crudely-hewn stones indicated a hurried exit from this place of horror and death. Names and ages told a frightening and depressing story.

Using grass to wipe the stones, he noted the inscriptions were not as old as he had first imagined. Winter storms had played havoc with the roughly carved inscriptions, making them appear older than first thought. An uneasy feeling consumed him hitting the pit of his stomach as he frantically searched for the name Connor. He rubbed stone after stone, his knuckles chaffed and bleeding, tears rolling down his face and nipping his eyes as he methodically moved from one to another, not pausing to rest until he had covered the entire area.

It was hopeless. Eventually, Archie sat on the wet grass and wept copious tears that ran down and stained his already grubby face.

29

He was distraught. His stomach rumbled like a gurgling waterfall. He needed to be free from the horror of this place before darkness struck and plunged him into even more misery, but exhaustion took over.

Archie struggled as far as he could from the nightmare and horror of the place, and once again attempted to sleep under the stars. The night was colder than the previous one, and drops of rain threatened to add to his despair. He no longer cared about his appearance; his mission had failed. He was beyond grief-stricken.

All he wanted was to return to the warmth and comfort of home with his sisters and substitute parents. He trudged on, retracing his steps onto the makeshift road where Vin had dropped him off what seemed like a lifetime ago. Overcome with weakness, shouting aloud and sobbing inconsolably into the dark, empty stillness of the countryside, he collapsed onto the ground. It was there, several hours later, that Vin spotted him.

'Oh Archie! Oh, poor lad,' the farmer lamented as he lifted the young man into the back of the cart. He covered him with sacking, gave him water, and headed off for home. Sandy, sensing the urgency, trotted as quickly as he could.

Archie slept for most of the journey. When he awoke, he lay in the cart listening to the clip clop of the hooves and the soft singing from Vin.

'Ah, so you've decided to join the world again?' chuckled Vin, as Archie raised himself into a sitting position.

He waited until Archie was ready to relate his unsuccessful search at the empty Moorland Mansion.

'It was awful, Vin. The place was closed up and neglected, but the worst thing was the graves...' He burst into tears, more from exhaustion than anything else. His heart was heavy as lead as he described the graveyard and its inscriptions.

'I wiped every one of the stones with grass and leaves looking for my brother's name. I don't know how I feel at not finding it,' he admitted. 'Relief, perhaps, that his name wasn't among them and that he might still be alive somewhere. But where? Vin, they were so young, just kids.'

Back at the farmhouse, Lottie immediately took charge. She fed him hot food, then packed him off to sleep in the warm barn.

'Poor boy,' she remarked to her husband. 'He had his hopes set on finding his brother.'

Archie remained at the farm until the next market day and travelled there with Lottie and Vin. He did not relish the tedious journey home. The journey there had been full of hope as he'd anticipated a fruitful outcome. But his failure to find the Nipper clouded his soul like a black veil that covered his entire being.

Even the jolly couple with their songs and stories of market life did little to ease his pain. Lottie insisted he eat a hot meal to prepare him for the long hours ahead. Her heart went out to the boy; she could find no answer to ease his pain.

At the close of market, she hugged the distraught lad as she bade him farewell. A farmer friend of theirs would give him a ride to where he was to pick up the train that would take him back to London.

'Never give up hope, Archie,' said Vin, as he waved him off. 'Methinks you might have looked in the wrong place. Your brother is out there somewhere. God speed your search.'

Determined not to go near the squalid tavern, he waited in the shadow of a building near the railway station for several hours until it was time to board the train. In his rush to leave the mansion, he had dropped some money from his pocket, leaving him with very little funds for the return journey – enough only to purchase a ticket. A biting wind funnelled through the alleyway, and he shivered as he sat on the cold earth and hugged his arms across his body to generate heat, pulling his jacket tightly in an attempt to protect himself from the elements. The wait seemed endless, and he ate the food that Lottie had packed, leaving none for the remaining journey. Archie felt miserable both in body and in spirit.

When the train arrived, he was pleased to note there was room enough for him to sit in the corner and rest his head on the window. The wooden seats in third class were hard but, overcome with exhaustion and with his jacket wrapped around as best he could, he settled to sleep for the entire time. A fellow traveller, noticing how the boy shivered and mumbled incoherently, wrapped his own cloak around him.

Archie finally returned home, wracked with pain, and sobbed as he told of his failed quest. Doris's heart ached for the lad who was grieving for what was lost.

'Come now, Archie,' she gently urged him. 'It's not like you to give up.'

'Doris, I've failed Mam. I haven't been able to keep the family together. Stupid, stupid me for wandering off to look for them and ending up at sea. If I'd stayed here, I could have got us all out of the workhouse.'

'Don't fret, lad,' consoled Stan. 'We know how much time and effort you've put into searching for them, and look how happy the girls are. You've done all you can for the moment to find the Nipper. Don't be disheartened, there's always hope.'

'Even if I find him,' Archie argued, 'he has no knowledge of our existence, and how can I prove he is my brother?'

The lad rambled on, muttering at time incoherently; he was fevered and his body ached, but it was nothing compared to the pain in his heart.

'Let's get you warmed up and into bed,' comforted Doris, as she served him warm soup. 'As for identifying the Nipper, have no fear. He has the same birthmark as you, on your right buttock. Don't forget, I bathed you when you were with us after your mam died. I noticed a similar mark on you and the baby.'

Archie looked up at her with interest. 'Da had a birthmark there, too,' he said. 'I saw it when he was bathing in the tin bath at home; there wasn't much privacy.'

*

Despondency turned to anger and misery for young Archie as he attempted to concentrate on his work at Oscar Nash's hotel. Stan and Doris despaired of ever bringing him out of his overwhelming grief, and his normally good appetite appeared to have abandoned him as he missed meals and picked at others. His sleep, too, was erratic. He tossed and turned, and when exhaustion took hold of his troubled soul, he dreamt of graves of young children opening to reveal monstrous, zombie-like sculls. Ruby and Betsy were confused at the change in their normally cheerful brother.

I've failed Mam. I've failed my family, became his guilty mantra.

Over breakfast one morning, the grief-stricken youngster announced, 'It's no use, Stan. Our Nipper is dead, either buried under rubble or dead from influenza.' He put his head on the table and sobbed uncontrollably. 'I'm going out to clear my head.'

He had a few days off work, and spent hours walking around, oblivious to the rain and wind that seemed to pound at the darkness of his soul. As darkness fell, loud voices brought him out of his reverie and he entered a tavern and drank until he could hardly stand. The inn was so crowded that no-one noticed the plight of the lad who was hardly able to keep upright at the counter without holding onto the ledge that ran along the front of the bar area.

He somehow staggered home into the arms of Stan, who helped him into bed.

'You'll have a thumping headache when you wake up in the morning,' he whispered to the comatose lad.

Stan lifted Archie's clothes that smelt like a saloon. 'I'll clean them,' he told Doris. 'We can't have him going out stinking of beer.'

After sleeping late, Archie surfaced and sat sheepishly at the table as Doris served a meal of rabbit stew and gently reprimanded him. 'Drink don't solve anything, Archie,' she said sternly. 'Look what it did to your da.'

Memories of da surfaced and he remembered the strain on his beloved mam's face as she had tried to feed her hungry brood while their hapless father drank every penny needed for food.

'You're right,' he croaked. 'I don't want to end up like Da. No more drinking for me. Sorry. That won't happen again... it's just that...'

'It's okay, Archie, we know you feel bad. You don't need to feel guilty. You've done your best.'

*

Some weeks later, a letter arrived from Dan with news of his latest sea voyage. The family gathered around the table as Archie read to them.

'When are we going to 'merica?' asked an excited Betsy as she sat close to her brother as if attempting to read the letter with him. Her pretty curls fell over her face, and she flicked them away with her hand as she continued to help Archie read his correspondence.

There was silence for a few minutes while Archie looked at the face of his sweet, innocent sister, and in that moment he made a decision that was to bring him out of his black mood.

'As soon as we find our Nipper.' Looking across at Stan and Doris, he announced, 'I'm *not* giving up. He's out there somewhere, and I'm gonna search to the ends of the earth.'

Betsy piped up, 'Is he hiding? Is our Nipper hiding?'

Archie smiled down at her. 'He is that, poppet. He's hiding, but I'm going to find him.'

30

Life moved on for the family. Ruby, now enrolled at the local charity school, was proud of the clothes that Doris made for her. With her unruly curls dressed in ribbons, she felt the confident child she had always been as she soaked up lessons like a sponge. The little education she had received in the workhouse, and her own desire to learn, gave her a foundation on which to build her reading and counting skills. She developed a neat hand and took pride in presenting her work, to the delight of the master.

She advanced rapidly through school and, encouraged by Doris, excelled in needlework. Every spare moment was spent sketching frocks and costumes, some from her imagination and others copied and adapted from the occasional magazine that Doris was given from a friend.

'There's no point in me throwing these out when you can make use of them,' commented the friend.

'These will be well perused, and read from cover to cover,' Doris told the woman. 'Ruby has a flair for designing costumes, and adores the fashions in the magazines. Thank you so much.'

Betsy, who was considered too frail and vulnerable to attend school, remained at home under the care and love of the Youngs. Ruby taught her to read simple words and recognise numbers, Stan helped with gentle exercise to help strengthen her arm, while Doris showed her basic household skills. The youngster was content to shadow Doris around the house as they sang and laughed together. And the pair made daily visits to the local market, where she became well known to the stallholders.

'Here comes the prettiest girl in all of London town,' remarked one such seller, bringing giggles and laughter from Betsy.

The highlight for Betsy was an addition to the family – a puppy that was to be her very own. Doris remembered how enchanted the child had been when she'd visited the specialist.

'I'm going to name it Blackie, cos his colour is black,' said the delighted youngster, and she spent many hours grooming and playing with her new friend. The regular walks improved her confidence on stairs, as she trudged up and down to the yard, and life was good for the fragile child.

*

Engrossed in the busy life of the hotel, Archie temporarily left his troubled thoughts behind. Walking through the main dining room one morning, he noticed that one of their regular guests had not appeared for breakfast; his reserved table had not been used. Enquiries to the dining staff confirmed that the gentleman, normally a creature of habit, had not eaten breakfast nor requested room service.

'That's unusual,' Archie commented. 'I'll check his room.'

He took the elevator to the penthouse suite where Monsieur Hebert stayed during his frequent business visits, then knocked tentatively on the door and waited.

When there was no response, he knocked louder and called out, 'Monsieur Hebert, are you well, sir?'

Hearing faint groans, he used his master key and carefully opened the door, hoping he hadn't disturbed the gentleman if he was trying to rest.

'Monsieur Hebert,' he called as he looked around. But as he moved further into the room, he found the gentleman in question lying on the floor, clutching his chest and moaning in pain.

'Oh sir,' Archie gasped as he rushed to the ill guest. 'Don't worry, sir, I'll help you up from the floor.'

Archie used the intercom to contact the front desk and instructed them to call an ambulance while he tried to make the guest comfortable. Seeing the man's condition deteriorate, instinct took over and Archie pumped the man's heart and breathed into his mouth. His patient's skin was clammy, his pallor grey, his breathing laboured. But after what seemed an interminable time, Monsieur Hebert rallied slightly, held Archie's hand and mouthed, 'Thank you.'

When medical assistance arrived, the ambulance men checked the gentleman's vitals, and prepared to take their casualty to the infirmary.

'Well done. You probably saved this patient's life by your actions,' one of the ambulance officer's commented to the concerned lad.

'I did what I thought was right, sir.'

Word of the gentleman's illness reached Oscar Nash, and a few days later he requested Archie's presence in his office.

'That was fortuitous, Archie. Your timing saved the life of a grateful guest. I visited him earlier today in the infirmary and I'm happy to report he is out of danger and improving steadily,' said the hotel owner. 'His doctor told him had he not been found when he was, he would not have survived a heart attack. He hopes to return here to his suite and continue his recuperation for the foreseeable future with the assistance of a private nurse, whom he has employed.' He smiled at his young employee. 'Meanwhile, as a token of my and the hotel's appreciation for what you did for one of our respected guests, I intend to increase your wages with immediate effect.'

A rather sheepish Archie thanked his employer. 'Sir, I only did what anyone would have done in the circumstances. But I'm pleased to hear the gentleman is recovering well. Thank you, sir.'

With a spring in his step, he continued with his work with a calmer attitude, and grateful for the increase in wages that was to help his American fund.

Some weeks later, a rather frail Monsieur Hebert arrived back at his suite, accompanied by Martine, his nurse. A forty-something efficient lady, she took no nonsense from her patient, as Monsieur Hebert was to find out to his cost when he rose next morning, eager to get the day started. He was promptly returned to his bed and informed he was to rest.

'Madame, I wish to go in search of the young man who saved my life,' Monsieur Hebert told her. 'I desire to engage him in conversation.'

'Then I shall request the employee in question visit you here in your rooms,' she replied. 'You may sit by the window for a short time only, to converse with him.' The invalid muttered something under his breath which Martine chose to ignore.

Later that day, Archie arrived in the penthouse suite as requested. Monsieur Hebert's face lit up when the young man arrived. Sitting opposite each other in winged, upright chairs, with a glass of lemon tea served by Martine, the two men conversed as if they had known each other all their lives. Archie felt comfortable in the older man's presence, and once the formalities were over found himself telling his host about his own life.

'I want to know everything about my saviour,' requested the invalid. He settled to hear Archie relate his life story and remained attentive and did not interrupt the flow of rhetoric from Archie, although he allowed himself a chuckle when he heard of the initial sea voyage.

Archie finished with an up-to-date report on the futile search for his brother.

'There you are, sir,' he finished with a grin. 'The life story of Archie Connor, Esquire.'

'And what a tale, young man. What a tale!'

Martine, who had been busy in an adjoining room, arrived and announced that her patient was due to rest.

'Darn, woman,' her employer admonished, 'can't a man get on with his life without some interfering woman attempting to ruin it? Thank goodness I had the good sense never to marry... Women... the bane of man's existence.'

Despite his gruffness, Archie spotted him wink as he spoke.

'I think, sir,' Archie stood to leave, 'that I have tired you out, and I must return now to my duties. It has been a pleasure to be in your company.'

Monsieur Hebert nodded. 'I concede. I know when I am beaten, and I do admit to the need of rest. Archie Connor, please do me the pleasure of returning someday soon and save this poor invalid from the wiles of this wicked nurse.' He laughed as he waved his guest off.

Over the following weeks, Archie became a regular visitor to the penthouse suite and learned something of Monsieur Hebert's life.

'I'm a confirmed bachelor, married to the job,' the man chuckled as he continued, 'I own a shipping company in my native Canada and have only recently retired from day-to-day running of the company. But I intend to keep an eye on things.'

'Sir,' interrupted a confused Archie, 'I thought you were French. Do all Canadians speak French?'

'Ah. Not all. I think I have to regale you with a brief history of my country. The original explorers were from France, and brought their language and culture with them. They wished to make a better life for themselves and to conquer the world. My ancestors were, I believe, from Paris, and most of them settled around Quebec. My ancestor, Louis Hebert, was interested in agriculture, although he was in fact an apothecary. He and his family were among the first settlers in Quebec.'

'And you still carry his name, sir?

'Indeed, I do. Louis Jacques Hebert, although Hebert is a common name. My family were farmers, as I was in my youth. But I became interested in shipping crops to other countries, so I invested in a ship, the firm grew, and I am now the proud owner of a fleet of sailing vessels.'

Once more, the formidable Martine arrived to declare the conversation over. Archie, out of respect for his newfound friend, and slightly in awe of the fierce-looking nurse, prepared to take his leave.

'Before you go,' called the patient, 'do me the pleasure of returning on Sunday with your family – the people who care for you. Perhaps we can all have tea.'

'Thank you, sir. They will be happy to meet you.'

'Until Sunday then. *Au revoir.*'

Sunday being Archie's day off, the family travelled by omnibus to Oscar Nash's hotel. Doris had hurriedly adapted frocks for the girls, adding pretty decorative belts to enhance the attire. She wore her best frock and had adapted a hat, adding ribbons and flowers.

'We have to look our best to visit Archie's friend,' she remarked as she attempted to control the girls' excitement.

Although they eagerly awaited the prospect of a ride across the city, Betsy remained apprehensive about the journey. Archie held her close and pointed out places of interest as they rode along.

'Look, Betsy, at that big house. That's where the King and Queen live,' he told her.

'Oh, they have lots of rooms.'

'Yes, they do, poppet. They have lots of servants to look after them.'

She nodded thoughtfully. 'Hmm. I'd like to be a servant in a big house.'

Before long, they alighted at the hotel, to be met by Monsieur Hebert himself in the grand foyer. Betsy, in awe of the exquisite hotel and plush surroundings and the approaching gentleman, hid shyly behind Archie.

'My family, sir.' announced Archie. 'Unfortunately, Mr Young is unable to make the journey due to ill health, but he sends his best regards to you. May I introduce Mrs Young – Doris – and my sisters, Ruby and Betsy.'

Introductions made, Doris was overcome when the gentleman kissed her hand, saying, '*Enchanté* Madame Doris, welcome.'

Her cheeks were pink as she stuttered her reply, 'N-n-nice to meet you, I'm sure, milord.'

'And who are these two pretty princesses?' The man turned his attention to the girls.

Ruby giggled as her hand was kissed by Monsieur Hebert. 'Princess Ruby, I am delighted to meet you. And we have another princess here. Princess Betsy, I am enchanted by your beauty.' Betsy, too, giggled at being called a princess; the ice had melted.

The tea party was a success. Doris, in awe at first, eventually settled to enjoy a treat of tea, sandwiches, and cakes, and jovial conversation with a very interesting Monsieur Hebert. He told of his life in Canada, his shipping business and his adventures at sea, and the girls were fascinated by his accent.

Ruby, when asked about her schoolwork, was delighted when requested to recite a poem. She chose *Silver,* by Walter de la Mare.

'*Slowly, silently, now the moon…*' The room fell silent as she gave her clear recitation, broken only by Betsy's applause when she finished.

'Bravo, bravo,' congratulated their host. 'Such a beautiful recital, and word perfect, my dear. You must come more often and brighten an old man's day.'

Beaming with delight, Ruby graciously accepted the praise lavished upon her.

Betsy, too, with a little encouragement, sang a little song, *Oranges and Lemons,* and was rewarded with rapturous applause from her audience.

It was a jolly group who travelled home to tell Stan of their day and to share some sweetmeats that Monsieur Hebert had given them.

'Don't all talk at once,' laughed Stan, 'or I'll have a sore head.'

31

Life moved on for the family. Monsieur Hebert returned to Canada with Martine, who was grateful to be employed and looked forward to a new life in a foreign country. With paperwork in order and packed ready to begin the voyage, they said goodbye to Archie, who promised to write.

Monsieur Hebert pressed a considerable amount of money into his hand and whispered, 'Thank you for saving my life and for introducing me to your lovely family. Use this to treat them, with my grateful thanks for their company. You have made an old man extremely happy.'

Archie tried to protest, but to no avail. Monsieur Hebert was adamant.

That evening, he showed Stan and Doris the cash and insisted they took their share. Christmas was looming, and the three planned to take the girls to the theatre.

'Do you remember our trip there when you were a young'un?' enquired Stan. 'Why don't we repeat that?'

'Leave it to me,' said the excited lad. 'I'll make arrangements. Doris, I want to buy the girls red shoes with buckles. Ruby has always dreamed of owning a pair.'

'Then, they shall have it,' she replied. 'I know where to purchase them and what size to get. Let's keep it as a surprise until the day of the performance. Monsieur has been very generous; we can afford to get them new frocks, too.'

A frenzy of activity took over the little house, and a jolly atmosphere added to the excitement of Christmas. Archie put his plan into action. Unlike the previous theatre visit in the cold omnibus, he organised a private carriage to collect them and return for them after the show.

With the help of the carriage driver, Archie managed to carry Stan, who was becoming more disabled and struggled to walk any distance, down three flights of stairs. The girls were ecstatic about their shoes and outfits that Doris had made for them.

'I feel posh,' laughed Ruby, as she twirled around.

'Me, too,' echoed Betsy. 'Posh.'

Posh did not end there. Unknown to the others, Archie had booked a circle box near the stage, and there they sat in awe of their surroundings. Doris shook her head in amazement as she looked up at the area where they had sat on their previous visit. The adults were briefly silent as they remembered the absent Nipper, who had been with them that day, safely tucked up in Doris's shawl. The girls were too excited to notice the sadness, and looked around in wonder at their surroundings, pointing out interesting objects to each other.

'Well, Archie, you certainly did us proud,' remarked Stan. 'I remember you saying that one day we would sit in the posh seats, and here we are. God bless the day you met Monsieur Hebert. He must be a wealthy gentleman to give so generously.'

And with that, the music started, the curtain rose, and the show began.

Some days later, Archie penned a letter of thanks to Monsieur Hebert, detailing how he had spent some of his money, and related the thrill of the theatre visit, the ride in the carriage, and his sisters' excitement. He sent greetings from Stan and Doris, and pictures that the girls had drawn for their Canadian friend. They eagerly awaited a reply.

Christmas 1920 was a delightful time for the family. Doris, with help from the girls, produced a meal fit for a king, while Stan fashioned dolls for them, evoking memories of a previous Christmas.

Doris knitted a warm muffler for Archie that Betsy took delight in wrapping round and round his neck until he teasingly pleaded for mercy. As on a previous Christmas, remembered by everyone but Betsy, they sat by the fire singing carols and listening to Stan as he read the story of Tiny Tim. Something in the deep recess of her mind triggered a memory as Betsy, to the surprise of everyone, called out, 'God bless us, one and all.'

*

Several weeks later, a letter with a Canadian stamp arrived at Oscar Nash's hotel, addressed to Archie. He did not recognise the writing.

Rue du Jardin,
Quebec
February 1923
Archie Connor Esquire,
London
    Sir,
    It is with deep sadness that I inform you of the death of my employer, Monsieur Louis Jacques Hebert. After a pleasant sail home to Canada, he succumbed to a serious illness and passed away one month later. He was aware of his limited time and wished to return to his homeland.

During our voyage, he spoke fondly of you and his delight in meeting your family. Your letter relating the details of the theatre visit pleased him greatly, as did the pictures from your dear sisters.

I remain, in sorrow,

Respectfully,

Martine La Blanche

Archie shared the missive with his employer, who had known Monsieur Hebert for several years.

Oscar Nash bowed his head in respect before saying, 'He was a fine gentleman with whom I was privileged to have several interesting conversations. Before he left, he confided in me that he knew he did not have long for this world and wished to spend his remaining days in his native Quebec.' He sighed. 'We have lost a valued customer and friend.'

It was a rather subdued family who sat around the kitchen table that evening when Archie shared the letter from Martine.

Doris wept into her apron, Stan lowered his head, and the girls, catching the mood of the others, hugged their brother and sobbed. The clock on the hearth ticked softly, as if echoing the passing of time with the passing of Monsieur Hebert.

32

Despairing of ever finding his brother, and unwilling to dismiss his sisters' hope of meeting the baby they vaguely remembered, Archie gave serious thought to returning to New York. Time had moved on and the girls were now maturing into young ladies requiring their own space. Even Betsy had grown in stature, if not in mind. Although much improved in speech and mobility, she remained vulnerable and required adult guidance.

Archie faced several dilemmas: he had sufficient funds to purchase a passage for himself, with a view to sending for Ruby and Betsy at a later date. But that in itself would raise difficulties. He could not envisage leaving the girls to travel alone.

He considered asking Stan and Doris to accompany them to make a new life in America. But no sooner had the idea entered his head than he dismissed the absurd thought; Stan was in no fit state to make such an onerous journey. With the older man's declining health and the girls outgrowing the small room they shared with their brother, Archie knew he had to act.

He worked every hour he could, saved every penny, and became more and more stressed as the months went by. Something required to be done to ease the over-crowding and afford the Youngs the privacy they deserved but never voiced.

Archie could see no way out of his predicament. Unknown to him, things were about to change.

Doris had noticed the slumped shoulders, the red eyes, and the quiet demeanour of the boy she considered her son. She wished she could take his burden from him. He arrived home late most evenings, having walked from work to save a few pennies. He looked worn-out and desperate to sleep.

'There's a letter arrived for you, Archie, with a foreign-looking stamp,' she announced one evening, hoping the correspondence would bring the lad out of his miserable frame of mind.

Thinking it was a correspondence from Dan, he took the letter, turned it over and studied the writing and the stamp. Then he frowned. 'It's not from Dan. It's marked Canada.'

'Are you going to stand there holding it all evening, or are you going to put us out of our misery? We've been looking at that envelope all day,' laughed Stan, as Archie carefully opened and read the missive.

It seemed an endless wait for the Youngs as they watched Archie shake his head, raise his eyes, then look at them in stunned silence.

'Not bad news, I hope?' said Stan.

'No, Stan,' Archie replied, clearly shocked. 'On the contrary... Oh, I have to sit down.' His hand shook as he re-read the missive.

'Listen to this. I think I'm dreaming.'

Rue Citadelle
Quebec
January 1924
Archie Connor Esquire,
London

　　Sir, it falls to me to impart news to your advantage. As full executor of the Last Will and Testament of the late Monsieur

Louis Jacques Hebert of Quebec, I have been instructed to inform you that in the terms of the Will of the aforesaid Monsieur Louis Jacques Hebert, you are to be the recipient of Eight Thousand

Canadian Dollars ($8000), in appreciation of your genuine kindness to my client, to be paid immediately, and a monthly allowance to be arranged at a later date.

Should you accept this bequeath, I shall arrange for transfer of monies forthwith. I await your reply.

Respectfully,

Emile Gagnon

Stan and Doris sat in stunned silence as Archie passed the letter over for their perusal. A grinning Archie shook his head in disbelief, his mind in overdrive as to how the generosity of Monsieur Hebert would change their lives.

'Oh Archie, you are rich beyond belief!' exclaimed Stan, and he wiped his spectacles to take a clearer look at the document that he held in his shaking hands.

Doris, for once lost for words, wiped the perspiration from her hands on her well-worn apron and re-read the missive with Stan. She moved round the table to hug the bemused youth.

'Your dreams can all come true now, Archie,' she told him. 'What a generous bequeath from that lovely gentleman. Eight thousand dollars! That must be a mighty amount of pounds.'

As if emerging from a dream, Archie replied, 'It is indeed a generous gift that I must use wisely, as he would have wished. We have plans to make, all three of us... well, all five of us. Shall I wake the girls?' he asked, as he rose from his chair.

'Let them sleep.' Doris shook her head. 'I don't expect any of us will sleep much tonight. Oh my goodness. Archie Connor, a gentleman of means.'

He laughed. 'Tomorrow, I shall contact the bank. They will advise me on the value of this bequeath.' He hugged Doris again. 'You're right. I don't think I will sleep a wink tonight.'

*

The next morning, Archie asked to speak to Oscar Nash; he wanted to tell his employer about his good fortune. He was ushered into the plush office, and offered a firm handshake from his employer.

Oscar Nash spoke first. 'I can see by your face that you have received an important correspondence from Quebec, as have I.'

They discussed the generosity shown by their friend.

'How do you plan to use your windfall?' enquired Oscar Nash. 'I, for one, intend to retire a few years earlier than planned and take my wife and daughter to Europe.'

Archie replied, 'I haven't worked out details yet, my head is still in a foggy state, I fear. But I intend to take my sisters to America. I have much planning to do, sir, and would be grateful if I could be released from my work here.'

Nash laughed. 'Of course. As of now, you have no need of employment.'

The two conversed, laughed, and shared plans. Archie thought he had never seen his employer so animated. When they parted, Archie promised to correspond and inform the older man when arrangements were in place for his voyage to the New World.

It was a light-hearted young man who entered the London Library. He immediately headed for the writing room and penned letters to Dan, Jimbel, and to C.J. Croft, informing them of his intended plans. He then went to the bank to discuss his gift, and left the interview in an exhilarated state.

Returning home, he shared his news with the Youngs.

'Oh, Archie! So much money! Archie, you are indeed a gentleman of wealth.'

He wanted to discuss his future plans with the couple who meant so much to him, and whom he looked upon as surrogate parents.

'I have enquired about a ship sailing to New York in about three months from now,' he told them. 'That will give me time to put arrangements in place.' He looked fondly at the couple and took Doris's hands in his. 'Will you come with us to America?'

Stan and Doris looked at each other, then at Archie.

'Archie, that is a generous offer, but you can see that a long journey would not bode well with my failing health,' Stan told him sadly. 'Doris and I appreciate your invitation. And were I a man of younger years, I would have jumped at the opportunity to see the great America. You must live your life now as you see fit. You go with our love and our blessing.'

Doris sniffled as she thanked the boy who had become her son in all but name.

'We will miss you all,' she said through her tears, 'and will not stand in your way.'

Archie had considered that they might refuse, and had an alternative plan to present to them.

'It has been some time since you saw your daughter and grandchildren,' he said 'Allow me to indulge you by purchasing a small cottage near them, and see you settled in before we sail. We could spend some time there together,' he smiled, 'and the sea air would be good for the girls before we return to the city to set sail.'

Stan and Doris spoke well into the night to ponder Archie's generous plan, and weighed up the pros and cons of a move to the coast. In the morning, they spoke to Archie, who nervously awaited their response.

'Dear Archie,' began Doris, her voice quivering with emotion, 'Stan and I have spoken at length and would like to accept your generous offer.'

'We're not getting any younger,' admitted Stan. 'I'm almost a prisoner up here; if it wasn't for you helping me downstairs, I would never see daylight. We would like to see our days out with our Mabel and the children. Her letters are good to have, but to spend time with them would make us both very content. We will miss you all more than we can say, but we don't want to stand in the way of a new life for you and the girls.'

The three hugged as if they didn't want to break contact.

'Let's tell the girls then,' said Archie, relieved that they had accepted his offer. 'We have so many preparations to make, the first of which is for me to book a cabin on the steamship *Porteous*, and to instruct an estate bureau to begin a search for a suitable house for you both.'

For the following few weeks, the little haven that had been home to its occupants for so long became a frenzy of excitement as Doris, with Ruby's help, adjusted, mended, and sorted suitable clothes for the journey.

'You are becoming a real proper seamstress,' commented Doris, as Ruby's finger nimbly sewed and mended.

'I'm going to be a proper seamstress in America, Doris, and make fine clothes for rich ladies.'

'And that you will, my little darling,' Doris whispered, as she wiped a tear from her eye at she thought of their impending separation.

Betsy, unable to contain her excitement, got in everyone's way as she tried to help with packing and cleaning.

'A hot drink and early night will do you the world of good. You don't want to be sick for the journey ahead.'

Correspondence had arrived from Mabel, who had viewed and approved a cottage two doors down from where she resided. She was thrilled at the prospect of having her aged parents living nearby. She wrote,

> *'Mam, Da, it's been too long since we saw you. The children know you only from letters. They are excited about having you nearby. Seagull Cottage is ideal. It belonged to a good neighbour, Jinny Blake, who sadly died from consumption. It has been cleaned and emptied ready for you to bring your own furnishings. We are looking forward to seeing you and to meeting the Connor family. As you know, Bill is now home with us and is doing well. He spends time in the garden and goes for long walks with our dog, Bunk. Bobby is a strapping lad, almost as tall as his da. He loves messing about in boats and wants to be a fisherman. Our Hilda is a livewire, there's no stopping her. She sings and dances around the place, a proper little actress she is. We can't wait to have you here with us.'*
>
> *Your loving daughter,*
> *Mabel Wynne*

Before they left London, Archie had one more task to complete. He made enquiries as to the resting place of his parents and discovered that as his father had died in prison, his body was interred in the prison graveyard – a grim setting for inmates to observe on the rare occasions they were allowed in the exercise yard. Those serving life sentences must have realised that they too would be laid to rest in the overgrown area, where only a wooden cross marked the final resting place of those unfortunate inmates. No-one visited, and flowers were non-existent; burials took place in the night, with only gravediggers and a cleric in attendance. Archie had no desire to visit.

With Ruby and Betsy in tow, he found the last resting place of their beloved mam. A graveyard attendant pointed him in the direction of the paupers' plot.

'I can't tell you, sir, where exactly your mam is buried; our records show she was buried somewhere in this area here.' He waved his hand across a large section, and left the three standing there looking at a vast mound of earth.

'Girls, we'll scatter these flowers over the area,' Archie told them. 'I'm sure Mam will know we've been here.'

The poignant trio moved silently along the path, tossing flowers as far as they could. Betsy had little understanding of what was happening, but Ruby remembered her mother's face as she scattered the flowers and wiped a tear from her eye. Elsie's children paid their respects.

'Is this a sad place, our Ruby?' whispered the awe-struck Betsy.

Ruby nodded.

With the task completed, Archie held his sisters close to him, said a prayer, then turned to return home to the Youngs.

33

The day of the move to the coast saw the family leave London for the last time. Archie had arranged a carrier to transport such furniture as Stan and Doris required, and sent it ahead of them.

'I *must* have the big table,' said Doris firmly. 'I ain't leaving without it.'

Stan and Archie laughed at the determination on her face as she scrubbed it as if there were no tomorrow, her face red with exertion.

'Oh, well then,' teased Stan, 'we'll leave you here with it, will we?'

Underneath the excitement of the move was a bout of nostalgia for the humble place they had called home.

A carriage arrived to take them to the railway station, and Stan locked the heavy door for the last time while the girls ran ahead to deposit the key with a neighbour for collection by the landlord. Doris followed with a basket of food for the journey while Archie, with help from the carriage driver, helped Stan downstairs.

Betsy carefully carried her beloved puppy in a basket. He was to live with Stan and Doris, and they'd assured her that he would be well looked after.

'Bunk will enjoy having a doggy friend to play with,' Stan told Betsy, who was struggling to cope with parting from

Blackie. 'He will have lots of fun running along the beach and splashing in the water.'

Betsy nodded and acquiesced to the arrangements for her pet.

'I won't be sorry to see the last of these stairs,' Stan commented, as he took one last glance at his former residence.

Excitement mounted as they drove towards the railway station. Doris sat back in the luxurious coach, closed her eyes, and sighed inwardly at the thought of the change that lay ahead for her little adopted family. Stan pointed out places of interest while Archie added his knowledge of the city, and Betsy nodded her head in time to the clip clop of the horse's hooves.

At the station, and with first class tickets purchased, a porter appeared to offer assistance.

'We are travelling light,' began Archie. 'There's only this hamper of food to be taken to the carriage.'

'Right, guv,' replied the porter, as he accepted a generous tip. Noticing Stan struggling to walk, he offered to wheel him along to the carriage. 'Sit here, sir, on this board. It's quite safe. What about you two young ladies? Hop on.'

Giggles and squeals of delight came from them as they were gently wheeled along the busy platform, linking arms with Stan. Safely on board, the family looked in awe at the carriage with its plush red seats, overhead netting racks, pretty seaside pictures on the wall, and little armrests.

'Archie Connor, you've done us proud, lad. Who would have thought we would ever travel by train, let alone in luxury?' Stan's appreciation was echoed by Doris.

Archie shook his head. 'It's the least I can do for you both after the sacrifices you made in caring for us for most of our life. I'm sure Monsieur Hebert would approve of us having a little luxury.'

The girls checked each seat in the carriage before settling on their choice for the excursion, then Betsy placed Blackie's basket on the floor by her feet. He was to prove an excellent traveller.

As the journey progressed, Ruby and Betsy, noses to the cold windowpane, took in every detail of the passing scenery. They jumped at the change of sound of the engine as it gathered speed, laughed when a train passed by on another track, like the iron horse it appeared to mimic, and coughed as smoke billowed from the engine and drifted in the tiny open window. After a time, weariness overtook the travellers, and one by one they dropped off to sleep. Only Archie remained alert, his mind full of thoughts of his past life and plans for the future. He still despaired at his failure and guilt at being unable to find the Nipper; in his subconscious, he felt sure the boy was alive somewhere and waiting to be found. The reality of his failure hit him hard.

*

The train pulled into a station where, to their delight, a tea trolley awaited thirsty passengers. A guard arrived to announce a fifteen-minute stop.

'Quick,' called Archie, 'let's get some tea.'

Doris accompanied him to the door where kind volunteers were already pouring out the golden nectar.

'Five cups, please,' requested Archie.

'The guard will collect your empty cups and hand them to our helpers at your next stop,' the server explained.

'Let's drink while the train is stationary,' suggested Stan, and with Ruby's help he lifted the hamper from the rack.

The travellers soon made inroads into Doris's picnic. Fortified with food and hot drinks, they relaxed and enjoyed the remaining journey. To relieve the tedium for the girls, Stan devised games like 'I Spy' and led them in a jolly singsong.

The iron horse pulled into its final station with a deep sigh, as it expelled its powerful energy into the air. A pillar of smoke rose and vanished, as if announcing the end of a job well done.

Waiting for them was a very excited Mabel; she could hardly contain her eagerness at the thought of being reunited with her parents. She craned her neck in an effort to spot her aging parents among the throng of alighting passengers. At last, she spied them in the distance, and waved furiously before running along the platform into the arms of Doris.

The women clung to each other until Stan, brimming with love for his daughter, coughed to announce his presence. Mabel was at first shocked at the appearance of the man who had once been strong, tall, and confident, but now appeared stooped, grey, and aged. She hugged him and drew Doris into her arms. The three stood like that, absorbed in each other's presence, until Doris broke away to introduce the Connor family.

'Mabel, here are your adopted brother and sisters!' she laughed.

Without waiting to be properly introduced, Mabel lifted Betsy up into her arms and covered the giggling girl with hugs.

'I've heard so much about you all that I feel I know you really well.' Turning to Ruby, she gave her a hug and a wide smile that reminded everyone of a younger Doris.

Archie, always the gentleman, stood back observing the welcome, then held his hand out and announced, 'Archie Connor, ma'am. Pleased to meet you.'

'Oh, you don't need to call me ma'am, although that is kind of you. I'm Mabel, and I'm so pleased to meet you at long last. Thank you for all you have done for my parents.'

They talked together before Mabel commented, 'It's a bit of a walk to the cottage. Da, will you manage, or should we call a carriage?'

'I would like to walk,' he replied. 'It's been a long journey and I need to stretch my legs. If we walk slowly and you take my arm, I'll be fine.'

The family headed for their new home. Mabel linked arms with her parents, while Archie walked beside them, holding Stan's arm and the empty hamper. The girls skipped along in front, their excitement high.

Eventually, they arrived at Mabel's cottage where they were welcomed by her husband, Bill.

'Bobby and Hilda have taken Bunk for a run along the shore to tire him out,' he explained. 'They'll be home soon. Let's have tea and scones before we go along to Seagull Cottage.'

Doris and Stan's new home was similar to Mabel's cottage. Two rooms led off from a small entrance hall – a bedroom, and a sitting room with an open fire. Their furniture was already in place.

'Where's my table?' Doris called out, a look of concern crossing her face.

Mabel laughed. 'Here, Mam, open this door from the sitting room and there's your kitchen.'

The well-loved table took pride of place in what was a cosy kitchen, and Doris stroked it as if welcoming an old friend.

With the tour of the property over, Archie and the girls left to walk further on to a small hotel where two rooms had been reserved. The owner, a lady of middle age, greeted them warmly and showed them upstairs to where they would live for the next two weeks.

'You'll have privacy here,' she announced, as she showed them to a pretty bedroom with two beds and a stunning view of the sea. Across the hall was Archie's room, with a bathroom nearby.

'This is ideal,' smiled Archie, as he shook hands with his landlady.

'I'll serve supper at six o'clock,' the woman told him. 'You must be tired after your journey.'

They were indeed weary, and Betsy almost fell asleep over her plate of fish pie.

In the following days, the girls revelled in their time by the sea, splashing in the water and letting it ripple between their toes. The movement of the tide fascinated them both.

Betsy enquired, 'Where does the sea go, Archie? Does it go all the way to America?'

'It does that, and we'll soon be sailing way out there,' he replied, as he pointed into the distance.

Archie kept the girls occupied and limited their time with the Youngs so as to ease their final separation, which he knew would be painful for them all.

The night before their departure, as the girls slept, Archie sat with Doris and Stan for the last time. Emotions were running high.

With a final hug, Archie told them, 'We have an early start in the morning, so I'll say goodbye now. It's best for the girls if we just leave quietly. I don't think I could cope with copious tears.'

His final gift was to purchase a wickerwork bath chair which allowed Stan some outdoor freedom. Bill and the grandchildren took turns to propel him around the town and along by the shore.

Early next morning, with a final glance towards Seagull Cottage, Archie and his sisters travelled in comfort to the port where they were to board the steamship that would take them to a new life.

34

Archie had reserved two adjoining cabins – the best on board – which allowed the girls a certain amount of privacy and space to move around during the long voyage. They were no longer children, and required their own space.

As the ship moved off, Archie stood by the rails watching the coastline fade from view and taking in the smell of the sea. He wondered whether he would ever see those shores again.

The trio explored the ship, laughing as they swayed to the rocking motion of the vessel and tried to avoid the spray from the waves. They copied Archie as he showed them how to walk like sailors.

'We have to find our sea legs,' he instructed, as they copied his swaying gait, laughing with him as they rocked back and forth.

After a few days of *mal de mer*, they settled into a routine that was to see them cope commendably with the long voyage. Archie devised board games, joined with other passengers for deck games, and set up a regime of exercise and walks around the decks.

'We need to keep our strength up,' he told them. 'We want to arrive in New York as fit as fiddles.'

'What's it like in America?' asked Ruby, as they sat on deck watching the waves toss and gently rock the vessel.

Archie gave them a description of New York, including the skyscrapers, food, and the many accents they would experience. He told them all about Granny Peggy and Dan, who they were to stay with until he acquired accommodation for them.

A fellow passenger, leaning on the deck not far from them, turned and walked towards them. He addressed Archie. 'Remember me?'

For a second, Archie looked at the man before recognition dawned on him. 'Roon! Is it you, Roon?'

The men grinned at each other, then hugged and laughed at the unexpected reunion.

'Roon, it is indeed. Archie lad, it does my heart good to see you again. I observed you from a distance, unsure at first until I heard your voice. And these young ladies? Are these your sisters?'

'Yeah, Roon,' Archie said with a grin. 'Let me introduce Ruby and Betsy, my sisters. Girls, this is the man I told you about. We shared a cabin when I came back to England to find you. He's a good friend, and great fun to be with.'

'Ah, so your search was successful then?' Roon frowned. 'But wasn't there a brother?'

Archie's smile faded. 'Sadly, Roon, he couldn't be traced. We had very little detail about him. I searched several establishments, even a remote country house where some boys were sent during the influenza epidemic, but to no avail. I failed in my search.' Archie shrugged. 'I fear he must have succumbed to the influenza or died during an air raid. But in my heart, Roon, I feel he is alive somewhere and we will be united someday. I live in hope.'

Roon kept his thoughts to himself, feeling that Archie's search had truly ended. While the girls went off to join in deck games with some fellow passengers, he and Archie sat on the deck and renewed their acquaintance.

For the remainder of the voyage, the older man regaled the girls with tales of his travels and his description of New York. His cheerful company helped the voyage pass quickly, and before long land was sighted. The group stood with what seemed the entire ship's company, watching New York come into view.

They were packed and ready to go when disembarkation was announced. As the ship docked, Archie spotted two people he knew well – Jimbel and Dan – who both waved their hats vigorously. Archie responded by waving both arms and encouraging the girls to wave their scarves in the direction of the two strangers.

Glad to be on land, and with formalities over, they made their way to where Dan and Jimbel waited to welcome them.

'Oh!' exclaimed Betsy. 'My legs feel like jelly.'

Archie laughed, 'Now we need to find our land legs. Here, hold on to me.'

A much older and weather-worn Dan hugged Archie, while Jimbel grinned from ear to ear as he waited to welcome his former colleague. The girls stood in awe of the strangers. Jimbel, taller and more robust, looked stronger and healthier than the scrawny bellboy that Archie remembered.

'Dan, Jimbel, meet my sisters, Ruby and Betsy.'

Jimbel could not take his eyes from the stunning beauty that Ruby had become. 'Welcome, welcome, ladies, to New York,' he told them.

Betsy giggled at being called a lady.

Dan asked if they required a carriage to take them the short distance to Peggy's home.

Archie shook his head. 'Let's walk, and get our land legs working again,' he replied, then instructed a porter to deliver their luggage to Peggy's house. 'We need to feel the ground under our feet.'

Betsy held her brother's arm and Dan's as she struggled to walk properly.

'You'll be fine, poppet, when we get used to walking on firm ground again,' Archie assured her.

Seeing Ruby wobble slightly, Jimbel held out his arm and said, 'Allow me to escort you. It's always strange to change from sea to land.'

Ruby held onto the arm of the most handsome man she thought she had ever set eyes on. She was captivated by his accent as she walked along, craning her neck at the first sight of skyscrapers and hanging on to his every word.

Before long, they reached Peggy's house.

'Archie, my boy, come in!' she squealed when she saw them arrive. 'Let me see you, you young scoundrel! My, how you've grown and filled out. Hey, aren't you the handsome one! And these pretty gals. Come and give Granny Peggy a hug.'

Dan made coffee as the girls sat in awe at the good-natured chat going on around them. Jimbel carried the luggage along to where they were to sleep then joined everyone as they sat around the table.

Archie noticed how frail and stooped Peggy had become, and wondered at the wisdom of inflicting the three of them on her.

As if reading his mind, the wise woman spoke, 'I've waited so long for this day and want you to stay here for as long as you like until you've gotten yourself settled. Dan has been looking after me now that he doesn't go to sea very often.' She smiled at the other man. 'He's semi-retired. He's my right-hand man.'

'You mean your worn-out slave?' was the response, much to the amusement of the company.

The effect of the long sea voyage soon took its toll with Betsy almost falling asleep on her feet and Ruby attempting to stifle a yawn.

Seeing how weary they all were, Jimbel took his leave of them with a request that they visit the hotel soon where C.J. Croft eagerly waited to meet them.

35

Archie's long-awaited return to the hotel was emotional as he renewed acquaintances with colleagues. Jimbel summoned Greta, who welcomed them with open arms. Ruby and Betsy stood in awe in the foyer just as Archie had done as a twelve-year-old boy all those years before.

'Would you like a tour of the hotel?' Jimbel asked the overwhelmed girls.

Suddenly a friendly voice boomed across the lobby, and CJ Croft approached them. 'Not until I have made the acquaintance of these lovely ladies!'

He shook hands with Archie, hugging him briefly. 'It's about time you came back to us, young man. Look at you! A sight for sore eyes and very different from the ragamuffin who entered these doors… how many years ago?'

Archie laughed. 'Almost a decade, sir. It's good to be back. May I introduce my sisters? Ruby, Betsy, this is the man who gave me a job when I first arrived in New York. Mr C.J. Croft.'

'Welcome, ladies, I'm delighted to meet you. And what do you two charming ladies do?'

Ruby, unfazed by the great man's position, replied confidently, 'I'm a seamstress, sir, and Betsy is my assistant.'

Unknown to them, CJ already knew the girls' life story and about Betsy's health problems. Both Archie and Oscar Nash had kept him informed over the years. He was determined to assist Archie's family in any way he could.

'A seamstress? Well now, it just so happens that Greta requires an assistant or two. If you are interested in working here, I would be delighted to employ you.'

Ruby looked at Archie, who grinned his approval.

'Yes please, sir,' she replied, then nudged Betsy, who whispered, 'Thank you, sir.'

CJ smiled. 'Right, that's settled then. Jimbel will show you around the hotel, and no doubt Greta will give you a guided tour of her department, while I catch up on years of news from your brother.'

The two awestruck girls were shown around the premises, gasping in wonder as one exquisite room after the other came into view.

'This is like a palace,' commented Betsy.

'Yeah, it is. It's one of the best, if not *the* best hotels in New York,' Jimbel said proudly. 'CJ makes sure we keep high standards.'

'Is he scary to work for? He frightens me a little.'

'No, Betsy, he's a real nice guy,' Jimbel assured her. 'He just comes across as scary, but he's a real pussy cat underneath, with a heart of gold.'

'Our Archie speaks highly of him,' commented Ruby, who was starstruck, not only at the opulence of her surroundings, but of the handsome Jimbel.

The tour ended in the basement where Greta ruled supreme. Ruby was amazed at the number of workers attending to mending laundry, and the machinery they used; she had only ever seen Doris's old treadle sewing machine.

Greta explained the workings of the department to the excited girls.

'When you start work, Ruby, I'll allocate a machine to you, show you how it functions, and give you a few samples to complete. Betsy, I need someone to fetch and carry the reels of thread that the workers need, and to see that they always have a supply of threads, wool, and needles. Do you think you would like to do that?'

Betsy looked to Ruby for approval. 'Yes, please,' she replied. 'I can manage that.'

With the tour over, they returned to the foyer where soft drinks and cookies were ready for them. They sat chatting to Jimbel as they waited for Archie, who was still engaged in deep conversation with CJ.

'I was saddened to hear that your brother could not be traced,' CJ told him. 'Oscar kept me informed, as did your beautiful written letters. I could use a personal secretary, as the previous one moved away from the area and I've never quite gotten around to filling the post. Would you consider dealing with my correspondence?'

Archie responded with a grin. 'I would be honoured, sir.'

'Let's get to the basics now of salary for you all and decide when you should start work. I guess your sisters need time to get acclimatised to the city, like you did all those years ago.' CJ thought for a moment. 'Shall we say, one month from now? As for accommodation, we have space in the staff quarters where you once lived. There's a single room for you, and the ladies can share a room in the women's quarters. How does that sound?'

Archie nodded. 'That would be good for us all, sir. We don't want to impose on Peggy any longer than necessary, although we will make a point of visiting her regularly. She's very frail now, but still has that indomitable spirit.'

The two men shook hands on the deal, then Archie joined the others for refreshments and related his conversation with CJ.

Jimbel was elated to have his old friend working nearby again. Turning to the girls he said, 'I'll get one of the girls to show you around the female staff quarters. Guys are not allowed there,' he grinned, 'more the pity. You folks eat up and I'll go fetch someone to take you there.'

'Archie,' began Ruby, through a mouthful of crumbs, 'this is a dream world. I feel I'm going to wake up and find it was all a dream.'

Jimbel returned with one of the seamstresses. 'Ruby, Betsy, this is Patsy, who will show you to the accommodation area while I take Archie to his.'

Patsy chatted as she rode the elevator and climbed the remaining two flights to the women's section. Like the men's quarters, several rooms led off from a long corridor.

'This is my room, number eleven. I share with Carly, who you'll meet soon,' she told them. 'Here you are, number twelve.'

'This is lovely, isn't it, Betsy?' Ruby said, her eyes shining. 'Look at the view over the roof. We've never been as high up as this.'

'The sun shines in each morning,' Patsy told them, 'and it's as good as an alarm clock. Come, I'll show you the shower and bathrooms.'

With the tour over and Patsy promising to be good friends with them, the Connors left the hotel to return to Granny Peggy's house.

Archie asked the girls, 'Do you think you will like your new life in America?'

'Oh yes,' they replied in unison.

36

Months turned into years as the family settled into a work routine. Each Sunday they visited Peggy and Dan. And when Peggy felt well enough, a car was sent to bring her to the hotel, where she was attended to by the staff who enjoyed listening to her tales of her early life in Ireland. CJ, when on the premises, enjoyed nothing better than a chat with the older woman. He teased her until tears of laughter ran down her cheeks.

Dan confided in Archie, 'She seems to recall events from her past but forgets what she has done earlier in the day. I've decided to make my next voyage my last one so that I can be here for her.' He looked concerned. 'She's getting on a bit, and doesn't ask for much, but I owe her for years of friendship.'

Archie nodded in agreement. 'I've noticed she has memory problems. I'll do what I can to spend time with her, Dan, and I'll send the girls over as often as I can. They love their new granny.'

During quiet spells in the sewing department, Ruby often made sketches in her scrapbook, which Greta greatly admired.

'Ruby, you have a unique talent for designing clothes. You should harness that talent. May I borrow this sketchbook? I'll take good care of it.'

Mystified as to why Greta wanted the sketches, Ruby agreed, and was surprised a few days later to be called to CJ Croft's office along with the other woman.

'Ruby,' began the imposing man, putting the bemused young lady at ease with his smile and affable nature, 'Greta showed me your sketchbook. These designs are stunning; you clearly have a talent and skill that you should use to your advantage. I've discussed a plan with Greta and Archie, so here is my proposal.

'We have a large room to the left of the foyer; it has been closed for years and used for storage. I propose we open it up as a dress shop for guests, and organise an area for you to work in and make your unique creations. You can give it an eye-catching name like, Gowns by Ruby.'

Ruby was stunned at the proposal.

'You don't need to agree to anything yet,' CJ assured her, seeing her shocked look. 'Take time to digest what I've said, discuss it with Archie and Betsy, and Greta of course, and give it serious consideration. It would benefit you and set you up as a businesswoman of repute, and I know the guests who visit the hotel will be charmed by you and love your creations.'

Finally finding her voice, Ruby stammered, 'I-I don't know what to say, sir. I'm stunned.'

CJ laughed. 'I can see you are bemused. This has happened too quickly for you, but go ahead and give it serious thought. You have our total support in this venture.'

With that, he shook hands and left the startled young woman in Greta's care.

Ruby turned to the older woman, looking worried. 'Oh Greta, do you think I can really do this? Make fine gowns for posh ladies?'

Greta patted the girl's hand. 'Have faith in yourself,' she told her. 'Of course you can pull this off. We'll set aside an area where you can lay out your patterns and cut and sew to your heart's content. I'm sure Betsy will enjoy her new position with you.'

While the gown room was being made ready, Ruby busied herself – with Greta's help – to produce a few outfits to display in the windows. A stunning sign had been designed and placed in a prominent position. It read: *Gowns by Ruby, from the school of Doris Young of London.* Business cards were placed in little silver dishes in the salon, which was exquisitely furnished with comfortable chairs and sofas. A selection of gowns hung around on rails to be perused by clients, and a private, curtained-off area was available where Ruby could measure and discuss her client's requirement. Betsy welcomed the guests by showing them her sister's books of sketches and describing the unique designs.

Within a few months, it was clear that Ruby's venture was a resounding success – to the point that she could only be contacted by appointment. Word soon spread among the hotel's guests, who commissioned her for ball gowns, wedding outfits, and trousseaus for the discerning bride.

Her wealth increased as her reputation soared among society ladies. She extended her premises and took on more staff, including Patsy, who worked with Betsy to ensure the smooth running front of house.

Romance blossomed between Ruby, now installed as a businesswoman of some standing, and Jimbel, who admitted he had been besotted with her from the moment she stepped off the boat in New York. After months of stepping out together, and four years after Ruby had arrived in America, Jimbel asked Archie's permission to marry her.

Before long, she had made not only her own wedding gown, but Betsy's stunning bridesmaid's dress. Betsy had blossomed into a confident, attractive woman, totally at ease with the New York society ladies who visited the salon. As the sister of a wealthy designer and a highly successful businessman brother, she was sought after by young men keen to make her acquaintance.

Archie, however, kept her firmly grounded and, with Patsy's help, guided Betsy safely away from unscrupulous suitors. On their time off, the two women would visit Granny Peggy and take her for strolls around a nearby park, always stopping at her favourite coffee shop. Occasionally, Jimbel would accompany them and help with Peggy, who adored the handsome man who she told everyone was her grandson.

Although he had the means to purchase an apartment, Archie remained living in the staff quarters. He preferred to be on hand in the hotel, and to be near Betsy. Over the intervening years, he had taken on more responsibility, which included visits to other hotels that CJ owned in other parts of the country, to audit, interview staff, and generally report back on the standards of the entrepreneur's empire.

CJ's most recent interest was in Canada, and he was keen for Archie to check out a property there.

'I've been told of a hotel near Halifax that is in some financial difficulties,' he explained. 'It's a prime spot, and sounds like something I'd be interested in adding to our portfolio. I'd like you to make an unannounced visit as a tourist, then return with your findings as to the possibility of pursuing it as a business venture. It will involve a long, possibly tedious journey, and will mean you will be away from your family for some time. Sleep on it, Archie, and give me your answer before the week is out. Discuss it with your sisters.'

Over supper with the Ruby and Betsy, Archie related CJ's request and listened as they agreed he must take up the offer to visit Canada.

'It will be an exciting experience for you to visit another country. What tales you will come back with! Archie, you must go. I feel it is the right thing for you to do,' encouraged Ruby, while Betsy nodded her assent.

There was plenty to be arranged before Archie could finally set off on his journey. CJ had already planned everything out for him, detailing train times and overnight stops.

'You must keep in touch by wire telegraph whenever you can,' CJ explained.

Before he set off, Archie bade goodbye to Peggy, and wondered if he would ever see the frail lady again. A tearful Ruby and Betsy saw him off, shouting *bon voyage* and waving handkerchiefs until he was out of sight.

As Archie settled in a comfortable carriage, he pondered how life had changed for him and his family over the years. Unknown to him, there were more changes to come.

37

Refreshed after his journey, Archie discreetly studied the hotel set-up. He could see plenty of potential for improvement to meet the standards CJ would demand before putting his name to the establishment. But he wanted to explore more the following day.

After dinner, he got into conversation with a guest who was there to finalise some business matters and had chosen to stay in the hotel for a few nights. A pleasant gentleman, Carsten Pike introduced himself and explained something of his farming business. 'I'm here for a few days to stock up on provisions for the farm before winter sets in,' he said.

Archie explained he was in the property business, but did not reveal the true nature of his stay at the hotel.

'Archie Connor, you say?' queried the farmer. 'We have a young guy on our farm, one of several who came over on the British government's child migration movement some, five, maybe six years ago. He was from London; said he was in an institution type of place there.' Carsten Pike looked closely at Archie. 'You remind me of him. Same mannerisms, and there's something about the eyes, too. In fact, now that I have had a good look at you, you are very alike.'

Archie's heart leapt. He could feel it race and pound in his body as he took in what the man was saying.

Seeing the colour drain from Archie's face, the farmer asked, 'You okay, sir? You don't look too good to me; you've gone a bit pale. Hey, can I get you a glass of water?'

Archie nodded as the Carsten Pike fetched a bar tender and helped Archie to a chair. 'You sure you're okay? Do you want to call for medical assistance?'

Archie shook his head. 'No, I'm fine. Just a bit shocked.' He paused before continuing, 'Can I speak to you in confidence in a quiet corner?' The bar area was beginning to fill up, and Archie didn't want to draw any more attention to himself.

'Sure,' replied a rather bemused Carsten Pike.

They found a couple of seats in a corner recess, and Archie wiped his brow, took a deep breath, then asked rather abruptly. 'Tell me about the guy. How old is he?' He felt his pulse race as sweat ran down his face.

'Oh, I reckon he's about fifteen now – maybe less, maybe more. Nice guy, hard worker. Goes by the name Herb Connor, Herbert. They named him in some kind of orphanage where he was abandoned with no name; called him after the then British prime minister, so he was told.' The farmer went on, 'He and another child, Nobbs Norman, came to us as young kids, and they still live with us on the farm. We couldn't do without their help – two great guys they are, and the best of friends. Etta, my wife, mothers them and they have thrived under her care. They were scrawny kids when we collected them from the charity folks that helped run the scheme to settle British kids in Canada. To be honest, we weren't sure about taking strangers in, but we ain't getting any younger, and it turned out the best thing we ever did. Those young guys are now real gentlemen, hard workers and polite. Yeah, best move we ever made.' He paused and took a closer look at Archie. 'Hey, here I am rambling on while you, sir, look unwell.'

PART 2

38

In an effort to ease overcrowding in workhouses and other charitable establishments, and with the hidden agenda to populate the colonies with cheap labour, the 1922 Empire Settlement Act passed by the British government allowed for immigration of children from Britain to Canada and Australia. Ex-servicemen and women returning from the Great War were given free passage, either through public or private schemes where migrants were expected to find employment, settle in a new land, and remain there for the duration of their lives. Included in the exodus were fit, young orphan children from various workhouses under the British Child Emigration Movement.

A young Herbert Connor was included in this scheme.

One evening, after what passed as supper in the workhouse, the master – a fierce-looking, overweight man with a penchant for young boys – called for attention and silence. There was rarely any noise to be heard in that room, with silence broken only by the slurping of gruel from tin bowls in an effort to extract the last drop of nourishment.

'The following boys await my presence in my office,' he instructed. 'Move in an orderly fashion.'

He then proceeded to call out the names of twelve boys, who moved smartly for fear of being whacked for dawdling.

Among those scared inmates was Herbert Conner – the Nipper. He had never experienced harsh treatment at the hands of the master, but had heard plenty of tales. He walked with his head down so as not to be singled out, but sweat formed in his clenched fists as he followed the others out of the room to face whatever fate awaited.

'Boys, after much consultation with the guardians who have provided food and shelter for you ungrateful inmates for many years, you have been chosen to go forth from here to a new life,' the master told them. 'An opportunity, an opportunity, I repeat, that you will grasp with both hands and accept as a means of becoming good citizens of our colonies.'

The pompous man talked at length, most of his speech going over the heads of the bewildered boys whose ages ranged from seven to fourteen. When he finished, he called for staff waiting nearby, who scurried along as if on cue.

'Take these boys, these chosen few,' he told them 'to be bathed, deloused, and properly dressed for a journey of some length. Ensure they are ready within four hours, when they will be collected by carriage and escorted to the docks to be met by social reformers who will see to their passage to the colonies.'

Turning to the confused boys, he bade them farewell with a warning to keep a stiff upper lip in situations of adversity.

Herbert's head buzzed with questions: questions he knew not to utter aloud; questions that would no doubt remain unanswered, even if he had the courage and foolhardiness to voice them.

A frenzy of activity began with rough handling from the servants who were afraid of not completing the master's instructions in time.

'Stand still. Stop wriggling.'

'Keep your head still.'

'How can I get rid of bugs if you keep moving?'

'Next, over here. Don't linger. We have no time to waste.'

Finally, Herbert Connor, now ten years of age, waited in line inside the door of the workhouse with the other boys – all suitably dressed, and with labels showing their name and age pinned to their coats. Not a word passed their lips. Such was their incarceration that they knew nothing but blind obedience. They certainly knew nothing of the fate that awaited them.

The boys' eyes darted back and forth from one to another, as if supporting each other in an unspoken pact of acceptance. A band of brothers thrown together in an unknown cause, they stood in silence, as was the way of life in the establishment.

A rattle on the door with a heavy stick or some sort of implement, startled them, making them jump. They stared at the door as it opened to admit a burly coachman who wore a full-length coat with the collar turned up against the elements and a severe, no-nonsense look on his blotched face.

'Right, let's be having you. Is the paperwork in order?' he called to a nervous servant girl who curtsied and handed over an envelope.

'Yes, guv, sir.'

'Get in the carriage, prompt like,' he addressed the boys. 'We don't have time to waste.'

Cold air hit Herbert with a shock as he walked the short distance to the carriage, which turned out to be no more than a farmer's cart pulled by a heavy-set horse. Space was tight as the twelve boys jostled for room to sit on the floor.

With a crack of the whip on the poor beast's back, the carriage moved off with a shudder that tossed the boys around. Night was falling as the motley crew rumbled on towards the sea. Herbert was fascinated as he watched the dark clouds flit across the sky, occasionally showing a gap where he spotted an occasional star.

The only sound from the boys was the occasional cough, as cold night air caught the back of their throats. Most of them were undernourished and unhealthy, some had narrowly escaped the influenza that blighted the country. The steady clip clop of the horse lulled some to sleep, but not Herbert. His gaze was focused on the night sky, where an occasional glimpse of the moon could be seen – the face smiling at him as if to reassure the lad that he had a friend.

The cart came to an abrupt halt, throwing some of the boys on top of a sleeping neighbour.

'Out you get. On the double, no loitering there at the back. Wait in line.'

In the semi-darkness the boys could make out the outline of a large, wooden construction – a warehouse of sorts, that was to be their home for the night. Two sailors escorted them to the building that was surprisingly warm. They were given bread, soup, and milk – a real luxury after years of watered-down gruel – then directed to an area where they were to spend the night among bales and sacks full of merchandise which would be loaded onto the ship at first light.

'Bunk down, we have an early start, gotta catch the first tide,' one of the sailors told them. 'Sleep well, me hearties.'

Most of the boys soon fell asleep huddled together, with their workhouse jackets gripped tightly around their frail bodies for warmth and security.

'Herb,' a voice whispered to the wide-awake boy. 'What's happening to us? Where are we going?'

'Dunno, Nobbs. Don't think we're ever going back to the workhouse, though. I think we're going far away.'

Nobbs, as he was referred to, had arrived at the establishment as a four-year-old waif, having been deserted by a young girl to live on the streets. He had been rescued by a charity worker whose job it was to walk the streets looking for young neglected children to rescue.

'Come on, lad, let's get you somewhere warm. What's your name?'

'Nobbs.'

'Just Nobbs? What's your other name?'

'No name, just Nobbs.'

'Well, we need to give you another moniker, a surname. How about, let me see, how about Norman? Nobbs Norman. How does that sound to you?'

Nobbs had nodded and accepted his new name.

During his time in the workhouse, Nobbs had failed to learn the basics of reading, and suffered many a beating for his lack of skills. He had eventually been removed from the learning programme; only pupils who showed some ability to learn were educated, to show the guardians in a favourable light to the authorities.

Now he whispered again. 'Herb, you know a lot, getting educated-like by the masters. What's colonies?'

Herb shrugged. 'Dunno, Nobbs, but I think it's a faraway place.'

The two finally fell asleep and were soon to learn about the colonies.

39

A ship's horn sounded close to where the boys had spent the night. Those who were still asleep woke with a start, looked around as if trying to recall the events that had brought them to this strange place, then recognising their fellow inmates, sat up in bemused silence and waited. They were used to waiting. They were used to silence.

After a while, the door creaked open, letting in shafts of light that flicked across the warehouse like a searchlight. A sailor instructed them to get up, use the bucket, then wait outside the building.

What lay in front of them was a massive dockyard that appeared to have come to life with a cacophony of noise; sailors were shouting commands to each other, bales and sacks were being passed from one to another along a line, then loaded onto a sailing vessel. A captain, or some such person in authority, stood on deck, counting cargo as it was loaded.

The smell of the sea was refreshing to the lads who had been almost imprisoned during their time in the workhouse. They stood in wonder, watching, listening, smelling, and tasting the saltwater as it reached them.

Two charity ladies, dressed in long pinafore dresses that reached to the ground, approached the boys and handed out food that they carefully carried in their aprons.

'Eat up before you set sail, boys. Best to have something in your stomach before you hit the high seas.'

'Some of them look so young,' whispered one to her companion, as they walked along the line of stupefied children offering bread and a smile.

'From what we hear, they are going to a better life,' said the other

'I hope so. I do hope so. Poor mites. Poor nippers.'

One of the ladies wiped the boys' faces with a damp rag. 'There yer go. Fed and watered, and ready for a great adventure.'

One of the boys plucked up courage to ask, 'Ma'am, where are we going?'

The women looked at each other before the older one replied, 'Hmm, didn't no-one tell yer? Yer going on a long sea journey to the other side of the world. Australia, methinks.'

A passing sailor corrected her. 'No, mistress, not this ship. It's heading to Canada. I've to collect these lads, if you're finished with them.'

A motley line of lads followed the sailor up a steep gangplank. 'Hold on there, me lads,' he warned. 'It moves with the sea. Yer don't want to fall in.'

Any fear the boys had immediately increased as they glanced over at the dark menacing swell of water as it lapped the wharf and rocked the ship to and fro.

Herbert loved the sights and sounds, and determined in that moment that he never wanted to live indoors again. Further along, they saw adult passengers boarding onto a different deck of the ship.

Once everyone was on board to the satisfaction of the captain, the ship set sail to a racket of shouts and instructions, as sails were hoisted and adjusted. Two sailors assigned to looking after the young human cargo, instructed them to sit on deck and hold onto whatever they could until the ship was well away from the wharf.

'There'll be a bit of rocking 'n' rolling for a bit, then she'll steady up,' one explained.

The twelve young boys sat on deck, holding each other with linked arms, as they watched in awe as the vessel that was to be their home for many weeks was made ready.

Young Herbert soaked up the scene. His eyes were full of wonder as he watched and listened while the crew sang sea shanties in time with each other as they worked the sails. Some of the boys succumbed to seasickness, while others held their stomachs or noses during the few nautical miles it took before they were allowed to move.

'Right, let's be having yer,' called out one of the minders, whose name they were to learn was Mickey. 'First things first. Clean this sick mess, all of yer. Fetch buckets, collect sea water, and splosh the decks. Here, I'll show yer how to do it without falling overboard. Captain gets right angry with folks that fall into the sea.'

The next hour or so was spent with the boys learning how to clean the decks.

'Okay, me hearties,' he told them. 'Now yer to find yer sea legs. Me and Larry will walk yer round the deck and up and down ladders till yer have got the feel of the ship and can walk like sailors.'

Herbert quickly caught on to how to splay his legs and walk like a sailor.

'Yer been a sailor in another life young 'un,' his minder said admiringly. 'What's yer name?'

'Herbert Connor, sir, but everyone calls me Herb.'

'Herb, it is then, and yer don't call me sir. I'm Larry.' He laughed. 'Yer seems to be a quick learner.'

The first days at sea passed quickly, with most of the migrants free from stomach ailments. They sat on the deck as their mentors distributed food.

'Best we've ever had,' whispered one lad, still in awe of his minders.

Their lifetime of being restricted from talking to others was still ingrained in them. But it wasn't long before they found they were allowed to talk freely – a new freedom that they relished and thrived on.

As night fell, they made their way to the deepest deck on board, where Mickey had shown them how to set up their hammocks. Much hilarity was heard as one by one, boys tumbled and fell from the swaying makeshift bed.

'Here, I'll show yer. Ye hold this bit taught, right, like this and lay yersel in the middle of the hammock,' Larry had explained. 'Yer'l fall out if you don't get right into the middle.'

It was many days, and with several bruises, before some of them mastered the skill of climbing into the hammocks.

Days turned to weeks as the ship, blown off course in a high wind, made for safe shelter to sit out the worst of the storm. With sea air in their lungs, food in their stomachs, and freedom to talk to each other without fear, the boys thrived. Their minders were kind and regaled them with sea stories, some of which were doubtful in authenticity.

'Where are we going?'

'What's to happen to us?'

'Will we be on this ship forever?'

Questions tumbled from them as they sat listening to Larry tell of how he had single-handedly fought off pirates and saved the ship and its crew from pillage.

'Four more days, me hearties, if the weather is favourable, we'll berth in Canada,' he told them. 'Captain says we'll be heading for Halifax. Then yer get taken somewhere. Don't ask me no more, I don't know what happens after yer leave the ship.'

Indeed, Larry had no knowledge about what lay ahead for the boys he had cared for since leaving England. He blanked rumours from his mind of tales of harshness and abuse that he had heard as being the fate of so many children once they disembarked.

40

The ship docked at first light with a frenzy of activity, noise, and apparent organised chaos that brought the port to life, as cargo was unloaded and passengers disembarked. Herbert found himself back on dry land, and struggled to walk without swaying.

Larry told the boys they would soon find their land legs, but some of them suffered for a time until they got used to being back on solid ground. They were ushered to an area outside the port to a campsite, where several charity ladies attended to them. They were showered, given fresh clothes, and food.

'We'll get the salt and smell of the sea off you,' said one lady, in an accent that was both new and fascinating to the boys. 'A good scrub-up will make you feel more human.'

'Now what?' whispered Nobbs.

Herbert shrugged. 'I reckon we'll soon find out.'

Before long, several officials arrived to disperse the children to various locations. The boys shuffled nearer to each other for safety.

One official called out, 'Stand!' – a demand the boys responded to immediately.

The imposing man walked up and down the line of worried boys and asked them to confirm their names, which he ticked off on his sheet of paper. He then conferred with his colleague, who nodded in agreement at whatever was discussed between them.

As if on cue, a few people entered the building. They would decide the youngsters' fate for many years.

'The following boys step forward,' they were told.

The boys were then dispersed – some singly, some in twos – until all twelve had been claimed by their new guardians. There was no time for goodbyes.

Nobbs held Herb's hand in the hope they would not be separated, and was relieved when they were both chosen to follow a cheery-looking man who introduced himself as Pike, and led them to a wagon drawn by a heavy horse.

'You're to live with me and Etta on our farm,' the man explained. 'I hope you guys are hard workers, we've a harvest to get in before the weather changes. You look scrawny, but my Etta will soon feed you up.'

Pike hardly drew breath as he drove on, describing the set-up at the farm that was to be their home for the foreseeable future. Herb and Nobbs were mesmerised by the vast expanse of countryside, the uncomfortable vehicle that tossed them around when driven over rutted roads, and Pike's strange accent. They held onto the sidebar as they rode along, neither had uttered a word since the journey began.

Arriving at a large wooden gate, Pike called out, 'Down you go, lads, and open the gate. Mind now, it's heavy. When I drive through, close the gate and jump back on.'

'Where are we?' whispered Nobbs to Herb as they wrestled to release the latch and swing the gate open.

'Dunno.'

Pike eventually brought the cart to a halt outside a large farm building, then blasted a makeshift horn and jumped down.

'Welcome to our farm – your new home for as long as you are to stay with us. Here comes Etta. I call her the boss.' He laughed as he hugged his wife and patted two excited dogs before introducing the boys.

'Here they are, Etta. This lad here is Herbert Connor, known to all as Herb, and the other fellow is Nobbs, Nobbs Norman.'

Unused to physical contact, the boys were taken aback as they were engulfed in the arms of the farmer's wife. It felt good.

'Welcome, guys, welcome to our home,' she said cheerily. 'Let me have a look at you... Hmm, you need a good feed if you're going to be helping old Pike here with the harvest.'

'Hey, less of the old,' chuckled Pike.

Etta brought them indoors to a warm kitchen with enticing smells. It was a homely room, the flagstones scrubbed clean, and the table almost bulging with food.

'Right, guys, first things first. Wash those grubby hands and sit here, all three of you. Pike, you ready to say grace?'

'Yeah, mother. Bow your heads, boys, and give thanks,' he instructed.

After a short prayer that they were to find out was the norm, they were served a feast of chicken pie with home-made bread, fresh milk, apple pie and fresh cream. Being used to silent meals, it took the boys some time to realise they were now free from the restrictions of the workhouse and were encouraged to talk about their life in England.

'We need to get to know each other if we're to live like a family,' began Pike. 'First, let me tell you about us. This little ol' farm is small by Canadian standards. We're part of a large area of farmland that belonged to Etta's father. When ol' Zak died, the land was divided among his six sons and one daughter. Etta here, being the youngest, was allocated only a small section. But you know, guys, it suits us fine. We manage to run it just fine with occasional help from her brothers. We were encouraged to apply to be guardians to British kids who were being transported here for a better life.'

Etta commented, 'I tell you, at first I was against the idea of having strangers here, since we knew nothing about the people who were coming over by steamship. But the committee folks who arranged it assured us we would be sent good living, God-fearing helpers, so I said okay. We ain't getting much younger and could do with a bit of help.'

Pike continued, 'Hey, we didn't expect you guys to be so young. The work can be tough at times. Do you think you're up to hard work?'

Herb, who had taken an instant liking to the couple, was the first to respond.

'Me and Nobbs will work hard for you. We're stronger than we look, sir.'

'We're real strong,' piped up Nobbs, not sure what to make of the whole surreal situation.

'Good to hear that, good to hear. How about you tell us a bit about yourselves and your life in England?' suggested Pike.

Herb began, 'There's not much to tell, sir. Me and Nobbs are orphans and were brought up in a workhouse. We've known each other all our lives.'

'Don't you have any family at all?' enquired Etta, as she blinked a tear from the corner of her eye.

'No, ma'am,' said Nobbs, who was beginning to feel more comfortable with their hosts. 'They told me I was found on the streets where I'd been living for some time. I don't know how I got there, but there were lots of kids. We stuck together and looked out for each other. The older ones stole food and shared it with us. I don't remember much before then, but one of the older guys said my name was Nobbs, 'cos the woman who dumped me there told him that before she ran off.'

'Oh, my poor child. How awful for you.' Etta turned to Herb and asked his story.

'All I know from what they told me in the workhouse is that I had no parents,' he replied. 'I think my mam died giving birth to me, and I was taken to the workhouse. I had no name except the surname Connor and a date of birth, so they called me Herbert after the Prime Minister of the day. Me and Nobbs have known no other life.'

Pike sighed. 'You guys are wise beyond your years. Well, I can tell you, you have a home here with us, and you can drop the sir and ma'am. It's Pike and Etta from now on. Okay, guys?'

With supper over, they sat by the fire as Etta, refusing help from the boys, cleared up while Pike fussed over the dogs.

'Let's get you guys to bed,' he said. 'You look half-asleep.'

Etta showed them to a room they were to share for several years. It was small but cosy and clean – a real luxury for two waifs. Within minutes, they had fallen asleep from exhaustion and excitement.

'Poor boys,' said Etta, returning to the fireside with Pike. 'They've had it tough.'

'From now on, we'll give them a better life. Etta, did you see how their eyes lit up when they saw the food? I have a real good feeling that they are good boys and won't give us any trouble. They sure are young, so we can't expect too much heavy work from them. I'll ease them in gently after a day or two of rest.'

Over the next few days, Herb and Nobbs were introduced to the workings of the farm and met their workmate, Vance – the workhorse who pulled the plough like a two-year-old yearling instead of a mature heavy horse who had served Pike well over many years. Vance, they were told, helped prepare the land for sowing, hay making, carting heavy logs, and whatever else was needed on the farm.

'Don't it hurt him to pull heavy things?' enquired Nobbs, who had an instant rapport with Vance.

'Not at all, Nobbs. Vance here is well suited to working. Look at his broad shoulders and his strong hindquarters. He's very placid is Vance, and I'm sure he enjoys his work. Don't you, Vance?' soothed Pike, as he nuzzled the beast. 'He works hard for me and has to be looked after. He needs fed, just like we do, and kept clean and warm. When he's not working, he likes to graze in the paddock where he can run around as much as he likes. In the winter he has a warm barn.'

Nobbs was totally smitten with the animal. 'Can I help look after him, please?' he asked the farmer. 'He's a beautiful creature.'

'Well now,' Pike said, as he stroked his chin thoughtfully, 'I'm sure with a bit of training you'll do right good by our Vance. He needs more time spent with him than I can spare. Tomorrow, I'll show you how to look after him.'

Nobbs was ecstatic at the thought of having such responsibility. Over the next few weeks, Pike took him through the care of his beast. Vance, sensing a friend in Nobbs, responded to his every command.

From then on, Nobbs talked and confided in the horse, and spent every moment he could brushing, chatting, cleaning his stall, providing fresh hay and water, and generally looking after his new friend.

41

The boys soon settled into a routine that was a million miles, in every way, from the existence they had lived for the past eleven or so years. Part of their weekly routine was attending Sunday church service. They donned their best clothes that Etta prepared for them, while she fussed, adjusting collars and neckties and generally making sure her men were fit to be seen among godly people.

Weeks rolled into months. Herb found he enjoyed the church service and especially singing in tune with Pike's strong voice to guide him. Singing was a new and exhilarating way for him to use a voice that had been silenced for so long. Etta smiled proudly as she listened to his tuneful voice.

The boys were regular participants in the service, and became acquainted with their fellow churchgoers, among whom was one of the lads who had sailed with them from England. Herb spotted him cowed in one of the pews, dwarfed by a burly man and his equally stern-looking wife and son. At the end of the service, the boy was roughly yanked away by his minders. Herb would have liked to speak to him, but the child was rushed away with the adults without waiting to talk with the pastor.

Once outside, Pike and Etta joined with other worshippers to speak with the pastor, while the boys joined the other children who ran around the grounds chasing each other, or sat on the grass catching up with friends.

'Nobbs, did you see little Alan in church?' Herb asked. 'You know, the littlest kid that came over with us?'

Nobbs shook his head. 'Can't say I did.'

'He looked scared of the people he was with, and I'm sure the big boy kicked his ankle as he left the pew.' Herb frowned. 'The kid looked as if he was still wearing the same clothes we last saw him in, and looked real neglected to me. I'm going to let Pike know. I'm sure us kids are meant to be looked after properly.'

Sure enough, Pike was concerned when he heard what Herb had observed. 'That's not so good,' he said. 'I know the man you mean. He and his wife are unfriendly; they never hang around after church to speak to any of us, and that son of theirs is just as mean as his father. So, you're telling me there's a young immigrant living with them?'

'Yeah, Pike. His name is Alan and he's only a little kid about seven of eight. He cried most of the way over on the ship. He was too young to make that journey,' said Herb with a maturity that never failed to surprise his guardians.

Pike nodded. 'Leave it with me. One thing I can't put up with is cruelty. There's no need for it.'

As part of the migration scheme, regular spot checks were made on the welfare of the boys. That week, two charity workers arrived unannounced at the farm while Pike and the boys were out in the field gathering the last of the harvest for the day. Etta was busy in the kitchen preparing supper when the two inspectors knocked heavily on the door.

Wiping her hands on her apron, she opened the door to the inspectors, who announced themselves and asked to be allowed in.

'Of course, come on in,' she said. 'The boys should be back very soon from the fields.'

The female inspector, who announced herself as Prudence Shire, explained that she had a list of checks to make and would begin immediately, while her colleague, Joshua Nicol wandered around the house, checking on cleanliness and ticking his notebook as he went from room to room. Etta was taken aback at what she saw as an invasion of her privacy, with every cupboard and drawer opened and inspected. But she kept quiet, unwilling to antagonize the people who could remove the boys from her charge at the stroke of a pen.

While the man moved from room to room, his colleague inspected the boys' room, opened cupboards, pulled back bed covers, and ran her fingers across surfaces looking for signs of neglect and dirt. Thanks to Etta's thorough training and insistence that the boys keep their room and possessions as tidy as possible, no fault was found by either inspector.

'Everything seems to be in order, ma'am,' the woman said eventually. 'All we need now is to see the two boys who are billeted here.'

While they waited, Etta served the pair coffee and home-made bread and jam. As they ate, the sound of singing was heard as the workers approached the house to the clip clop of Vance's hooves.

'Ah, that will be them now,' announced a relieved Etta.

Seeing a strange vehicle by the door, Pike instructed the boys to see to Vance as quickly as possible and wash at the yard pump.

'Be as quick as you can. I reckon we have important visitors,' he told them. 'Herb, do something with that hair of yours; you have half a field of wheat in it.' Herb's unruly hair had caused him much trouble in the workhouse. However many times he tried to flatten it and however many times it was cut, it remained a tangled mess.

Nobbs led Vance to the stable, quickly rubbed him down and saw to his water and hay. He left the animal, but not before whispering in his ear, 'I'll be back as soon as I can, I promise.'

He ran to the water pump, where Herb had finished splashing water on his face and dried it with the rough cloth left there for the purpose. Nobbs washed quickly and followed him into the house.

'Ah, here they are, sir, ma'am. Herbert Connor and Nobbs Norman,' announced Pike, as he introduced them to the visitors.

One of them wrote in a notebook before addressing the boys.

'We wish to talk to you individually. Herbert, go with Mr Nicol. Nobbs, come with me. We'll walk around outside a bit.'

Turning to Pike, she explained, 'It's part of the inspection, sir. We won't be long. I can see these boys are well cared for.'

Once out of earshot, Prudence Shire asked Nobbs to tell her about his everyday routine. Warming to the lady and sensing he had nothing to fear, Nobbs related his daily routine.

'Tell me about the food,' she said. 'Do you have enough to eat?'

'Yes, ma'am. Etta is a good cook. We get lots of food, and we get to help with baking.' Sensing an opportunity to say more, Nobbs continued, 'Me and Herb love living here. Please don't take us away. I don't want to part from Vance.'

Flicking through her notes, Prudence Shire questioned, 'Vance? I have no note of anyone here called Vance.'

Nobbs smiled. 'Ah, I should explain. Vance is the farm workhorse and he's my special charge. Would you like to see him, ma'am? He's in the barn.'

Catching the boy's enthusiasm, she followed him to the barn to be introduced to Vance who, on seeing his friend, nuzzled up to him and accepted a titbit.

'What a beautiful creature.' The inspector asked, 'Tell me, what do you do to look after him?'

Needing no encouragement, Nobbs regaled her with his routine of caring for Vance.

'Well, Nobbs, all I can say is he is a lucky horse to have such a loyal friend.'

Nobbs shook his head bashfully. 'Ma'am, I'm the lucky one to be given the chance to look after him. Next to Herb, he's my best friend in the world.'

The inspector made a few final notes. 'Talking of Herb,' she said eventually, 'we'd best get back or they will be sending a search party for us.'

Herb's interview with Joshua Nicol was conducted along similar lines. The charity inspectors had a list to complete and were satisfied that all was well with the boys.

'Before we return indoors, is there anything you want to ask or tell me?'

Herb hesitated. 'There is one thing, sir.' He related his observation of young Alan's treatment, only to be halted by the inspector.

'You need not concern yourself about Alan. We've already had a report about the boy, and he's been removed to a safe home out of harm's way,' the man assured him. 'The people who were supposed to care for him will never have another child placed with them. Your friend is quite safe now.'

The inspectors sent the boys to attend to the horse while they reported their findings to Pike and Etta.

'We are pleased to say how grateful we are for taking such good care of these two good boys,' Joshua Nicol told them.

'We will present a favourable report to the committee. My only concern is schooling. I appreciate the difficulty for them travelling to the nearest school, especially as winter is approaching, but they do need some kind of education.'

'Sir,' replied Pike. 'We feel they will learn more from nature, the changing seasons, and such like. They have enquiring minds, especially Herb, and we try to answer their questions as best we can. Etta is teaching them to read from her family book of illustrations of wonders of the world, and they are soaking up information and reading some by themselves. Herb had a bit of education in England. He has a neat hand and keeps the farm journal up-to-date by recording measures and weights.'

Etta added, 'They help with planting crops for our cottage garden for our own use. They sure are learning from the outdoor life.'

The inspectors made final notes before taking their leave, but not before assuring Pike that his concern for a young immigrant had been dealt with.

'The couple have been charged with neglect and face a hefty court fine. The court deals harshly with people who take these kids in for the pittance we give for their upkeep,' Prudence Shire informed them. 'They will be blacklisted from ever having a child in their care. I wish all our guardians were like you; those guys are thriving.'

In bed that night, Nobbs could hardly sleep for mulling over the inspectors' visit.

'Those folk seemed happy with everything, didn't they, Herb?' he whispered. 'Herb, are you awake? Are you listening to me? Wonder what would happen if they weren't okay with everything. Do you think they would send us away? I'd hate to leave Vance. Herb, are you listening?'

Herb rolled over to face Nobbs, whose bed faced his.

'There's not much chance of sleep with you prattling on,' he whispered back. 'Yeah, I'm glad it went well. I don't know where they would send us if they weren't happy with our care. Now, get some sleep, we've work to do in the morning. There's fencing to be mended. Good night, Nobbs.'

Herb curled up, pulled the blankets up to his chin and tried to sleep, but Nobbs wasn't finished.

'Herb, do you ever wonder where we've come from? I mean, really come from, like who our parents are and stuff like that, and how we got to be orphans. Do you ever dream of being found by real parents? I do. I dream of rich parents who've searched for years for me and whisk me off to live with them in their posh place where there are servants to look after me and lots of horses. Yeah, there's got to be lots of horses.'

Herb gave up any attempt to sleep. He knew that once Nobbs was on a roll, he would chatter on for ages until sleep took over. He turned over towards his roommate, who was lying with his arms above his head, wide awake, and watching the wind blowing the branches of the old tree that gently hit the window.

'Well, I guess it don't do any harm to dream,' he told Nobbs. 'And yeah, at times I wonder about things, too, but I guess it ain't gonna happen… No rich parents or servants, nothing like that. We are orphans and that's that. Now, can I get some sleep?'

'At least you know your date of birth, Herb. I don't. It's kind of Etta and Pike to mark your birthday with a fruit cake, and mine, too. They made my birthday the anniversary of when I came to live with them. You listening?'

There was no response this time. Herb was sound asleep.

42

As the years progressed, both boys learned to deal with the changing seasons. Canadian winters, which could be harsh, were a particular challenge for them. Preparations were essential, so they were taught how to prepare for being cut off for several months. Logs were cut and stacked in the lean-to; meat salted and placed in barrels; vegetables harvested and stored; oil lanterns primed and ready should power fail; apples and other fruits harvested for Etta's marathon cooking of pies; extra bedding and warm clothes made ready; and finally, and more importantly for Nobbs, Vance's barn was replenished with fresh hay and fodder, and horse blankets.

During their first winter preparations, Nobbs was distressed at the thought that he might not be able to attend to his beloved animal should the snow be too deep for him to reach the barn.

'I could clear a path from the house,' he pleaded.

'Once the snows come, the path could be covered for days on end,' Pike told him. 'You would need a snow plough to shift a mountain of the stuff, and it would be covered over again as fast as you could dig. That's why we have to have Vance ready for whatever the elements throw at us. His water trough could freeze over, so we need a heater there, somewhere safe where he can't inadvertently kick it over.'

As Pike spoke, Nobbs eyes widened in astonishment at the thought of what lay ahead of them.

The seasons changed, winters came and went – some fiercer and more difficult than others – but the boys learned from Pike and Etta to adapt to each challenge.

The year 1927 witnessed a formidable feat, when Charles Lindberg made his historic nonstop flight across the Atlantic Ocean between New York and Paris. People were greedy for news of the event, and the boys gathered with the others around the old wireless for daily progress reports. They pored over a map that Etta had found in an old book, and traced the daring adventurer's historic solo journey. It was a historic year for aviation, and unknown to them, other events elsewhere in 1927 would change their lives forever.

Pike often made a trip to a town some twenty miles or more from the farm to deal with farm business matters and collect provisions for Etta; the list seemed to grow with each trip. He was absent from home for a few days, and regularly stayed in a hotel while his old vehicle was serviced, and provisions were ordered and packed for him. It was an arrangement that suited them both, as Etta felt he needed a break from the farm.

'Why don't you take the boys with you on this trip?' she suggested. 'They've seldom left the farm over the years. I'm sure they would enjoy a change of scene. A few days away from here would do them the world of good, and they could help with provisions.'

Pike shook his head. 'The timing is bad, Etta. There's too much to be done before winter hits again. We need to start preparations, as the forecast is for another harsh one. I'd rather they stayed here with you. I promise once winter is over, I'll take them camping for a few days.'

Etta nodded in agreement. 'I reckon you're right as usual, and they will enjoy camping.' She smiled. 'Herb told me how much he loves being outdoors.'

During Pike's absence, Herb helped Etta gather in what was required for winter storage, while Nobbs attended to Vance's needs.

'Vance, I hate when winter comes and I don't get to see you as often,' he told the horse. 'You understand, don't you, that I'll never leave you? Next to Herb, you're my best friend in the world.' Vance nuzzled into Nobbs, as if agreeing with him.

As Herb helped Etta with preparing vegetables, he asked about her life.

'You know this was my home all my days, well, I mean this farmland. I was brought up in the big farmhouse Pike took you boys to last year to pick up some fenceposts from Chick, my eldest brother, who still lives in the family home.' She laughed. 'He never married, *married to the farm,* he would say. It was a happy life, hard but loving. My mom was the homemaker and as the only girl I spent lots of time with her, learning to cook and clean and look after the menfolk. Boy, could they eat! It was just as well we grew our own produce. There was no filling those brothers of mine. There were six of them: Chick that I mentioned, then Jake, Tommy, Isaac, Billy, and Greg. My mom was delighted when at last she had a daughter, and we were close, my mom and me.' She paused briefly, remembering.

'Sadly, she had a massive seizure and never recovered. Da was distraught and never really recovered from his loss; they had been childhood sweethearts. Anyhow, when he passed, the farm was carved up and me and Pike were given this plot. Suits us just fine. We don't often see the others as farming is a full-time job, as you know, and we only farm a tiny bit compared to the others.' She turned her beaming smile on the young boy she'd grown to love. 'You and Nobbs have been a great help to us. Are you happy here?'

'Oh, yeah, we are,' Herb assured her. 'It's a different life from the one we had in England. But yeah, me and Nobbs love the life here.'

Suddenly, the kitchen door opened and Nobbs burst in, out of breath and excited about something.

'Sounds like Pike is coming home,' he announced. 'I heard the roar of the old Ford and ran up the hill to get a better view. Sure enough, it is him, and looks like he has a passenger with him. I'll run and open the gate.'

With that, he took off at speed, leaving Etta wondering who could be visiting.

'Best put the coffee on,' she said. 'Whoever it is will need some sustenance after Pike's driving. Herb, set the table for me while I heat up some scones.'

When they heard Pike cut the engine then blast the horn in his usual way of announcing his arrival home, Etta went to the door, wiping her hands on her apron in readiness to welcome the visitor.

A tall, well-dressed man climbed down from the vehicle with his back to her. But as he turned around, Etta gasped as she stood dumbfounded and stared: he was an older version of Herb.

She trembled as she approached the truck. 'Oh, sir,' she began, 'I'm sorry to stare, it's just… well…'

A grinning Pike came to her rescue. 'Etta, meet Archie. Archie Connor.'

43

Nobbs closed the gate, stared in awe at the passenger, then ran to the house. He reached there just as Etta was being introduced to the visitor.

Herb, unaware of the commotion, was still indoors finishing his task of setting the table. Pike hugged Etta, reassured her that all was well and called for Herb to join them.

'Herb!' he shouted. 'There's someone here to see you.'

Time seemed to stand still as the brothers stared in astonishment at each other.

Archie grinned. Without doubt, he was looking at the Nipper. He felt calm, unlike the way he had imagined he would feel when, and if, he found his brother. Somehow, he had always imagined he would sweep a young child up in his arms and cry with emotional relief.

Now, though, he stood facing a younger version of himself – a youth, tanned from outdoor work; a well-cared for young man, with an inquisitive look and an air of confidence about him. Apart from the unruly hair that his sisters possessed, Archie could have been looking in a mirror.

The stunned silence was eventually broken when Pike, his arm around Herb, spoke to him quietly.

'Herb, this gentleman believes he is your brother. Let's go indoors out of the cold and hear his extraordinary story.'

Herb looked confused. 'I don't have a brother,' he replied, shaking his head. 'I'm an orphan with no family, except you and Etta and Nobbs.'

Emotions raged within him, questions tumbled around his brain, words stuck in his throat, as he fought to make sense of what he was seeing and hearing. He was totally confused.

Pike turned to Archie. 'Would you like to be alone to talk to Herb?'

But before he could reply, Herb spoke abruptly. 'No, I want you all here with me. *You* are my family.' He felt threatened by this stranger; his security was in danger of being whipped away from him, and he was struggling to think straight.

Etta, always the practical one, stepped in. 'Let's not stand around looking bemused,' she said. 'Come inside and sit down everyone, while I serve coffee.'

Nobbs sat close to his friend, his eyes seldom leaving the man with Herb's unmistakable features sitting opposite them.

Pike spoke first. 'I was in the hotel bar and got chatting to this gentleman, and was struck by his similarity to you, Herb,' he explained. 'And when he introduced himself as Archie Connor, originally from England, I almost fell off my barstool. Please listen to what he has to say. I know you are in shock, but give our guest an opportunity to share what he revealed to me.'

There was silence in the kitchen, broken only by the ticking of the clock. Herb was sure his racing heartbeat must be heard by the others as he waited to hear what this stranger had to say.

With a nod from Pike, Archie began

'This is a long story, so I'll start at the beginning. In 1913, at the time when war was threatened, my family lived in dire poverty in a rundown area of east London. Our hovel, for that is what it was, was in the basement of a derelict tenement that was due for demolition. It was grim. We had no furniture to speak of, and I slept on the floor covered in newspaper – that's if I was lucky to find any. My da, like most men at that time, worked in the docks loading and unloading goods. He was a weak man who couldn't bear the situation his family was in, and could see no way out of it. Everyone was poor, so we didn't think we were any different from anyone else. Da was an alcoholic who spent his wages on drink.

'Our mam was a gentle woman, a saint,' Archie smiled as he remembered his mother, 'who did her best for us – that is, me and my sisters, Ruby and Betsy. She gave birth to a baby boy, but she died three days later. There wasn't even time to name him. Before she died, she made me promise to keep the family together and to look after the Nipper, the baby. I was only twelve years old, frightened and grieving, but determined to follow her wishes.' He looked straight at Herb as he added, 'I've spent my entire life searching for my siblings.'

All eyes were on Archie as he continued his story, apart from Pike who had heard the account in the hotel and who watched the others' reactions. Nobbs was wide-eyed and puzzled as he listened to the visitor with Herb's features relate a story that could have passed for a bedtime tale; Etta, engrossed in what she was hearing, could not take her eyes off Archie; Herb, though, was difficult to read. The young lad seldom blinked as he listened to the stranger who he clearly felt was a threat to his security, his way of life, and messed with his emotions.

When Archie drew breath to sip some coffee before continuing, Herb stood up.

'Excuse me,' he said politely, 'but I need some air.' He left the warmth of the kitchen, the opening and closing of the door causing a cold draught to enter the room.

Looking worried, Nobbs stood to follow his friend, but Pike held his arm gently and said, 'No, Nobbs. Herb needs to be alone for a time. Let him go.'

'I guess I've upset him,' said Archie. 'I'm sorry. Will he come back?' His own emotions were tumbling around his head and heart, causing confusion and tension.

'Yeah, don't worry, it's a lot for him to take in,' Pike assured him. 'Herb is a deep thinker. He'll be fine when he's had time to himself.'

Etta, the practical one, spoke. 'You all must be famished. Here, let me serve some food. Mr Connor, I'll make up a bed for you for the night, or for however long you wish. You can't travel back tonight.'

Archie smiled gratefully. 'Thank you, but please call me Archie. Mr Connor sounds too formal.'

They ate in almost total silence, other than the sound of them scraping their plates and the dogs snoring comfortable by the roaring fire.

When he'd finished, Nobbs asked to be excused. 'I know where Herb will be,' he said. 'I want to talk to him.' Pike nodded his approval.

*

Nobbs pushed open the barn door gently, trying to prevent the penetrating cold filling the area. 'Hey, Herb,' he called.

Vance neighed on hearing his friend's voice and the promise of a titbit, but when Nobbs reached his box, he found Herb sitting with his head in his hands. He settled down beside his friend and waited until Herb was ready to pour out his feelings. The boys had shared so much over the years, and had always trusted each other with their thoughts and emotions.

'Has that guy gone?' Herb asked eventually.

'No, he's staying the night. Tell me what you're thinking.'

'Nobbs, I don't know what to think. I'm confused and a bit frightened. He looks like me, it's scary. He even knows my date of birth. Who is he?'

'He says he's your brother, and I kinda believe him,' his friend admitted. 'He seems an okay guy, and he has a lot more to tell. Hey, let's go in and hear him out and get a bit more information.' He nudged Herb. 'Etta has made your favourite hot pot. Come on in.'

After a goodnight nuzzle with Vance and the inevitable titbit, the boys left the barn and returned to the warmth of the kitchen. Archie was standing by the fire with a cup of coffee in his hand, deep in conversation with Pike. They stopped talking when the boys came in.

'Sorry to shock you, Herb,' Archie said immediately. 'I've dreamt of this reunion now for fifteen or more years and tried to imagine what it would be like to find you, but I seem to have messed up by coming into your life without any warning. I didn't mean to scare you.'

Pike intervened. 'Why don't we all sit down and listen to what Archie has to say?'

With everyone seated, and Etta filling a plate for Herb, Archie cleared his throat and picked up his story again. He kept his eyes firmly on his brother, hoping the youth would show a modicum of acceptance.

'When Mam died, we were looked after for a while by kind neighbours. It was a confusing time for us and our da proved totally inept at caring for us. He was so distraught that I don't think he was even aware of our presence. We lived with Stan and Doris Young, who were kind. In fact, we are close friends to this day. The baby wasn't expected to live as he was so poorly, but Doris nursed him and arranged for a wet-nurse to tend to him. And the Nipper, as we referred to him, thrived, much to everyone's surprise.' Archie smiled. '*A miracle baby*, Doris called him. However, with war on the horizon, we couldn't continue to live there and were to be sent to the workhouse. I remember screaming, *No, we're not going to any workhouse*, when I was told.'

Archie took a gulp of coffee, his guilt at leaving his family all those years ago still troubled him. 'I was distraught and confused, and ran screaming from the house. It was a wild night. The rain soaked me and I could hardly see where I was going, but I kept on running. Eventually I went to our old house, which was long boarded up for demolition, but I broke in and sat on the cold, damp floor, overrun with rats, and cried myself to sleep. I wanted Mam. I didn't know what to do. I didn't know how I was to save us from the workhouse and look after you all. We had nowhere to go. I remembered before Mam died she told me she had hidden some money away under the floorboards, so I found it. Here, let me show you.'

Archie withdrew a ragged piece of cloth from his pocket, untied it, and placed some coins on the table.

'I keep them with me all the time to remind me of my humble beginnings and Mam's sacrifice in storing the money away before Da used it for drink.'

Pike picked up the coins then handed them around for the others to see.

Nobbs turned them over in his hand. 'We never had any money. I've not seen these before.'

'Me neither,' said Herb.

Engrossed in Archie's story, Nobbs asked him to continue. 'If you were so poor, how come you look rich now?'

Archie laughed, 'That is another long story.'

Turning to Pike and aware of the lateness of the hour, he asked, 'Should I leave the rest until morning?'

'Yeah, that might be best.'

They stood to move from the table, when Herb spoke directly to Archie.

'If you say we are brothers, can you prove it?'

It was the first reaction Archie had had from Herb.

'Yes,' he laughed, 'but maybe not in the way you want. I have a birthmark on my right butt, reddish colour about the size of this coin,' he said, as he picked one from the table. 'You have a similar one? Correct? Our da had the same.'

Nobbs looked at Herb and nodded excitedly. 'Yeah, Herb, you have. Remember we used to call you red bum, until one of the wardens overheard us and put an end to the name-calling. Remember?'

Herb's face went a shade of pink as he mumbled, 'Well, yes I do.'

Archie's hearty laugh lightened the mood of the evening, easing the earlier tension. 'Hey, we could show everyone if you like!' he suggested, and they all joined in the laughter.

'I don't think we need to go that far. I won't have guys dropping their pants in my kitchen.' Etta's mock scolding brought a smile to the face of everyone present. 'I suggest we all need to get to bed. Nobbs, check on Vance; Herb, take the dogs out while I clear these dishes. Dropping pants in my kitchen, whatever next?'

Still smiling at Etta's embarrassment, Archie said, 'I'll say goodnight then and thank you all for listening.' And he headed for the snug that Etta had prepared for him.

44

The two boys spoke long into the night. Despite being emotionally drained, Herb listened as Nobbs prattled on.

'Herb, man, looks like you have a brother. I believe him, he's got an honest face, just like you, and he knows enough about you to convince me. Wonder how he got to be rich? And how did he get over here? I can't wait to hear more from him. Herb, I like him. What are you thinking?'

Herb had turned over, deep in his own thoughts, the questions tumbling around his head preventing sleep.

'Nobbs, if it is true, will he take me away from here?' he said. 'This is the only family we've ever had.'

'No-one can make you go anywhere if you don't want to,' Nobbs told him, then as a sudden thought struck him, added, 'Herb, please don't leave me. We've always been together.'

It was Herb's turn to offer reassurance. 'Don't worry, we will always be together. Remember the pinkie promise we made years ago: *Together, forever, through thick and thin.* I won't be going anywhere with him, brother or not.'

*

Archie woke late to the sound of rain and sleet battering on the tiny window. The room in which he'd slept was used mainly for storage, but it was clean and comfortable. Looking

243

outside, the grey sky looked menacing and heavy with the threat of snow. For a moment he wondered where he was, then smiled as he remembered he had found the Nipper – a reluctant Nipper, perhaps, but undeniably his brother.

He climbed out of the cosy makeshift bed, shivered as cold air hit him, then dressed quickly and headed to the warmth of the kitchen. It was empty of people. A handwritten note lay on the table: *Help yourself to coffee on the stove, there's bread and other food in the larder.* After making himself some breakfast, he heard Pike's old Ford pull up at the door.

The farmer came in, shook himself free of snow that had settled on his jacket, and declared that winter had started.

'The boys are having some difficulty putting fence posts in to shore up one of the outhouses, but the wind is hampering progress, I've come back for some more tools. I dropped Etta off at her brother's house,' he explained. 'She likes to keep him stocked up with food.'

'Let me help, please,' Archie offered.

'Not dressed like that,' commented Pike, as he gathered some heavy outdoor clothes. 'Here, don these. An extra pair of hands will always be welcome. Let's go before the weather gets worse.'

They drove a few miles before spotting the boys huddled together by the side of the outhouse.

'Here's the van,' cried Nobbs. 'We'll have the outhouse shored up in no time at all now. Hey, he's got your brother with him.'

'Don't call him that,' was Herb's curt reply.

With a nod to the workers, Archie took instructions from Pike and they worked together as a team to steady the fence posts against the bitter wind that seemed determined to obstruct them. Putting his whole strength into the task, he used his body to steady the post while Herb attacked it with a heavy hammer, hitting the post as if releasing the tension he felt in his body.

The group moved from one post to another, shoring up the wooden structure as best they could, while the wind blasted its full power at them and threatened to thwart their progress. After a lengthy time, Pike was satisfied that the job was done.

'That should see us okay,' he told them. 'The shed seems firm enough now, and with a bit of luck it will survive the winter. Thanks, everyone. Thanks, Archie, an extra pair of hands did the trick. Climb in, guys, we need to go fetch Etta before she's snowed in at Chick's and we have to fend for ourselves.'

A few miles on, with the wind shaking the vehicle and making it rattle even more than normal, they arrived at Chick's farmhouse. The house was not unlike Pike's, but slightly bigger.

'Come on in,' called the owner, who was a ruddy-faced male version of Etta. 'Looks like you all need some coffee to heat you up.'

Shaking snow from their boots and jackets, they welcomed the invitation.

Etta served them coffee as Chick welcomed them.

'No need to tell me who you are,' he smiled, as he addressed Archie. 'Peas in a pod, if ever I saw any. So you must be Archie, Herb's brother. Etta's been telling me about you. Welcome.'

Introductions over, they sat around near by the fire having a welcome hot drink. Herb remained quiet, his defences up. He was determined not to acknowledge this man who had come into his life, threatening to disrupt his happiness, confusing him by his presence. Only Archie was aware of the antagonism directed towards him.

When they'd all finished, Pike told them they better head off before the weather deteriorated any further.

As they piled into the vehicle, Herb found himself crushed between Archie and Nobbs and, unable to shift position, had to contend with the closeness to his brother. No-one spoke much as Pike struggled to keep the vehicle on track while the wipers struggled to clear the windscreen.

Pike tensed as he fought desperately against the elements. He felt the vehicle rock then suddenly it hit a boulder and shook vigorously before toppling onto its side and skidding to a halt. Nobbs and Etta were thrown out onto the snow-covered road; Pike hit his head on the dash, a deep cut formed on his brow.

Still inside the upturned vehicle, Archie reacted quickly and grabbed Herb by the arm to prevent him from falling.

The young man pleaded, 'I'm scared. What can we do?'

'Keep still for a moment until I see what needs done.' Archie looked around. It seemed an eternity since the car had overturned. 'Right, we need to help the others. Climb down carefully so as not to rock the van. Here, hold onto me.' They made their way slowly out onto the snow-covered track.

'Help me see to Etta,' Archie instructed. 'She hasn't moved.'

Nobbs, who had been momentarily stunned, came to and looked around. As he attempted to stand up, he let out a scream of pain. 'Oh my arm! My arm. I think it's broken.'

Wiping snow from his eyes, Archie looked at the distraught youth, took off a scarf, and carefully wrapped the injured arm in a makeshift sling.

'Nobbs, that will have to do as a temporary measure,' he told him. 'We need to help the others.'

Archie struggled to get near Etta, who was still lying prone, groaning quietly. When she attempted to stand up, her legs buckled under her.

'Herb, help me steady her. We need to get her off the wet ground.' The two brothers managed to prop her up by the shelter of the truck, which seemed steadier now that it had come to a halt. Archie removed his outdoor jacket and wrapped it around the shivering woman.

Turning to Pike, Archie called his name. 'Pike, stay with us. Don't sleep. Herb, Nobbs, have either of you got a clean kerchief or cloth? We need to stem the flow of blood from this wound.'

'Here,' called Herb, as he reached for a cloth from his pocket. 'It's clean.'

As he handed it to Archie, their hands met and their eyes locked in a moment of understanding.

'Can you hold me steady while I climb up and move Pike from the dash?' Archie asked. 'I need to cover the cut.'

Herb held his brother steady as Archie reached into the vehicle and carefully lifted Pike's head to examine the injury. He pressed the cloth to it and fumbled for a strap of some kind to hold it in place.

'Here's my muffler,' offered Herb. 'Will it do?'

'Perfect, just what we need.'

Pike rallied as Archie put the scarf in place. 'What's happened? Where's Etta?'

'I'm here,' replied a muffled voice. 'I'm fine, honey.'

Archie turned to Herb. 'Looks like we're the only able-bodied ones. If we carefully move the others out of the way, we could try to right the van. Are you able to do that?'

Herb wiped snow mixed with tears from his face and nodded. The two worked quickly and carefully as they helped the others to the side of the road, away from danger. Herb followed his brother's example and wrapped his jacket around Pike's shoulders as he placed him near Etta.

'Okay, Herb, let's give it a go. Everyone is well out of harm's way. So, on a count of three, let's right this old thing,' Archie shouted. 'One... two... three.'

The vehicle did not shift.

'It's no use,' Herb told him. 'It's too awkward.'

'Come on, Herb, don't give up,' Archie urged. 'We're the only two that can do this. Try again, and use as much force as you can.'

It took three more attempts before the vehicle was finally back upright again.

'Well done, Herb, I'm proud of you.' Archie grinned. 'Help me get them back into the van and out of the cold.'

Nobbs, who was sitting on the ground beside Pike, called out, 'The tyre, Archie. Look at the tyre, it's burst.'

Archie looked down. 'Oh no. Is there a spare?'

The snow hampered his vision, and he shivered as the dampness seeped through his body. Herb, too, was without an outdoor jacket. He wiped the snow from his face and watched as Herb located the spare tyre and, with great difficulty, rolled it to him.

But despite their best efforts, they struggled to remove the damaged tyre.

'This is a nightmare,' Archie groaned, his teeth chattering with the cold. 'We need to shift these wheel nuts, but they're solid and rusted.'

'Here, try this oily rag. It might lubricate them enough for us to force them away from the wheel,' suggested Herb, as he handed over a piece of cloth.

It took some time before the tyre was finally changed, and while they worked, Archie kept looking in the direction of the injured passengers for any signs of deterioration. Finally, he wiped his brow on the rag, stood up and declared the vehicle ready to board.

Herb shivered as he blew his hands together and stamped his feet on the ground to generate some heat. With difficulty, they placed Etta, Pike, and Nobbs into the back of the truck – the latter stifling a scream as Pike's heavy body fell on him.

'How far are we from home? Archie asked Herb, who had climbed into the driving seat. 'You sure about driving this?'

'I know the road better than you, so I'll drive. I'm used to this old piece of junk.'

Herb drove slowly and carefully as the swirling snow threatened to conceal his view. There was no heat from the engine as it chugged along, and Archie prayed it would not break down before they reached the farmhouse. At one point, the snow was coming so thick and fast that the wipers laboured then ceased working. Archie jumped down, cleared the snow with his bare hands, and managed to release the wipers enough to get them working again.

After a fraught journey that seemed to take hours, the house came into view and they heard the dogs barking as the vehicle approach.

'What do we do about getting medical help up here?' Archie asked.

Herb shrugged. 'It's almost impossible in these conditions. There's a well-stocked medical kit in the kitchen, so that will have to do until we can get help. I'll fix up the radio transmitter and leave word for a medic to get in touch.'

'Herb, you are one great guy,' Archie told him, and together they assisted, first Pike, then Etta into the house, and sat them by the fire. Archie threw on more logs to provide some well-needed warmth. Then they returned to the vehicle and helped a white-faced Nobbs down and into the house.

45

'Herb, can you boil some water, please? I think we all need a warm drink,' Archie told him. 'And bring me the medical kit, I want to see what we have.'

Archie rubbed Etta with a towel, then removed her wet jacket and wrapped a warm housecoat around her back. He dealt similarly with Pike, and washed the grime from the man's head wound before applying iodine and a fresh dressing. Pike winced at the discomfort, but was alert enough to know what was going on.

'Thanks,' he whispered. 'Thank you both. You've saved us all from a dangerous outcome.'

Herb distributed hot drinks, which they all cupped their hands around to try and restore some feeling into their cold hands.

Pike whispered, 'There's whisky in the cupboard. Add it to our drinks; it will help with the pain.'

Nobbs, meanwhile, rocked back and forward on the seat by the fire, holding his arm as he waited his turn to be helped.

Herb held the warm, bitter drink to his lips. 'Sip this, buddy, it will put some heat in you and ease your discomfort. Archie will see to you as soon as he can. Hang in there, Nobbs.'

Nobbs muttered something to Herb, who pressed his ear nearer to catch the request. 'See to Vance for me.'

He nodded. 'Sure, as soon as we have sorted everyone here.'

Herb shared his brother's instinct to do what he could to help. He heated some soup and helped feed the invalids, and was relieved when Etta and Pike recovered sufficiently to be helped to their warm bedroom.

Etta, much more composed, hugged Archie. 'You two boys have been so good, thank you. A good night's sleep should see us all fine.'

'Call out if you need anything,' he told her. 'I'll be nearby.'

He turned to Nobbs, 'Right, let's see what damage has been done to this arm of yours. With a bit of luck, it might only be bruised.'

Archie carefully removed the muffler that held the arm in place, then shook his head. 'Sorry, Nobbs, looks like a break on the forearm,' he told the lad. 'Herb, is there anything lying around, like bits of wood, that I could use for splints?'

While Herb searched, Archie eased the wet clothes off Nobbs' shivering body, rubbed him carefully with a warm towel, and helped him into dry clothes. The boy whimpered despite Archie's gentleness.

Herb returned with a selection of sticks. 'Will any of these do?'

Archie nodded. 'Should be fine. Help me put a splint on. Nobbs, I'll be as gentle as possible, but this may be painful,' he warned.

Nobbs nodded as the brothers worked together to immobilise his damaged arm.

'This should ease things a bit for you until we can get proper medical assistance. Let's get you to bed,' Archie suggested. 'The hot drink should knock you out for the night.'

The brothers carefully helped him to bed then Archie went downstairs, leaving Herb to change into dry clothes.

Nobbs, drowsy and almost asleep, whispered, 'Your brother's an okay guy.'

Herb smiled. 'I know, Nobbs. He is.'

When he had changed and had seen Nobbs settled, Herb went back to the kitchen where he tinkered with the radio box. 'There's no signal, nothing,' he announced after a while.

'Keep trying,' Archie urged. 'It's our only chance of getting help.'

After what seemed an eternity, a crackle was heard, then a voice asked for identification. They were connected.

Herb identified himself and gave his location, then he turned to Archie and asked, 'What do you want me to say?'

'Tell them we have three injured – one with a suspected broken forearm, one with a head wound, and one with possible concussion. All are in shock.'

With that done, Herb disconnected the radio and sighed. 'They will send someone as soon as the road is passible. It could be day or two. I need to check on Vance before I head for bed. Won't be long,' he said as he headed out, letting a cold blast of air into the room.

With Vance settled for the night, Herb let himself back into the farmhouse. He yawned, rubbed his eyes, and announced he was heading to bed.

Archie smiled wearily. 'Yeah, it's been a long day. Sleep well. Nobbs might moan in the night if he moves his arm. Call me if you need me. I'll check on the others before I head for bed. You've been terrific, Herb. I couldn't have managed without you.'

'I was scared,' the young lad admitted. 'If you hadn't been there, I don't know what I'd have done.'

He started to climb the stairs then paused, turned, and looked at Archie. 'So, we *are* brothers?'

'Yes, Herb, we are.' Archie opened his arms wide to engulf the exhausted young boy, and the two held each other tightly. At last, Elsie's boys were together. One was relieved that his long search was finally over; the other was coming to terms with the fact that his life was about to change.

'Goodnight, brother,' Archie said. 'We'll talk tomorrow.'

Now that everyone appeared settled for the night, he checked on Pike and Etta once more before heading for a wash and to change into dry clothes. Still shivering, he sat by the fire sipping a good measure of Pike's whisky.

He was totally exhausted but elated at finding and connecting with Herb. *Ruby and Betsy will be delighted at the news,* he thought to himself. Gazing into the flames, his thoughts flicked like a slow-moving movie over his life: the search for the Nipper; his journey from poverty to wealth; how fate had brought him here to this snow-covered country; and finally to his future plans.

Archie slept deeply and woke with sunlight creeping through the window, making dust particles dance and swirl. He was still in the kitchen; someone had covered him with a blanket and placed logs on the fire.

Etta, alert and busy, was preparing breakfast.

'Oh, Etta, you shouldn't be out of bed,' he told her, jumping up. 'You need to rest until a doctor has examined you.'

'Nonsense, Archie, I'm perfectly well enough to look after my brood,' she assured him. 'Really, I feel just fine. You and Herb were remarkable last evening. I dread to think of the consequences if you hadn't been there.'

Archie, with his experience of life with strong women like Peggy and Doris, knew there was no arguing with such formidable females.

'I checked on Pike,' she told him. 'He's snoring like a pig and should sleep for a bit yet. His wound looks dry. You've dealt with us like a professional doctor. Where did you pick up those medical skills?'

Archie gave her an abridged version of his encounter with Monsieur Hebert and how he'd saved the elderly man's life. 'After that experience, I decided to learn some basic first aid skills.'

'It sure helped us last night,' Etta said.

'I couldn't have managed without Herb's help.' Archie frowned. 'Nobbs is a concern now, as I'm sure his arm is broken. Herb helped me strap it up, but he will need to be seen soon by someone who knows about bones.'

As if on cue, Nobbs came slowly downstairs assisted by Herb. The boy's face was ashen, his pain clear for all to see.

'We heard voices and smelled cooking,' smiled Herb, as he helped his friend to settle by the fire. 'We're hungry.'

'You guys are always hungry,' Etta said with a laugh. 'Nobbs, let me have a look at you. Hmm, Archie has patched you up real good, but you need to rest that arm and not move it about like that. Have some food then get right back into bed.'

Nobbs shook his head. 'I need to check on Vance,' he said softly. 'He'll think I've deserted him.'

Herb spoke firmly. 'Vance is just fine. I'll see to him.'

'But... but...'

Nobbs never finished the sentence. Pain seared through him, and the smell of food made him feel nauseous; he wanted to vomit. Etta helped him back to bed and put a pillow under the injured arm to give him some relief.

Returning to the kitchen, she was about to serve breakfast when Pike appeared, ready for food and company.

'Now,' he said, taking his seat at the table, 'I want to hear more of Archie's story.'

46

Archie cleared his throat, looked at Herb, then picked up where he had left off.

'After the shock of hearing about the workhouse, I ran back to Stan and Doris's house, soaked to the skin, hungry and angry, but determined to take the four of us away from threats of the workhouse. My mind was in a mess, what with losing Mam and feeling livid that our security with the Youngs was being whipped from under us. Blaming the war and the entire world for our plight, I ran into the house to find I was too late – the authorities had taken you all away and were coming back for me.

'Doris and Stan were openly crying and apologising that it had come to this. I was so angry I remember thumping Stan's chest in frustration. Poor Stan, he had shown us nothing but kindness, and there I was, this twelve-year-old boy blaming him for not saving you all,' he told Herb. 'I ran from the house, my head in a total a muddle, and I had no idea where I was going. A creepy down-and-out vagrant tried to take money from me and shouted that I'd never find you unless I headed to a workhouse near the river. I didn't know then that he had deliberately sent me in the wrong direction. It was getting dark, the rain never stopped, and eventually I found myself at the docks.

'It was frightening with the noise from ships and shouts from sailors as they loaded and unloaded stuff from the ships anchored there. A pieman gave me some pie and porter, so I had to part with some of Mam's precious money, but I knew she wouldn't want me to starve. He told me to take cover as night was falling and the loud crazed sailors were out in force heading to the beer shops. So, I climbed up among a pile of bales and settled among sacks to keep the worst of the wind off me, and fell asleep.'

Archie stopped to sip his coffee, while the others waited in silence. Herb had not taken his gaze from his brother while he was speaking, his eyes widening in wonder as the strange tale progressed.

'What happened next?' he asked, almost reverently.

Archie's grin made the others curious as to where the tale was heading. 'This is hard to believe,' he told them, 'but I slept soundly and woke to find that I was on a ship, way out to sea, and heading for America.'

'America?' gasped Etta 'Oh, what a turn up. What did you do?'

'I was hauled by the scruff of the neck to the captain, who whipped me for stowing away on his ship. I yelled at him to turn the ship around and take me back to the docks. But he just laughed, as did the sailors who had gathered to watch the whipping.'

'Poor you!' exclaimed Etta. 'That was awful.'

Herb, his eyes wide with amazement, asked, 'Did they turn the ship back?'

'No, Herb, they sailed on. So, I spent over six weeks on that sailboat, sleeping under a tarpaulin at night, and scrubbing the decks by day until my knuckles were raw. Weeks of seeing nothing but water and wild waves scared me, and at times I thought I would never see land again, let alone England. One of the sailors was assigned to look after me and check that I didn't do anything crazy, like jump overboard. His name was Dan, and to this day he is a very good friend. If it wasn't for Dan, I would have lost my mind.'

Etta studied the young man then glanced at his brother. They looked so alike, their mannerisms so similar in many ways. Turning to her husband, she noticed he looked tired, and suggested he go back to bed.

'I don't need to rest. I'm fully recovered,' Pike replied, rubbing his head where Archie had patched him up.

But Etta was having none of it. 'Husband, we are going to rest. These guys have a lot to talk about. Let's give them some privacy.'

'Ah, I see. Fine by me.' He stood up slowly. 'I guess I do need to rest.'

When the elderly couple left the room, Herb sat quietly, his mind trying to take in everything he had heard. He knew now that Archie was indeed his brother, but so many questions were tumbling around his head.

'Tell me what happened when you arrived in America,' he prompted.

For the next hour, the brothers sat by the fire as Archie regaled him about life with Dan and Peggy, the chance meeting with CJ Croft that changed his fortune, his friendship with Jimbel, his work at the hotel, and his determination to return to England.

'I spent six years working every hour I could to save every dollar to purchase a ticket to return to England, in a cabin this time, and to save what I could to gather our family together. Meanwhile, my employer CJ did some investigation on my part to locate you all. He had several contacts working for him. Because of the destruction brought about by war, things were difficult, people were moved from one workhouse to another, and records were almost non-existent.

'Eventually, CJ called me with news of where Ruby and Betsy were living. I was ecstatic on hearing they were near where we had lived in London. I was eager to take them home – not that we had a home, but I knew I'd figure something out. My mind raced ahead as I planned and worried and longed to get back to England. Sadly, though, there was no word about you. I was devastated, but CJ told me never to give up hope, and I held on to my resolve to find you.'

He paused to study the youth in front of him – a younger version of himself with a quizzical look on his face. The boy deserved more.

Archie recounted his sail home, his encounter with Roon, and his eventual arrival in England. 'I was unprepared for the devastation and chaos in the city, with derelict buildings, fallen masonry, and dangers all around, which made moving around the city treacherous and foolish. It was so dull and grim. I'd forgotten how dismal England could be.'

Herb interrupted, 'We were in the workhouse when a bomb fell nearby. I've never been so scared in my life. We had to run to the cellar, it was horrid.'

Archie went on to explain how he'd met Jake, then found Doris and Stan. He told of his meeting with Oscar Nash and his work in the London hotel, when suddenly Nobbs appeared, claiming to be starving.

Archie found some of Etta's hot pot and some bread, which Herb helped his friend to eat, feeding him at times when he struggled to lift his arm.

'Are you feeling better?' he quizzed as he looked at Nobbs' ashen pallor.

'A little. The pain isn't as bad as it was yesterday. I just want to get better and get back to normal life. Vance will be missing me.' He yawned. 'I think I'll go back to bed now. Thanks for the food. I heard you guys talking. What was that all about?'

Archie helped him to his feet and assured him he would be filled in on their conversation as soon as he could stay awake long enough to concentrate.

When he'd gone back to bed, the brothers wrapped up in warm jackets and went to check on Vance. Together, they mucked out his stall, refreshed his water, laid fresh straw, and declared him as well looked after as the invalids.

They returned to the warmth of the farmhouse, where they settled again by the fire and talked like they had known each other all their lives.

47

That night, Archie slept better than he had in a long time. As he slept, a wide-awake Herb related Archie's story to Nobbs, who fought sleep to listen, enthralled at how events had unfolded.

'Hey, I wish I had someone search for me for years and years,' he said sadly.

When Nobbs eventually gave into sleep, Herb lay awake, mulling everything over in his mind. He felt a strange contentment, coupled with a little anxiety, at what the future had in store. His sleep was disturbed by images of sailing vessels struggling against waves, and scary sea captains brandishing swords ready to cut off the heads of a line of mariners. He woke to a damp bed, his nightwear drenched in sweat.

It was three days before medical help arrived at the farmhouse, by which time Etta had recovered sufficiently to continue her fussing over the others. The doctor checked her over and declared her fit, but insisted she pace herself and take regular rest periods. He knew she would agree to his request but, without doubt, ignore his instructions as soon as he left the premises. He smiled as she sat him down at the table and served him hot food.

'Even doctors have to eat, especially after driving through heavy snow,' declared Etta, changing the subject.

Pike's wound was healing nicely, and the doctor pronounced himself pleased with the treatment Archie had delivered.

'You did the correct thing in cleaning the wound and treating it with iodine,' the doctor told him. 'I feared it might require sutures, but it has closed by itself. As for this guy here,' he turned to look at Nobbs, 'the splint has helped hold the arm in place, but I fear you need a trip to hospital to have it set properly.'

Nobbs paled. He felt sick at the thought of hospital. To him, it conjured up images of the workhouse.

The doctor continued, 'I can take him back with me, now that the roads are reasonably passable. But one of you will need to accompany me to attend to the patient during the journey.'

In unison, Archie and Herb said, 'I'll go.' They smiled at each other at the similar way they had responded.

'Herb,' Nobbs said quickly, 'come with me. Please don't leave me.'

Herb looked at the adults for approval before agreeing to accompany his friend.

Etta, as always, turned her thoughts to the practicalities of them being away for several days, then went about gathering and packing clothes.

'I have to see Vance before I go,' mumbled the patient, and accepted Archie and Herb's assistance to take him to the barn, where he snuggled into the horse's mane and whispered secrets to him.

While he was busy with the animal, Archie spoke to his brother. 'I'm coming along too, with the doctor's permission. I need to get back to civilisation and send a few telegram messages. My employer must wonder where I've been. You can stay with me at the hotel while Nobbs is being attended to.'

Nobbs was carefully lifted into the doctor's car, which was a much more comfortable vehicle than Pike's old truck. Etta wrapped pillows around him to hold him secure and comfortable, then stood with Pike at the door of the farmhouse to wave them off.

The doctor spoke little, saving his concentration for the road ahead, and before long Archie nodded off, though he was aware of the conversation between the two friends in the back seats.

'What you gonna do, Herb?' Nobbs asked quietly. 'You going away with your brother?'

Herb hesitated before replying. 'I dunno, Nobbs, I'm real mixed up. It's all been too much to take in.'

'Please don't leave me, Herb, you know I won't cope without you,' the injured lad pleaded. 'We've been together forever.'

Herb was silent for what seemed to Nobbs to be an eternity.

'Don't worry,' he said eventually. 'Remember our pinkie promise, *together, forever, through thick and thin.* No-one can take us from here unless we choose to go. Pike told me we can live with them until we are sixteen, then the charity would need to be informed of any development in our placement. Seems like they are our official guardians until then.'

Nobbs was silent for a time, as if working something out in his mind.

'But, Herb, you'll be sixteen before you know it. Then you can go wherever you like. If you wanted to, you could go back to England. I don't know my birthdate, so I could be stuck here alone forever.'

Herb shook his head. 'We know you're about my age, don't we? You came to the workhouse when they reckoned you were about four years old and I was about five. I guess they could be wrong about your age and you might be even older.

Who knows if we will ever find out the truth? But don't fret. I ain't gonna leave my best buddy. We're like brothers; always have been, always will be.'

Herb found he was talking to himself; Nobbs had fallen asleep. The rest of the journey was made in silence, with only the occasional question from the doctor as to how the patient was faring.

Eventually, they arrived at a one-storey building that looked welcoming and clean inside. The patient was transferred to a chair and taken through bright corridors to a room where a nurse welcomed him.

'Let's get you settled here before Doctor Tasse arrives to examine that arm,' she said.

Nobbs secretly enjoyed being fussed over. And to his surprise, his stay in hospital proved to be a better experience than he had imagined, with staff caring for him and seeing to his every need.

After they'd seen Nobbs settled into the hospital, Herb went with Archie to the hotel.

Archie's first task was to wire a telegram to his sisters and CJ:

SNOWBOUND IN CANADA-STOP-FOUND OUR NIPPER-STOP-ARCHIE

During their stay together, Herb asked many questions. Secretly, he was hoping to find a flaw in Archie's story so that he could catch him out and have him admit they weren't related. But in his heart, he knew that would not happen; he and Archie were undoubtedly brothers.

Arche told him that a home was available to them with Stan and Doris, should they return to England, but that he had always harboured a wish to bring the family to New York to make a fresh start. At that point, Herb asked about his sisters. Even saying *my sisters* felt strange, yet comforting to him. But he was horrified to hear of their plight in the workhouse and of the cruel treatment meted out to them.

'Our life was strict in the workhouse, but we didn't know any other life,' he told Archie. 'Some of the lads were hurt and whipped, but I escaped all that as I was clever enough to be put in the education system. The guardians wanted to prove to the authorities that we were being treated well. Poor Nobbs couldn't get the hang of his ABCs and was put to work in the building, cleaning and stuff like that. I know he was beaten. I often heard him crying at night, but he wouldn't talk about it. Sounds like my sisters weren't so well treated.'

Archie's heart burst with pride as he heard Herb say *my sisters*. How he longed for them to be a family again, but he knew from the conversation he'd overheard in the car that he still had a mountain to climb to make that happen.

Archie told him all about Betsy's plight at the hands of the cruel woman in the workhouse, and how it had left her physically damaged and mentally impaired.

Herb interrupted, his brows furrowed with an anger that Archie recognised as a family trait. 'I would give that woman some of her own medicine,' he stormed. 'How cruel of her to treat children like that.' He looked furious; his fists clamped together as if ready to take on the world.

'I heard she is left badly damaged after a fall and will never walk again, let alone be near children,' Archie assured him.

'I must say I'm pleased to hear that,' Herb replied. 'Tell me more about my sisters.'

48

'Ruby is almost twenty, and she is engaged to be married to my best friend, Jimbel,' Archie told him proudly. 'She is a talented dressmaker and has her own establishment where she makes beautiful clothes for wealthy women. She learned her trade from Doris when we lived in London. Betsy is her assistant and thrives on the work. She has a room in the hotel where I live, too, so that I can keep a brotherly eye on her.' He smiled, thinking of his youngest sister. 'She is a bit vulnerable, and I won't have anyone take advantage of her lovely nature.'

Herb's questions then turned to their parents. 'What were they like?' he asked.

Archie described a kind mother who struggled with ill health and poverty.

'She did her best for us, and we were loved and cherished. There were three more babies, born dead, which must have broken her heart. Our da...' Archie sighed, 'Well, there's not much to say about him. I've told you of his drinking that led to prison, where he died of some strange illness. His name was Albert, known as Bertie, Bertie Connor. Your name is not far short of his. I'm sure if Mam had lived she would have named you after him.' He shook his head sadly. 'He was the love of her life when they married at first, but poverty had its casualties. I took the girls to visit her last resting place; we were so poor that she was buried in a pauper's grave. I feel sad whenever I think of that.'

Archie paused to draw breath and recover from the emotional toll of relating his life story to the Nipper. He had never envisaged how traumatic their reunion would be.

'We all called you the *Nipper* since Mam asked me to look after *our nipper* and we had no other name for you. During the years I was searching for you, Betsy, in her own mind, thought you were hiding; to her, the search was a kind of game, until she matured a bit and realised what it really meant,' Archie told him. 'When I got back from New York and settled with Stan and Doris, I was employed in a hotel owned by Oscar Nash – a kind man who took me under his wing. He, like CJ, found some information about various workhouses, and I tell you, I tramped the streets visiting each and every one. Sometimes I had the door slammed in my face, other times people were sympathetic and suggested places I might try. I was told of a country mansion, Moorland Mansion, in the parish of Lincoln and I planned to visit—'

'I was there!' Herb interrupted excitedly. 'Me and Nobbs and loads of other boys. It was a dreadful place, been left lying for years seemingly; it was cold and bleak, the bed covers were damp, and several of the boys succumbed to the influenza – the very thing they sent us away to protect us from. It was horrible to see dead boys being buried in a kind of grave-yard. It was a horrible place.' He shrugged. 'I don't know how me and Nobbs survived. We were scared we would be next. Those of us that were okay were taken back to London in an old wagon; it was a hellish journey that took two days. It was the most miserable time in my life.'

Herb screwed his eyes up as if wiping a memory that haunted him, one that had resurfaced at the mention of

Moorland Mansion. Archie waited until his brother seemed calmer before continuing,

'It was indeed a wretched place. It took me two days to travel there. I was almost assaulted in a hostelry, then fortunately met some kind farmers who gave me food and shelter and took me part of the journey. I slept in the open until morning then made my way to the mansion. I couldn't believe the depressing wreck of a place and doubted anyone would have brought children there to recuperate, that was, until I stumbled over a stone and realised I was in a makeshift graveyard.

'Herb, I was frantic with worry as I searched every stone and prayed your name wouldn't be among them. I sat down and cried myself to sleep, then made my way back to the track where the farmer had dropped me off two days previously. I was soaked to the skin, starving, thirsty, and just wanted to curl up and die. I felt I'd let Mam down, and it was only the thought of Ruby and Betsy's need of me that made me go on. I must have gone unconscious, as the next thing I knew, I was in a cart covered with blankets. Vin, that was the farmer who gave me a ride, found me on his return journey. Seemingly, I was delirious and would have died if it hadn't been for the care he and his wife Lottie gave me. I don't remember how long I stayed with them – until next market day, I guess. They saw me off on the train with a final message, *'Don't give up, your brother is out there somewhere.'* And I didn't.'

Herb stood up and hugged his brother, tears streaming down both their faces. They stayed like that, connecting, weeping, believing that they were meant to be united as family.

'You did all that to look for me?' he asked incredulously. 'I can't stop crying.' Archie nodded. 'Nor me. We have so much to catch up on. Let's get tidied up and visit Nobbs. We don't want him to see us like this.'

*

Nobbs looked much better when they arrived. He was sitting up in his hospital bed, and the ashen pallor had gone, to be replaced by a healthy pink glow. He grinned as the brothers arrived with some sweetmeats that they had purchased.

'How's the patient?' Archie asked as he patted Nobbs's head.

'The pain has gone,' he told them. 'The doctor mended my arm but I've to keep it like this for a few weeks. He told me I can go home tomorrow.'

Herb laughed, relieved to see his best friend looking so much better. 'You mean you can come home and watch me do all the work while you laze around?'

Their laughter was broken by the entrance of a nurse who, hearing part of the conversation, said, 'Yes, indeed. This young man can return home with strict instructions to rest. The doctor is pleased with him and has assured him the arm will heal well enough for him to use it as normal – thanks somewhat to the initial care he was given.'

She smiled at Archie and departed, leaving them to continue their visit.

'How will we get back to the farm?' asked Nobbs. 'Will Pike come for us?'

'I can't see how he can do that with a burst tyre that needs to be replaced,' Herb replied frowning. 'Anything could happen if he ventures out. If he burst another one, it would be disastrous. That old van is done.'

Archie smiled. 'Hmm, I have an idea. I'll leave you two to talk. See you back at the hotel, Herb. Nobbs, it's great to see you looking so well.'

With Archie's departure, the boys chatted freely about the events that had shaken their lives since Pike had returned from town with Archie.

'What's gonna happen?' questioned Nobbs with a worried frown. He had an ominous feeling that he was to be abandoned when the brothers left the farm.

'Nobbs, I'm mixed up in my head,' Herb admitted. 'I sat up all night listening to how Archie searched for me. He never gave up hope of finding me, and I can't tell you how much I admire him. He even trekked to the horrid Moorland Mansion and almost died from fever.' Looking his friend squarely in the eyes, he said helplessly, 'Nobbs, I don't know what to do, you have to help me here. I have two sisters that I'm desperate to meet. What should I do?'

For a while, the two sat quietly, each with their own thoughts: Nobbs, scared that he would lose his best friend; Herb, confused, and unsure of what lay ahead.

49

Archie had a plan in mind, but would it work? He desperately wanted his family unit to be together, and mulled over various scenarios to put to Herb. The last thing he wanted was to separate the two friends, but would it work? Would Nobbs be content to visit Herb should the latter agree to go with him? He thought of Pike and Etta and how his plan might affect them. But first, he had something more important to see to.

As arranged, the brothers met back at the hotel a few hours later. Despite his friend's obvious progress, Herb looked solemn and downcast.

'Something on your mind, Herb?' Archie enquired. 'Do you want to talk about it?'

'I'm worried about what happens now you've found me.'

Archie sighed. During the years of searching, he had dreamt of the moment he would find the Nipper and bring him home. But this was not the reunion he had expected; it was much harder than he'd thought. Nobbs was clearly an integral part of Herb's life, and the two had endured many experiences and stuck together. Could brothers be any closer?

He took his brother's hand, looked into the eyes that reminded him so much of his mam's, and asked quietly, 'What's your biggest fear?'

Herb's eyes filled with tears. 'I don't know what you plan for me. Until I know that, I won't be at peace. You've come into my life, and things will never be the same for me. I have a family I never knew or dreamt of, and I want to meet my sisters but...'

'It's Nobbs, isn't it?' Archie asked gently. 'You don't want to leave him?'

Herb nodded, and tears began to trickle down his cheeks. In his entire life he had not experienced such emotional turmoil, and he could not see any solution to his dilemma.'

'I've been thinking about that. Hear me out, then mull over my plan and give me your thoughts,' Archie told him. 'Sleep on it and we can talk tomorrow before we collect Nobbs.'

Archie detailed his plan.

*

The following morning the brothers spoke at length before setting off to the hospital.

'How are we going to get back to Pike's?' asked Herb as they headed out of the hotel.

Archie smiled and pointed to a truck parked a short distance from where they stood. 'In that!' He had purchased a more up-to-date truck and intended presenting it to Pike.

'Wow, that is handsome,' replied Herb, as he examined the shining vehicle in detail.

'Let's go fetch Nobbs,' Archie said. 'Do you want to tell him the plan, or shall I?'

'Hmm,' Herb mused, 'I'd rather you told him.'

With Nobbs securely seated in the truck after saying farewell to the hospital staff and thanking them for his care, they set off. Archie drove carefully so as not to jerk his passengers any more than necessary. The road was rough, the terrain in parts difficult, but the vehicle travelled well under the expert guidance of the driver.

'This is a better ride than we've ever had before,' remarked a smiling Nobbs, glad to recognise familiar territory.

Herb, who was sitting beside him, said, 'Nobbs, Archie has something to say.'

Nobbs sighed, believing this to be the moment he'd dreaded. 'Yeah, I'm listening,' he reluctantly replied, preparing himself for the bad news. He'd had time in hospital to think of the consequences of being parted from Herb, should the latter decide to make his home with his new-found family. And it was certain that he would find himself alone in the world when his time with Pike and Etta came to an end. The young lad had cried himself to sleep at the prospect. A caring nurse, thinking he was in pain, gave him a sedative, which only resulted in a restless sleep for the distraught youth.

'I'll pull off the road so we can talk without the noise from the truck forcing us to shout,' Archie announced. 'Here will do just fine, and I have some snacks we can have while we talk.' He cut the engine then turned to face Nobbs. 'Herb and I had a long conversation last night, and this is what we've come up with.'

As Archie explained his plan in detail, Nobbs listened carefully, then realising what was on offer, held Herb's arm and grinned. 'Really?' he breathed. 'Is this truly happening?'

'Yeah, Nobbs,' said an ecstatic Herb, relieved to see the strain lift from his friend's face – the same strain that had only a few hours ago sat like lead on his own shoulders, pulling him into darkness and gloom. But now, he felt light and happy. *Could life be so good?* he thought.

Archie continued the journey, answering a barrage of questions from the boys as honestly as he could. He felt full of hope for the future.

A blast of the horn brought Pike and Etta rushing to the door to welcome the cheerful passengers.

'Welcome back everyone,' called Pike. 'Nobbs, you look more human now. Come in and let me have a proper look at you.'

As Etta fussed over the boy, Pike admired the truck, examining it in detail before declaring it a fine piece of machinery.

'It's for you,' said Archie, handing the farmer the keys. 'I want you to have it to replace the clapped-out truck.' Taking in Pike's look of amazement, he added, 'Think of it as repayment for looking after Herb and for taking me into your home this past while.' He paused, then added, 'We need to talk with you and Etta regarding Herb's future.'

'And Etta and I have some news to share,' Pike replied. 'Looks like a serious pow-wow is called for.'

Before they all sat down to one of Etta's hearty meals, Nobbs, holding onto Herb's arm, went off to see Vance. Recognising his friend's voice, the horse neighed in delight as Nobbs snuggled into his mane.

During the meal, Nobbs asked, 'Archie, you never got around to telling us how you got to be so rich. How did that happen?'

Archie laughed. 'Okay, I guess I need to compete my story. It was after I returned to England to look for my family,' he explained, as he looked at Herb. 'I was employed by Oscar Nash, a wealthy hotelier in London. One morning I noticed a regular customer had not been for breakfast, which was very unusual as he was what you would call a creature of habit and stuck very much to routine. I knocked the door of his penthouse suite and heard groaning. When I let myself in with the master key, the poor man was lying on the ground, moaning in agony. I managed to get medical help for him, but while waiting for it to arrive, he took a turn for the worse. I pumped his chest and got him breathing again; I was told later I had saved his life.

'He was a delightful, French Canadian gentleman from Quebec, who sadly died several months later. He left me a massive amount of money in his will as a token of his thanks, and I was astounded at his generosity. During his recovery back at the hotel, he had met Ruby and Betsy, and enjoyed weekly visits from them. He also knew of my search for the Nipper. The bequeath made it possible for me to bring the girls to New York and, before we left, to purchase a cottage for Doris and Stan beside their daughter and grandchildren.' Archie shrugged modestly. 'So, there you have it:, the rags to riches story of Archie Connor.'

Nobbs continued to bombard him with questions, he was fascinated at Archie's life story, some of which had been related to him by Herb.

'And what does the future hold for you now that you have found Herb?' enquired Pike, looking serious.

Nobbs grinned. 'Wait until you hear this?'

Archie took a deep breath then began, 'Pike, Etta, I've had a long time to think. It's been an emotional journey for me for the past fifteen years, and I need to get this just right for everyone. I want, and need, my family to be together; I owe it to my mam's memory. The main hurdle was how Herb would feel about moving to New York and leaving Nobbs, who has been his lifelong friend. I couldn't justify separating them, so I asked Nobbs if he would come and live with us in New York. There is work for them both at the hotel, and accommodation.' His gaze moved from Pike to Etta, trying to gauge their reaction. 'But I need your permission and that of the guardians who placed them here, before I can remove them from your care.'

He paused to assess the impact of his plan on the couple who had been so kind to the boys for the past years, and treated them as family.

Leaning over to pat his hand, it was Etta who spoke first. 'Archie, you are a kind and honest man, and you deserve to have your family together with you. And as for Nobbs,' she glanced briefly at the young lad and smiled, 'well, you have solved a problem for us.'

They looked quizzically at her as she nodded to Pike to explain.

'Etta and me aren't getting any younger, and that accident back there took more out of us than we thought,' he admitted. 'We've had a long talk and decided to sell up and move into town. It will make life easier for us, especially in the winter months. We expected Herb would go with you, but we were in a dilemma about Nobbs. We didn't want to return him to the charity; he could be placed with anyone, anywhere, and we couldn't do that to him.

'Etta's middle brother, Isaac, will buy the farm from us, as he's keen to expand his farmland. But we didn't approach him about Nobbs, because he has a family of four and a wife who wouldn't welcome another mouth to feed. In the past they were approached by the charity to take a boy, but Olive, his wife refused. She didn't want strangers.'

Etta smiled broadly at Nobbs before picking up the story. 'There was no question that we would abandon you. We would have thought of something, like taking you with us until it was time for your charity placement to end. But this is a perfect solution – a new life. And in New York!'

They talked well into the day. A sudden thought struck Nobbs and he blurted out, 'What about Vance? Has no-one thought of him?' He was distressed and upset at the thought of parting from the animal.

Etta told him, 'Vance will be cared for by my brother. He loves him, because he used to ride him. He will be happy to look after him.'

'That's good, but I'll be sad to leave him,' sighed Nobbs.

*

The next week was taken up with everyone helping sort out what Etta and Pike required for their new house, while Archie returned to town to speak with the charity authorities and obtain permission to remove the boys from the programme and to arrange documentation for travel. Nobbs spent as much time as he could with Vance, as he was limited in how much help he could give with the move.

On moving day, Chick arrived to take the horse to his place, and assured a weeping Nobbs that the animal would be well cared for.

'I'll never forget you,' whispered Nobbs, as he took tearful leave of the horse, then hid in his room to avoid watching Vince being led away.

'Poor kid,' remarked Pike. 'Vance is one of the best friends he ever had. I guess he has to learn the pain of parting.'

Etta sighed as she watched Chick leave with the beloved horse. 'I know Nobbs will be fine when he gets going, and what an adventure awaits him. How life will change for those boys. It's a remarkable story of a brother's love for his family.'

With help from Etta's brother Isaac, and a reliable wagon, the furniture was loaded for removal. The others followed behind, Pike enthralled with his new vehicle. The few personal items belonging to the boys had been loaded on, and with a tearful wave to the old farmhouse, they prepared to meet up with Archie in town.

'A new beginning for us all,' remarked Pike, as he turned onto the road that was to take them all to a new life. For the final time, Herb jumped down to open the gate and secure it once both vehicles were clear.

Despite the excitement of moving to New York, Herb and Nobbs knew that parting from the elderly couple would be hard for them all. They had been treated as sons, and had returned the love by doing all they could to make life easier for Pike and Etta, both indoors and out on the farm.

As arranged, they met Archie at the house that was to be home for Pike and Etta, and they helped unpack and place the furniture; Nobbs did his bit by carrying light packages.

'It's not totally goodbye,' Archie assured the elderly couple, as they waited for the Maritime Express to whisk him and the boys off on the first leg of their journey to Montreal. 'CJ has intimated he wishes to purchase the hotel that I've been assessing, so you might find me on your doorstep if I'm assigned to check on things at a later date.'

With final hugs all round, the elderly couple waved until the train was out of sight. Only then did Etta resort to tears.

50

The twenty-eight hour journey from Halifax to Montreal gave the boys an opportunity to question Archie about what lay ahead for them. They were excited at the freedom to travel as Archie pointed out places of interest and regaled them with life in New York.

'We'll get you settled after the journey and, Herb, you'll meet your sisters. They will be so excited. They don't know we're coming; I didn't want to set a date in case we were delayed. I've spoken on the telephone to CJ who has offered employment and accommodation to tide you both over until you make your own decision about where you wish to live when you are a bit older. I want you to meet Dan and Granny Peggy, too.'

'Is she our real gran?' asked Herb, trying to get his head around all the people Archie had mentioned.

'No, but everyone calls her Granny Peggy. She's a wonderful old lady, getting on a bit now and not so sprightly. I try to visit as often as I can. She was kind to me when I arrived in New York as a twelve-year-old, very confused boy, and gave me a home with her and Dan. I owe her a debt of gratitude.'

Archie had spared no expense in purchasing first class sleeper and dining car tickets. He knew how tedious the journey could be, having travelled that line to investigate CJ's enquiry about expanding his business empire, and he was determined to give the boys an experience to remember. He was still amazed at how fate had brought him to this area and a chance meeting with Pike in a bar. He felt blessed.

For two boys deprived of simple things while incarcerated in the workhouse, the luxurious surroundings were incredible. Archie delighted in their excitement as they explored the train with him, amazed at the open seating section with its plush upholstery, ornate ceilings, mahogany finished carriages, its dining room with fine cuisine, and delightful sleeping area. *They won't sleep tonight for excitement,* he thought.

The travellers were enchanted by the scenery as they rode along, and gasped in awe as spectacular views unfolded before their eyes. Archie smiled with contentment that he had made the right decision to bring Herb home with his lifelong friend. The joy on their faces was well worth every dollar he'd spent, as the locomotive sped through the countryside, stopping at various stations on the way. At Point-Levi, several passengers alighted to continue their journey by way of the St. Lawrence to Quebec. Herb and Nobbs were enthralled at the sights and sounds of the port that they observed from the window.

Arriving in Montreal was another exciting experience, and Archie planned a few days' stay there before embarking on the long journey to New York. Eventually, the trio arrived in New York, tired, exhilarated, and anxious to reach the hotel.

Almost fifteen years after promising his dying mother that he would keep the family together and look after the Nipper, the time was approaching for a reunion that promised to be highly emotional.

Refreshed from their lengthy trip, the trio arrived at the hotel where Archie immediately took them to a private room where he planned to summon his sisters. Nobbs, feeling he should give them privacy, suggested he might explore the building.

'Better still,' suggested Archie, 'I'll call one of the staff to give you a personal tour.'

With Nobbs occupied, Archie called in at the boutique, where he found Ruby busy adapting a gown and Betsy tidying the room for the next day's clientele.

Archie stood for a moment observing them, bursting with pride as he reflected on how far they had come in life's adventure. Sensing someone had entered the room, Betsy was about to explain that the boutique was closed for the evening when she realised who it was.

'Archie! Our Archie! Ruby, Archie is back.' She threw herself into his open arms, and Archie's heart was full of love for his fragile sibling.

Ruby joined them, a wide smile on her face as she too was engulfed in his strong arms. 'We've missed you. You were gone such a long time. Did you find our Nipper?'

Betsy echoed, 'Did you find him? Our Nipper?'

He looked into their wide eyes, their faces searching his for an affirmative response. 'Yes,' he grinned. 'I have. He is here in the hotel and longing to meet you.'

He held Betsy's arm and gently explained, to the girl-woman, 'Betsy, he's not a baby any longer. It was a long time ago since you were all sent to the workhouse. You've grown up, so has Ruby, and so have I. We're all grown up now and our Nipper is a man now, not a little baby.'

Ruby looked affectionately at her dear brother as he prepared Betsy as simply as he could for the meeting with her younger brother.

'Shall we go along and meet him?' Archie suggested. 'His name is Herbert Connor; we call him Herb. Are you ready?'

Both sisters nodded then linked arms with Archie and crossed the foyer to the room where Archie's search was to end and Elsie's children would finally be together.

A nervous Herb was pacing the room waiting tentatively for them. He still struggled to get his head round the surreal situation. In a few short months he had gone from believing he was an orphan to finding out that he had a family. A family who, if the others were anything like Archie, would change his life forever.

He turned at the sound of the door opening, his heart pounding.

'Herb, allow me to introduce your sisters, Ruby and Betsy. Ruby, Betsy, meet your long-lost brother, our Herb, our Nipper.'

The three siblings looked at each other. Herb saw two very pretty young women sporting a wild hairstyle similar to his own, and with facial features not unlike his. He was rooted to the spot as though he was dreaming. *Would he waken and find himself back in the grim workhouse?*

Betsy stared in awe at the man who looked like, but wasn't, Archie. She shivered slightly with confusion, but Archie's protective arm and gentle hug assured her that this was a good situation to find herself in.

Ruby was the first to break the silence that had lasted only moments but seemed like an eternity. 'Our little brother! How we have longed for this day.' Without any hesitation, she approached and hugged the emotional youth. 'Well, aren't you the handsome one in the family?' she laughed. 'Let me have a good look at you. Oh, you look like our mam, doesn't he, Archie?' She turned to her sister, and said gently, 'Betsy, say hello to your brother.'

When the young girl hesitated, Herb smiled at her before remarking, 'You must be my pretty sister. Hello Betsy, come and give me hug.'

Drawn to his gentle manner and resemblance to Archie, she smiled back and hugged the Nipper.

Archie joined them in a family hug. Their emotions were mixed with tears, smiles, and a sense of relief, as Elsie's four children clung to each other as if wanting the moment to last forever.

'Let's sit down and talk,' suggested Archie eventually, as he rang for refreshments. 'We have so much to say and ask each other.'

For the next hour, they relaxed in each other's company as Herb answered the many questions that tumbled from Ruby. Betsy, too, feeling more secure, asked him where he had been hiding. Taking his cue from Archie, he gently explained about the workhouse. They shared experiences of those painful years but had no desire to waste precious time discussing it.

'I would never have survived the regime if it wasn't for Nobbs,' he told them.

'Nobbs?' questioned Ruby, looking confused.

'Yes, my best friend from when we were nippers. He's here with me,' he explained. 'He's going to live here, too.'

'I'll go fetch him,' said Archie he set off to find Nobbs, leaving the other three to converse among themselves.

'We have so much to catch up,' commented Ruby, as she warmed to her new sibling. 'Archie searched everywhere for you. He wouldn't give up on you, even when everyone said it was no use and you had probably died from the influenza.'

Betsy nodded in agreement. 'Archie cried at night for you. He didn't think I heard him, but I did.'

There was a lump in Herb's throat as he listened to his sisters' words, but his thoughts were interrupted with the arrival of Nobbs.

'Ruby, Betsy, meet Nobbs. Nobbs Norman,' Archie told them. 'Nobbs, here are Herb's sisters, Ruby and Betsy Connor.'

Nobbs shook hands with them, slightly in awe at the situation where not only Herb resembled Archie, but Ruby and Betsy did too.

'Pleased to meet you,' he told them. 'I've heard a lot about you.'

They were interrupted by the arrival of C.J. Croft, who had just returned from a meeting and was anxious to meet the newcomers.

'May I interrupt this happy gathering?' he asked, smiling broadly.

Archie stood, shook hands with his employer, and proceeded to introduce his brother and Nobbs.

'Sir,' said Archie, 'allow me to introduce Herbert Connor, known as Herb, and his friend, Nobbs Norman.'

CJ approached Herb. 'I think I am seeing double. You must be the elusive brother, although for a moment I thought I was addressing Archie.' He shook hands with both young men. 'Welcome. I believe you might be interested in working here for me, at least until you have time to make further plans at a later stage in your lives.'

'Yes please, sir,' Herb replied. 'We would love to work here.'

'Thank you,' mumbled Nobbs, slightly in awe of the great man.

'Good.' CJ nodded. 'We have accommodation ready for you in the staff area, and when you have recovered from the long journey from Canada, I'll discuss your employment.'

Turning to Archie, he commented, 'So, the trip to assess that hotel was successful?'

He laughed as Archie glanced at Herb then replied, 'Oh yes, sir. Extremely productive.'

'I'll leave you to catch up with each other.' Turning to Nobbs, he remarked, 'That's an unusual name, Nobbs. Is it a nickname or a short form of something?'

Feeling a little comfortable now that he'd had time to get the measure of CJ, Nobbs replied, 'Sir, I have no idea. I was abandoned, and lived as a street waif. An older boy told me that the woman who left me there told him, *His name is Nobbs,* and ran off. The surname Norman was added when I was taken to the workhouse.'

CJ looked thoughtful. 'That is interesting. I do like a challenge, as Archie well knows. Allow me to do some research. I feel there is more to your story.'

Nobbs smiled. 'Thank you, sir. I would like.'

The group chatted for some time until a waiter knocked on the door and spoke to Archie. 'Sir, the table you requested is ready.'

'Thank you, Symons. Right, everyone,' Archie told them, 'let's celebrate this reunion with a good meal, then we have to go and see Greta, who is anxious to meet you both.'

Over dinner, they discussed Ruby's forthcoming wedding to Jimbel, with the bride-to-be even more excited now that the Nipper was there to share her big day.

'And when do I get to meet the groom?' asked Herb. 'After all, it's only right and proper that I assess his suitability as a husband for my beautiful sister.'

As laughter filled the room, Archie thought his heart would burst with pride. He watched his siblings bond as if they had never been apart.

They were interrupted by the arrival of Jimbel, who declared, 'Well, isn't this the happiest gathering I've ever seen?'

He shook hands with Archie, planted a kiss on the cheeks of both his fiancée and Betsy, and was introduced to Herb and Nobbs.

'Gentlemen,' he said, as he looked at the two latest additions to the family. 'Welcome. I look forward to getting to know you.'

51

The hotel ballroom was decorated beautifully for the happy couple, and Archie had spared no expense to ensure they had a day to remember. CJ insisted on providing the meal, while Herb and Nobbs, both resplendent in frock suits, acted as ushers for the couple.

'Look at us, Herb,' exclaimed an excited Nobbs. 'Could you ever imagine when we were dressed in nothing more than rags in the workhouse that we would one day be dressed like toffs?' They laughed as they paraded up and down, perfecting their walk while Betsy scolded them for fooling around.

Dan and Peggy were guests of honour at the top table and Archie thought he had never seen the old lady look so happy. She was dressed in an exquisite *Ruby* gown as she watched the couple make their vows in front of the gathering of friends from the hotel and a few chosen clients. It was a day to remember and Archie watched the proceedings with a heart full of love and pride for his family. Later, he and Peggy danced a slow foxtrot, much to the delight of the guests.

That night, Archie raised a prayer of thanks to whichever god was listening, and whispered, *I did it, Mam. I've got the family together.*

After the nuptials, Ruby and Jimbel moved into a vacant apartment near the hotel – a wedding gift from Archie – while Betsy remained in staff quarters with her best friend Patsy. Life was good for Elsie Connor's children.

Herb and Nobbs, now trained by head waiter Symons, enjoyed serving guests and living and working for CJ. Herb was often sought out and feted as the brother of the talented dressmaker. And Nobbs, questioned often about his strange name, never tired of telling of his abandonment which drew gasps of astonishment and sympathy from New York ladies who slipped him a few extra dollars while dabbing their eyes.

One morning, CJ requested Nobbs pop into his office for a chat.

'I see you have settled well to the work here,' the hotel owner said. 'I'm really pleased how you have fitted in with us.'

'Thank you, sir, and for the opportunity to be included in the education programme. I enjoy the work here and meeting guests.'

'Now, to your name…' CJ began. 'I've been intrigued by it. I think Nobbs is a surname, not a first name. Do you think that could be possible?'

Nobbs stared at him, surprised at the thought. 'To be honest, I've never thought about my name, sir. I just accepted it. We weren't encouraged to think for ourselves in the work-house. I guess it could be a surname.'

'I would like to get my researchers onto it – the same people who investigated Archie's family. Do I have your permission to do so?'

Nobbs hesitated. 'I'd like to discuss this with Herb first, sir. I'm not sure at the moment whether I want my life turned upside down,' he explained. 'I'm settled and content with my life as it is.'

CJ nodded. 'I fully understand. There's no pressure on you to allow this investigation. Let me know when you have reached a decision.'

That evening, when they'd finished work, Nobbs discussed the conversation with Herb. 'What do you think I should do? I've never given much thought to where I come from, but when I see how things turned out for you, I guess I'm curious.'

'Yeah, we never gave much thought to our beginnings in life, and all that time Archie was searching for me. Wonder if somewhere out there someone is trying to find you. Let's find out what Archie thinks.'

Archie was duly summoned and told about CJ 's proposal. He let Nobbs do the talking before he commented, 'I guess it is up to you. Would it do any harm to indulge CJ's curiosity? You never know, something might come from it, and if nothing materialises, then what have you lost? Nothing. You have a family here with us, forever.'

'Hmm,' mumbled Nobbs, thoughtfully.

He pushed the idea from his mind until one day, passing through the hotel, he saw Herb with his family. They were laughing at something Betsy had said and looked a picture of contentment. Herb had confided in his friend that he never felt as happy as he did now.

The cosy domestic scene decided Nobbs, and he approached CJ and asked him, somewhat humbly, to go ahead and research his name. Later, he called into Archie's office, where he found him busy with some kind of picture frame.

'Come in, Nobbs. Here, hold this frame while I place these coins on.'

'Are those the coins you showed us at Pike's?' Nobbs asked.

'Yeah. I'm framing them as a reminder of my family's humble roots and my mam's sacrifice at hiding them for me when she needed ever farthing to feed us nippers,' Archie explained. 'When I look at them, I'll remember her and hope never to take my wealth for granted.'

'I've called in to tell you that CJ is researching my name,' Nobbs told him. 'He seems fascinated by it so I'll leave him to get on with it. I'm not bothered one way or another.'

Life continued at the hotel: seasons changed, guests came and went, many regulars returned, and Herb and Nobbs settled to a contented life. They often teamed up with Betsy and Patsy in their time off and, when time allowed, visited museums, shops, and theatres.

Betsy and Patsy adored dressing up for their excursions with the two handsome young men, and they became a happy foursome. Archie was pleased that Herb and Betsy were managing to spend time together. Although younger than his sister, Herb had taken took on the mantle of the caring elder brother and Betsy adored him. Occasionally she mistook him for Archie, so similar were they in looks and mannerisms, but her *faux pas* caused plenty of amusement.

Some months later, Archie requested that Nobbs call in at CJ's office at his convenience.

'He has some news for you.'

52

C urious, and a little nervous, Nobbs tidied himself up, combed his hair and thanked his lucky stars it wasn't as unruly as Herb's, then knocked purposefully on CJ's office door.

'Ah, Nobbs, the very man I want to see,' the hotel owner welcomed him. 'Sit down here and indulge me. Your name Nobbs is, as I suspected, a surname. So, Mr Nobbs, what do you make of that finding?'

Nobbs smiled. 'I don't think it will make much difference, sir. I've always been Nobbs and always will be, but that is interesting.'

'My researchers found it to be from an area of England called Norfolk. Do you know of it? It's in the east of England.'

Nobbs shook his head. Norfolk could have been at the other end of the world for all he knew of English geography.

CJ continued, 'Every ten years on a particular date, a head count is taken by the government and the records sent to the London census office. It seems that members of the Nobbs family were mostly employed as building labourers or domestic workers. And in 1911, a family by the name of Nobbs lived in an area of London near where you were abandoned to the workhouse. This copy tells us there were eight people in a one-room building.'

He handed a piece of paper to Nobbs. It read:
4168 Mile End Close, London, 1911

Edward Nobbs	Husband	Age 35	Labourer
Jemimah Nobbs	Spouse	Age 32	Domestic servant
Mary Nobbs	Daughter	Age 17	Domestic servant
Thomas Nobbs	Son	Age 15	Labourer
Jessie Nobbs	Daughter	Age 14	Domestic servant
Earl Nobbs	Son	Age 10	Scholar
Edward Nobbs	Son	Age 7	Scholar
Timothy Nobbs	Illegitimate son of Jessie Nobbs	Age 3 months	

Nobbs brow wrinkled as he studied the information. 'Interesting, sir, but what connection are these people to me?'

CJ looked steadily at Nobbs and replied, 'I think you are Timothy Nobbs.'

Nobbs looked stunned then examined the document in front of him. His hands shook as he scrutinised it.

'Are you saying the woman who gave birth to me was fourteen years old? I find this hard to believe. I need to know more.' He looked up at CJ. 'This would make me two years older than Herb.'

'It would indeed,' CJ agreed. 'I want you to look at this other census result from 1921. This extract is from an East End London workhouse. Check out the other names on it.'

Once again, he handed Nobbs a document to read.

Extract from workhouse, 43 High Street. Census, 1921

Alan Black	Age 11	Inmate of workhouse
Thomas Loos	Age 10	Inmate of workhouse
Timothy Nobbs	Age 10	Inmate of workhouse
Wilson Kelly	Age 14	Inmate of workhouse
Fred Malory	Age 11	Inmate of workhouse

Herbert Connor	*Age 8*	*Inmate of workhouse*
Alfred Smith	*Age 8*	*Inmate of workhouse*

Nobbs gasped. 'Herb and me, we were in the workhouse together all our lives. So this means...' he flicked the document with his fingers, making a swooshing sound in the silent room as CJ waited for reality to hit the young man. 'That means, I am who you say, Timothy Nobbs. Why did no-one in the workhouse tell me my proper name?'

'Unless there was another boy of the same name, I think we can safely assume, yes, you are indeed Timothy Nobbs, Esquire.' CJ smiled.

'I'm stunned, sir, but pleasantly so. I appear to have a family of sorts – an aunt, and three uncles. Whoa!' He frowned. 'But why give me away?'

'I expect circumstances in those days were difficult for a girl like Jessie Nobbs to keep her child. Perhaps pressure from the parents led to you being placed in care,' CJ replied kindly. "Here is another extract that appears to confirm the above. It is from the 1921 census.'

Extract from 4168 Mile End Close, London

Edward Nobbs	*Husband*	*Age 45*	*Labourer*
Jemima Nobbs	*Spouse*	*Age 42*	*Domestic servant*
Mary Nobbs	*Daughter*	*Age 27*	*Domestic servant*
Thomas Nobbs	*Son*	*Age 25*	*Labourer*
Jessie Nobbs	*Daughter*	*Age 24*	*Domestic servant*
Earl Nobbs	*Son*	*Age 20*	*Labourer*
Edward Nobbs	*Son*	*Age 17*	*Labourer*

'There is no mention of Timothy Nobbs,' CJ pointed out, 'so we may presume you are that child who resided in the workhouse in 1921.'

Looking at the shocked face of the young employee, CJ suggested he share the findings with Herb and Archie. Nobbs shook hands with him and left to seek out his friend and found him poring over staff work schedules with Archie.

Archie looked up. 'Nobbs, you look as if you have seen a ghost.'

'In a way, I have,' he replied. 'Lots of them.'

He sat down, showed the findings to the brothers, and waited as they perused the information. He pondered the meaning of it all as questions raced around his head: *Why was I abandoned? Has anyone ever searched for me?*

Herb was the first to look at the ashen face of his friend. 'This is extraordinary. Oh, and you are older than me by two years. Timothy Nobbs?' He smiled reassuringly. 'Gosh, what a find.'

Archie added, 'Nobbs, it looks like you have lots of relatives. What do you plan to do with this information? Is a trip to England to be undertaken?'

Nobbs retrieved the papers, folded them carefully in his pocket, and shook his head. 'No. I don't plan to travel to England,' he replied firmly. 'This is my home now, my new country with you two and your sisters. You are my life now and all the family I need. If my family abandoned me to a life in the workhouse, then I have no wish to seek them, whatever the circumstances.'

Archie suggested he sleep on things before making a rash decision.

With a twinkle in his eye, Nobbs turned to leave the room, stopped and turned to look at the two brothers, then grinned widely. 'I have no wish to leave here, and I may as well tell you,' he added, 'that Patsy and I are getting to know each other real well. Real well. This is my home now. My future is here.'

As he turned and left the room, Archie and Herb looked at each other and smiled with delight.

53

At a seaside resort on the south coast of England, a large letter arrived at the home of Stan and Doris Young. It was a balmy summer day when the envelope dropped onto the doormat, and Doris took it outside to where Stan dozed in his basket chair, a blanket over his knees.

Despite the warm weather, he felt the cold air from the sea penetrate his frail bones but relished sitting outdoors watching holidaymakers go about their pursuits. A cool drink sat on a little table beside him, with the local newspaper open at his favourite sports page. Betsy's dog Blackie lay by his feet, content to snooze and soak up the sun with his master.

Examining the envelope, Doris remarked, 'Stan, we have a letter with Archie's writing on it. I'd know it anywhere.' She looked at the stamp, turned the envelope back and forth and continued, 'It's bit heavier than his normal letters.'

She continued to examine the envelope before Stan, waiting patiently, eventually sighed and said, 'Open it, woman. Don't keep us in suspense.'

Doris pulled a chair over beside him, carefully opened the envelope and extracted the letter. Enclosed with it was a photograph of four young, smiling adults. She donned her glasses and studied it carefully. Her eyes filled with tears as she turned it over and read:

Elsie's family: Archie, Ruby, Betsy, Herbert (the Nipper) Connor

THE END

ABOUT THE AUTHOR

Terry H Watson qualified in D.C.E. and Dip.Sp.Ed. from Notre Dame College, Glasgow and Bearsden, and obtained a B.A. degree from Open University Scotland.

A retired special needs teacher, Terry began writing in 2014 and has published a mystery thriller trilogy, THE LUCY TRILOGY: CALL MAMA; SCAMPER'S FIND; THE LECI LEGACY.

She has written a compilation of short stories: A TALE OR TWO AND A FEW MORE; and a children's book: THE CLOCK THAT LOST ITS TICK AND OTHER TALES.

Her second book in a Novella trilogy – JULIE SINCLAIR INVESTIGATES – has recently been published, adding A BREAK for JULIE to the earlier A CASE for JULIE, to be followed in due course by A LETTER for JULIE.

She has since added BEFORE LUCY as a prequel to the highly acclaimed LUCY TRILOGY.

This latest work, OUR NIPPER, is a standalone novel set at the time of WW1.

Terry welcomes reviews for her books.

You can contact her at:

Twitter: https://twitter.com/terryhwatson1
E-MAIL: terryhwatson@yahoo.co.uk
Website: http://terryhwatson.com
Facebook: https://m.facebook.com/ramoanpress